*Abdirazak Y. Osman*

# IN THE NAME OF
# OUR FATHERS

HAAN PUBLISHING

Published in the UK by HAAN Publishing
P.O. Box 607, London SW16 1EB


Copyright Abdirazak Y. Osman, 1996

ISBN 1 874209 66 9


Typeset by Books Unlimited (Nottm) in Sabon 10.5/12.5
Printed and bound in the United Kingdom by Ipswich Book
Company

Cover photo by kind permission of the Foundation for Cross
Cultural Understanding, Washington D.C.

# DEDICATION

To my cousin Mohamed-Deeq, whose first-hand experience in the civil war provided the skeleton and the basis of my story, especially the war scenes, and to all young Somalis who were used, misused, abused, misled and betrayed by their fathers, uncles and leaders whom they trusted, respected and obeyed.

*Ratiga dambe ratiga hore saanqaadkiisuu leeyahay.*
The later camel follows in the footsteps of the one in front.

◆

Although the setting for the novel is a real period in Somalia's history, the characters, apart from the political figures of the day, are fictitious and are not intended to resemble any actual persons living or dead.

# GLOSSARY OF FOREIGN WORDS

anjeelo   –   a pancake, made from fermented dough, cooked on a griddle iron

bibito   –   small kiosk selling soft drinks and cigarettes

dafi   –   Ethiopian version of 'anjeelo'

diraa   –   a long, loose over-dress made of semi-transparent Swiss voile worn by Somali women, especially women from the northern part of the country

emma   –   man's scarf of fine white cotton lawn, worn loosely thrown over one shoulder

jihad   –   Muslim 'Holy War'

khat   –   the leaves of a shrub, popularly chewed in Somalia and Yemen as a stimulant

maawiis   –   tubular-shaped cotton skirt worn by men. It is folded at the waist and reaches the ankles. Equivalent to the Indonesian sarong and Indian lunghi.

shaheed   –   a soldier or civilian who dies in the cause of a holy war; martyr

Ugaas   –   title equivalent to Sultan

# BOOK ONE

# 1

Before I knocked on the big red gate in front of me I paused as I remembered the heavy artillery shots I had heard earlier that afternoon. It was while we were playing a very serious football match in the Hodan quarter of the city about seven kilometres from the Medina quarter where I lived. Those shots were really scary. It was the first time I had ever heard such heavy shells. We even stopped the game and wondered what the hell it was all about. We tried to go on playing but the sound got louder and louder until we decided to give up, though it was unheard of for the kids to stop a game which was part of a tournament, a 'sharad' game. There were ten teams altogether, and each of them had deposited an agreed amount of money. The overall winner would get all the money to share among its players. That game was one of our last two games, and if we had won it we would have had only one more to play to win the whole tournament. That meant that each member of my team stood to win more than a thousand Somali shillings. That tournament was a special one, with the finals set for New Year's Eve, which was only a couple of weeks away. Anyhow, today's match was cancelled. "It must be some kind of military exercise," somebody said of the commotion, and we dismissed the case and the game.

I heaved a sigh and knocked on the metal gate.

"Who is it?" asked the voice behind the gate. It was Mona, our maid, but what I couldn't understand was why her voice was so low. I could hardly hear it. I knocked again.

Mona was a young woman of about twenty. I use the term 'about' because people in my country in general, and those like Mona in particular, didn't know and didn't care much about their exact age. We didn't celebrate birthdays, and the day and the month you were born just wasn't considered important. One reason was that all of the people in my country who were above thirty, and half of those under thirty were born in the countryside or 'under a tree' as we city people like to call it. That meant they didn't have birth certificates and all that. And instead of knowing the exact year of their birth by number, they'd link it to something important that had happened around that time and that everybody knew about, so they'd say things like, "in the spring after The Revolution". Even though these dating systems were actually fairly accurate and dependable, it sounded a little funny to us city people.

Anyway, Mona was one of those people from the countryside whose age was about twenty. She came to our family as a maid four years ago when I was starting secondary school. She was our maid but she wasn't *exactly* a maid. She wasn't paid wages. That would have been an insult to her position in the family. She cooked, cleaned and pretty much took care of everything. In return she ate and slept with us. Her whole life and needs were taken care of exactly as for the rest of the family. She was one of us, you see. If your maid was related to you, and Mona was our relation in terms of clanship, you must not pay her a fixed salary. It's an insult, and it's slavery according to our culture. That's the culture. You only pay money to those who are not related, and you treat them as maids. Mona was not treated like a maid. She could have a day or a week off any time she wanted. She could, and she did, have a say about family matters. She could yell and fight with any one who treated her badly. Unlike most girls like herself, she could read and write. That's all due to my father who believed in education as the key to success. He made her take evening classes six days a week.

"Who's that?" she asked again, her voice still really low but clear.

"Will you open the damn gate or I'll break in!" I shouted in a half angry, half suspicious tone as I leaned against the closed gate, exhausted and dehydrated by the heat of the afternoon sun under which we had been playing. I could hardly wait to drink a lot of cold water and lie down, and my impatience increased as the girl took longer than usual to open the gate.

"I know what you're doing!" I yelled from behind the closed gate. "It's OK, I don't mind. Just open the damn gate!"

4

I was referring to her boyfriend. When Mona knew that none of the adults was going to be home she would sometimes bring her boyfriend to the house, and she would usually use my room to entertain him. She was too shy to meet him in the presence of others, and she didn't have a room of her own.

"Mona?" I said, feeling her presence behind the gate.

"Is that you, Ali?" she asked still keeping her voice down. "Are you alone?"

"No," I joked, for no reason at all, "I'm with a policeman."

"Police!" she exclaimed. "Uncle Farah! Uncle Farah!" I could hear her voice fading away as she ran back to the house. "Uncle Farah! The police are here!" She was calling my father. I banged at the gate to tell her I was only joking but she was too far away to hear me. I didn't know what to think. First I thought she had gone crazy, then somehow I knew something was wrong. Anyhow, the gate was flung open in a couple of minutes, and Mona appeared in front of me looking like a mad woman. She was not wearing her usual smile. She stepped aside as I entered, not saying a word. I was about to say something but the look in her eyes changed my mind. She was shaking and breathing hard, and she looked at me as though she had never seen me before. Then she looked behind me for my companion. For the policeman.

"Where is he?" she mumbled, and before I said anything my father appeared in the yard, coming out from the living room. Another huge dark man who resembled my father followed him.

"Oh," Father sighed, and signalled to the other man to relax. "It's only my son, Ali."

By now I could feel something wasn't right, but I couldn't tell what it was.

"Close the door, Mona," Dad instructed, and then added, "Didn't I tell you not to open that gate without my permission?" The poor girl nodded and closed the gate slowly.

"What's this all about?" I asked, puzzled, as I stretched out my hand to greet him.

"You'll find out very soon." We shook hands. "This is Alasow," he introduced his companion.

"How do you do, sir."

"How do you do, son."

"Follow me," Dad instructed me as he headed for the living room. I followed them silently.

There were three other men in the living room. I eyed them well to see if I knew any of them, and recognized Haji Ahmed and Haji Ismael, two business men who were our neighbours and very close family friends. They had helped the family by all means possible during my father's imprisonment. The third man, the only one of them who was thin and had a beard, was a total stranger to me. He also looked the youngest, and was the only one who was wearing glasses. Except for the thin one, they were all smiling at me. I managed a smile in return.

"You know Haji Ahmed and Haji Ismael," my father started when I had finished taking in the group, then added, "This is Dr. Osobleh," pointing to the thin man.

"How do you do, sir."

"How do you do." I realized he could smile too.

I didn't invite myself to a seat because I didn't know what I was expected to do.

"Sit down and relax, my son," said the huge man named Alasow, the one who looked like my father. I sat on the sofa beside Dad and managed another fake smile. Relax? How could I relax when I was being watched by all those strangers surrounding me? The worst thing, however, was the silence which fell as I slid down into the sofa. None of them spoke and they were all watching me as though I was from another world. I knew that the reason they had come together was political, because I had seen all this before. The only difference was the company my father had. But tonight I sensed it was more than the usual politics. A part of me wanted to flee the intimidating silence of the room, but another part of me was curious. Why don't they just get to the point? I asked myself. All old men are like that, I thought. They have to drag things out so before they come to the real issue. I suddenly thought of Mona. She must have some sort of idea of what was going on, I thought. Mona was always my friend, but more than that she was also my informant, and she was always there for me. She told me everything, and she usually knew everything, not just everything that was going on in the house, but also in the neighbourhood. Yes, I thought. Mona must know why on earth these old men were meeting. I decided to excuse myself and sneak out to Mona to get a hint of what was going on. The question, however, was how to excuse myself. I looked at my father who was sitting in the other corner of the sofa and smiled. I had the feeling Dad sensed that I was trying to leave.

"Why are you sweating like that?" Haji Ismael interrupted the silence.

"Why else!" my father said, seizing the opportunity to engage in the interesting pastime of scolding me. "He has nothing to do but to play football," he added sarcastically, "I hope you break your neck one of these days."

"Leave the boy alone," said Haji Ahmed. "He's not the only one. Every young man of his age is doing nothing else."

"What else can they do, for God's sake!" added the thin man. "They have no universities, no jobs, nothing."

"That's right," my father said still smiling, "but none of these things come just like that. They have to make it happen."

"What do you want me to do, father?" I asked. "You always talk about things I don't understand."

"I want you to fight for your rights. Do you know what I did when I was your age? I..."

"I know what you did, Dad," I cut him short before he started bragging about how he had managed to marry by the time he was eighteen without paying the hundred heads of camel, cattle, and horses like the tradition was. How he had stood up to Italian colonization. How fast he'd learned the Italian language and so on. "I know what you did," I repeated, "but what do you want me to do exactly? Do you expect me to do the same as they did a hundred years ago? Or do you want me to talk about politics like you do."

"That's at least a beginning!" he retorted. He had tried to interest me in politics a thousand times, and had failed at each and every attempt. "You just don't understand, Ali."

"I do understand but I'm not interested in politics. I'm interested in education and I don't have any, because my father's not rich enough to send me abroad to study, and he's not smart enough to find a place for me in the local universities!"

A little laughter followed. Dad smiled sourly.

"It's not being smart to do those things, it's being corrupt. Do you want me to take part in this corruption?" he asked angrily. His tone and expression became serious, like it always did whenever that subject corruption was mentioned. "For God's sake, I wouldn't have gone to jail for four years if I wanted to take part in the corruption that's rife! Do you know..."

"Calm down, Farah," said Haji Ahmed. "He's only a child."

"His ignorance drives me crazy and he won't listen to me."

"It's the same with my children, too." He looked at me. "Let's get to the point, my son."

The point? I waited with my ears open.

"First of all don't talk to your father that way. Secondly, I agree that politics is a dirty game in general, and in our country particularly. However, it's not bad to listen to grown-ups talking about something you don't know. It might be useful one day, you never know. Besides, ..."

"But Dad's always talking about tribalism, not politics!"

"Because that's what politics is all about in this country!" Dad interrupted. "What's devastating our country is tribalism!"

"And maybe the lack of real tribalism," added the man with the glasses, in a very relaxed and self-confident tone and in apparent contradiction of my father. Dad glanced at the man with a let's-talk-about-that-later attitude. I wondered what the man meant. It never occurred to me that lack of tribalism was a problem. Dad never mentioned that part. I hoped the man would explain himself but he didn't. That was all he said about the subject for the moment. I was really fascinated by that far-out-theory. As far as I knew tribalism wasn't any good. Our government said tribalism was bad. Our school textbooks said the same. Countless Somali poets and playwrights showed how devastating the thing could be. I wanted very much to discuss the idea. I really did. My country needed real tribalism, the man had said! Hmmm.

"You have to understand tribalism, Ali," Dad said at last.

"Your father's right, my son," agreed Haji Ahmed. "This country like many others is ruled by tribalism, and if you don't know the system you'll get lost. No matter how good a politician you are!" glancing at Dad and Alasow, "No matter how well educated you are!" glancing now at the thin man with the round golden glasses. "If you don't understand how this society's tribes are built, you'll never be able to do anything about it."

I didn't understand all that the man was trying to say but it seemed to be important.

"So I want you to listen to your father carefully without interrupting" he said, staring at me, "OK?" He turned towards Dad.

I nodded and looked at Dad who was watching me.

"Listen, Ali," he started, "I know you don't like my lectures, but you'll have to listen to me tonight." He stopped and looked at me to see if I had any objections. I had none.

"I'm not going to repeat my lecture about how this country is run because I'm sure you've had enough of it." He stopped and looked around for reasons I didn't understand. "Enough to hear but NOT enough to understand." He stopped again. "There's one thing, however, I want you to know." Once more he stopped but this time he looked at the others, seeking their approval. They all nodded encouragingly.

"Things are getting out of hand," my father suddenly said with great emphasis, "and this country of ours is on the verge of real breakdown." He looked me in the eyes to make sure I was following him. My expression didn't change because I didn't hear anything new. He was always saying that the country was in very serious trouble. Something I had never noticed.

"I mean it!" he continued. "We are about to have a civil war. Very soon."

"So that's what it's all about!" I felt so relieved "Who is fighting?"

They all laughed instead of answering my question.

"What's funny?" I smiled, too. Not because I was amused but I felt stupid.

"The funny thing is that you don't even know what a civil war is," said my father, looking very serious and not blinking.

"I know it means that two tribes are fighting. But what's the big deal? I mean it used to happen every now and then."

"I'm not talking about two or three tribes," continued my father. "I'm talking about the whole country. There's going to be a civil war in which each and every one of us is going to take part. Do you understand what I'm trying to say?"

How could I understand what he was trying to say? He was telling me that I was going to be forced to fight my neighbours. Or the military. Or whatever it might be.

"I mean it's going to be Hawiyas against Daroods!" he raised his voice. "Do you understand now?"

Hawiyas against Daroods! He was completely out of probability now.

"Do you understand what I'm saying?" he repeated, still unblinking.

I looked at the old men around me to avoid my father's eyes. They were all cool and expressionless.

"The government has been killing civilians publicly for the last twenty-four hours," Dad continued. "I mean the Hawiyas!" He pointed at all of us with his forefinger to indicate that we were the Hawiyas. "I don't think we can take it any more. We are going to defend ourselves, and that means destruction!"

We? Destruction? I didn't know exactly what these two horrible words meant and I didn't dare to ask. A part of me was already in pain.

"But why Hawiyas against Daroods!" I asked.

"Because the Marrehans are killing only the Hawiyas."

"And why is it not the Marrehans against the Hawiyas...I mean why generalise all Daroods?" I said stammering with words and wondering if I had suggested a better solution.

"Because the Daroods might defend the Marrehans," said Haji Ismael.

"They will for sure defend them!" shouted my father.

"But why?" I asked. It was the first time I showed willing to know about the political situation in my country. Not because it was interesting but because if what he said was true it meant I would be involved. It meant I would be fighting. "I mean... the Majeerteen-Daroods, for example, were fighting the Marrehan-Daroods for years and you're telling me now that they might defend them. I don't get it. I mean what were they fighting for, after all?" I liked this theory of mine and hoped it would do some good. "Isn't it because they don't like how this country is run just like you don't?"

"What do you think they were fighting for?" Alasow asked me.

They all laughed at what they called my innocence and ignorance.

"Let me explain this to you, my son," my father said. "True, the Majeerteens were fighting the Marrehan government, but the reason they were fighting was simply to get the power for themselves. Nothing else. They didn't fight because they wanted to change the injustice. They were simply looking for power. And what's more, they wouldn't like any Hawiya tribe, no matter how good they were, to replace this corrupt Marrehan government. Why is that so? Because they are brothers! They might fight one another or even hate one another but they would never, never let anybody who is not a Darood rule this country!"

"And that's why the rest of the Darood tribes would defend this corrupt Marrehan government?"

"Exactly." This time his voice was low, his face expressionless. "In the last twenty-four hours sixteen generals have resigned. Most of them were Hawiyas and Isaaqs but there are also a couple of Daroods. In another couple of days everybody who's not willing to fight the Hawiyas is expected to do the same. Do you get the picture now, young man?"

I nodded.

"A civil war," he said it so slowly and smoothly.

I watched my dirty feet.

11

"Do you think the people could divide, Farah?" asked Haji Ismael.

"Well," sighed my father as he took stock of the situation. "That depends, I suppose."

I was glad the old men had shifted their attention from me. I took a deep breath and looked around the room as though I was a guest. At one end there was a round table and four wooden chairs surrounding it. It was the place we used to read and eat, but now it was mainly used only for dining because I and my brother Hassan (he's in Canada now) had finished high school. At the other end, where we were now sitting, there were four armchairs and a big sofa. A couple of cheap paintings and two framed family photos were on the wall. One of the photos was the whole family standing in a green field. I think it was one of the times we were in Afgoye for a picnic. The other was my father in military uniform dressed as a major, taken just before he was kicked out of the army for what the government called dishonesty.

"On what?" Haji Ismael continued his inquiries.

"It depends on how Mr. President plays his game. I mean if he plays his usual way, which I'm almost sure he will, the people will divide into two – Hawiyas and Daroods."

I didn't want to hear this any longer. I looked at my wristwatch, meaning to try again to excuse myself, but my father noticed my gesture. It was what I always used to do when I thought I had had enough of his lectures.

"You may go now, Ali," my father dismissed me. "But before you go," he continued, "I want you to know one more thing."

All the men focused on me once more. I felt horrible again.

"I'm not telling you to stop seeing your friends, but..."

"I won't let you," I interrupted.

"For God's sake let me finish!" His voice echoed in the room. "I'm not telling you to. All I want to say is be careful and don't trust everybody. No more football. No more discothèques. No more late nights. At least until things settle down a bit. You hear?"

"OK" I said.

"Now you can go," he said and smiled.

That man could smile even if he was told he would die in a week. As I left the living-room I didn't quite know whether I believed his predictions or not.

2

My two stepmothers, Anab and Falis, my two little brothers, and Mona were in the courtyard, or the daash as we call it. Mona was sweeping the daash with a long broom. Anab was knitting as usual, Falis was preparing some tea for the guests, and my two little brothers were running about in the daash. None of them looked tense or upset like the men in the living-room. It was a relief.

"Get me some water to drink, Ahmed, will you?" I told my little brother, and sat on the ground close to where Anab was knitting. I was as wet as a well with sweat, so much so I could feel the sand sticking to my naked legs as I sat.

"I'll get it!" said Nasir and both of them ran to the fridge in Mona's room.

Our house had five rooms. Entering from the gate, two bedrooms were in the front, the one to the left Falis's and the one to the right Anab's. Adjacent to Falis's room were the living-room, and my room which had two doors – one which opened into the courtyard and one which opened directly to the street outside. Adjacent to Anab's room was the one shared by Mona and the children. The rooms were connected like three sides of a square, and the area between these five rooms is the daash, which, if it were covered would be equivalent to what some people call the hall. Unlike the rooms, the daash was sandy and had no roof. It was a place for the kids to play, but mainly it was a kitchen. We liked to cook in an open area because we used charcoal instead of a gas cylinder and stove. It often makes a lot of smoke.

"I got it! I got it!" The kids came running, each holding a glass of water. Nasir fell accidentally in the sandy daash.

"That's all your fault!" shouted his mother at me.

I didn't talk back for once. I just took the glass of water from Ahmed and called to Mona.

"Will you get my keys, please?"

"Yes," she answered and disappeared into her room. She usually kept my room keys when I was going to a football match because I was afraid to lose them like I had done a number of times before.

Luckily the boy wasn't hurt so Falis let the matter drop. Usually we would have ended up in a fight or something.

"I'll get another glass" said the little boy and ran back to Mona's room again to refill the empty glass in his hand.

"Here," said Mona as she handed me my keys.

"Thank you," I said and stood up to unlock my room. My whole body was as sandy as the daash itself. I was dusting myself off while Mona and my little brother, Ahmed, were chuckling at me.

"You look like somebody who's just come out of his grave!" said Mona leaning the broom against the daash wall.

"When did you see somebody come from the grave?" I asked.

Before she made any response Nasir came running again with the glass of water. This time he made it.

"Here's the water, Ali."

"Oh thank you Nasir. Thank you very much indeed."

I was kissing the boy when somebody knocked on the gate. Nasir ran to open it.

"Don't! Don't!" yelled Anab. The boy stopped in shock.

I stared at her angrily and said nothing. I headed for my room instead and unlocked the door while she herself went to open the gate.

"Is Ali here?" asked the newcomer. I knew it was the voice of my friend Musa.

"Yes, but he's sleeping," said my stepmother.

"That's a lie!" I yelled from my room and came out. "I'm not asleep!" Anab stared at me with hostility as I approached them.

14

"Don't go out, Ali," she advised. "You know your father will disapprove." I was about to tell her to go to hell when she revised her tone. "OK," she said. "I know it's none of my business – I'm just concerned."

"Hey, Musa!" I started talking to my friend instead. "Are you OK?"

"I'm fine." We were both outside the gate now. "What about you?" he asked as he sat on the steps of my outside door.

"I'm fine. Fine." I was about to sit with him when I remembered that the outside door was still locked. "Hold on a minute, Musa. I'll open the door from inside."

"Sure."

I went back to the house, through the daash and entered my room taking the keys out of the inside door lock. I grabbed a towel from my bed and opened the outside door to where Musa was still sitting on the steps.

In my country men always put a towel round their shoulders when they sit on the outside steps. In fact, they usually wear one when they're at home relaxing. The reason, I think, is because the weather is always warm and they don't want to stay dressed-up in the house, so they just wear their maawiis, which only covers them from the waist down, and they cover their upper, hairy parts with the towel. Anyway, it's one of those things I learned from Dad. It seems a cool thing to do, I think, because it's something only grown-ups did.

"So," I said as I sat beside him. "Where have you been today? Why didn't you show up? You knew we were depending on you to help us win." Musa was our best striker and he always scored goals. I was the worst to score but I was a good defender.

"Before anything else," he raised his hand. "I want to know about the result."

"We won."

"Of course!" he cheered. "Of course!"

I smiled.

"What was the score?"

"One, nil." That was the score, though I didn't tell him yet about the game not being finished.

"Mustapha scored the goal?"

"Bad guess." I smiled again. Musa was such a great guy to be with. We could always cheer each other up.

"Wait," he said raising his hand once again. "Let me guess again." He closed his eyes and concentrated. "Liban?"

"Wrong again."

He looked me in the eyes. "You!"

I smiled.

"I knew it!" He stood up and kissed my head. "I knew it!"

Somebody opened the gate. We waited to see who it was. Mona appeared.

"Do you guys want some tea?"

"Yes, please," I said.

"Why didn't you show up today?" I asked Musa as soon as Mona had disappeared again.

"It's a long story, my friend," he said sadly. "You know these old folks always exaggerate things."

"I'm not following you, I'm afraid."

"Here you are, boys," said Mona as she placed two cups of hot tea on the steps beside me. I noticed it was getting dark.

"Thanks, Mona," I said as the girl left us again.

"What's going on, Musa?" I asked again and handed him his cup.

"Did they tell you anything?" he asked.

"Like what?"

"I don't know."

"I mean," he said as I looked at him and remembered the little secret meeting in our living room, "didn't your parents tell you anything?"

I didn't know what to tell him exactly. 'Didn't your parents tell you anything?' Anything! What he said and how he said it bothered me, somehow. Was he talking about what I was thinking about, I wondered?

"I mean anything political?" he added.

"I'm not sure. Why?"

"I mean this civil war thing."

The words 'civil war' echoed in my ears. God it was true! Everything my father said might be true after all. Don't trust everybody! Hawiyas against Daroods! God! Musa was not only a Darood but Marrehan. Could I trust him? I wondered.

"My father told me not to go out any more." He stared at me. I could see the fear in his eyes.

"So did my father," I mumbled. But why? I asked myself as I sipped the hot tea. Why civil war?

"So you know what's going on?" he asked still nervous. "I mean the USC and the Government?"

"The USC?" I asked. I've heard the name before but I don't remember what it is exactly. "Who is the USC?"

"You must know this USC thing of yours," he said. He looked astonished. "It's the United Somali Congress."

"What are you talking about?"

"I'm talking about your father and his friends."

"Hey! Hey!" I stopped him. "What has my father got to do with this?"

"I'm sorry," he said. "I thought you knew…"

"Knew what?"

"That your father is one of the original members of the USC"

"My father? Original member?" I was lost. Totally lost. "Wait a minute now! Tell me first what the USC is all about?" I managed.

"It's a Hawiya rebel group founded in Rome a couple of years ago. They're planning a *coup*."

"You said Rome?" I stood up. "My father has never been to Rome!"

"Yes, he has."

"When?" I remembered when my father went to Germany about two years ago. My friend must be mistaken. "He's never been to Italy. He went to Germany." I took refuge in the sentence.

"And after that to Italy."

That sounded serious. I wondered if the guy was right. I wondered if Dad was right too. Has the guy been snooping on my family? How did he know all this? I didn't care about Italy but about Germany – how did he know that my father had been to Germany?

"And how do you know about this?" I asked still looking at his startled eyes. He somehow still looked like my friend. NOT my enemy.

"My father and mother told me. But it's top secret, you know."

"And why are you telling me all this, then?"

"Because you're my friend."

"Musa! Musa!" Somebody called. "Come here at once, will you!"

"Hey!" he said. "It's my mother. She doesn't want me to be here. I'll see you later." He stood up, took two mouthfuls of the hot tea, and departed.

"When?" I yelled as he made off.

"Don't know!" he yelled back as he disappeared in the darkness.

Musa was a Marrehan-Darood by tribe, but he was my best friend as a person. His family had lived right beside our house for many years. We grew up together, went to school together, and were friends for ages. We never kept any secrets from each other. Musa was living with his mother, Asli, who was divorced. I liked her, she was quite a good woman. All the neighbours respected her. His father was a Colonel in the army, the Commander-in-Chief of the 54th Division of the Bay region, which was about 150 miles from the capital. He had another wife and children but they lived with him in Bay.

I usually enjoyed the darkness, but not on this particular evening. It was also windy so I decided to go in my room and relax. I closed the outside door, opened a window, and put some good music on. I stood in front of a picture on my wall. It was a photo taken last year in a hospital after I had broken my hand during a football match fight with another team over a referee's decision. In the picture I was sitting on a bed all in white, and Dad was standing beside me with his hand on my head. We were both smiling. I got closer and stared at my father's smiling face as though I didn't know him. Is it true? I asked the picture. Could you be one of the USC founders as my friend said? I knew my father hated the Government but I never thought he would be stupid enough to establish a guerrilla group right here in the capital city. That would be too dangerous, and he knows that better than anyone else. It was not so long ago he had spent four long years in jail, and God knows what the family had been through then! You can't do this to us again, I told the picture. You just can't! I left the photo and lay down on my bed. I was suddenly aware of people talking. The voices came from the outside window. They must be in the street, I thought. I thought I heard my old man's voice so I jumped up from the bed and looked through the window. It was my father saying good-bye to his friends who were leaving. I drew up a chair and sat by the window to watch them leave. I hated all of them. They were five, including my father. Haji Ahmed and Haji Ismael walked away towards their homes. Alasow and the man with the golden glasses were in a Fiat 132 car. I could hear them talking but it was difficult to hear what they were saying. I couldn't see their expressions either, even though I could see their outlines. It was dark outside but the light from my window cast some visibility. Alasow started the engine and shook hands with Dad. He saw me as he did so and waved to me. As the others looked at me I forced a smile and waved good-bye. They drove off to the right where the main street was.

I watched my father come back to the house. He was wearing his maawiis, a vest, and a towel on his shoulders. He was always dressed like that when he was at home in the evenings, and in the mornings when he woke and had breakfast. It was what he wore for relaxing after the day's work and out of uniform. My inside door was ajar, and I could see my father close the gate as his friends left. Instead of going to the bedroom of one of his wives – depending on whose turn it was – as he always did, he headed for my room. I was still sitting on the chair by the window when he entered. My father hardly ever entered my room, and would rather call me to the sitting-room if he needed me.

"Hello, there," he said smiling as usual. I wondered how he could afford to smile in the middle of the mess he was in.

"Hi," I said as I looked away. I could see a woman and three kids walking in the road in front of our house.

"You don't look good, son," he suggested, still standing at the door.

I didn't answer. I didn't invite him in either. He invited himself in and sat on Hassan's bed which was just behind me. My bed was too full to sit on, as usual. There were piles of clothes, newspapers, cassettes and so on, but I loved my mess and I always had trouble with the maid about that habit of mine. I looked at the photo on the wall again. I remembered Dad wearing an ugly white prison uniform when he was in the Laanta Buure Jail. How we used to talk to him behind the bars. How the soldier always watched us and listened to what we were talking about. It was horrible. I remembered those days when we used to eat once every twenty-four hours if we were lucky. How we were rescued by Haji Ahmed and Haji Ismael and others. I remembered everything that had happened during his imprisonment.

"Hey, son," he reached for my hand. "You're crying?"

I said nothing. He waited.

"Have you ever been to Italy?" I managed to ask after a moment's silence.

"Italy?" he asked, in total surprise.

"You heard me. Have you ever been to Rome, the capital city of Italy?"

He was speechless for a moment.

"Who have you been talking to?" he asked in a low voice, though I had the feeling it wasn't because of fear that he lowered his voice.

"Have you?" I repeated. The words echoed in the room.

"Steady on!" he said in an even lower but sharper voice. He glanced at the part-open door. "Yes, but it's not what you think. Don't worry, nothing is going to happen to me."

"Don't worry?" I retorted. "What am I supposed to do?" I noticed I was shouting for he put his hand on my mouth to shut me up. I flung his cold hand away.

"Do you expect me to be happy when I know you're going to jail again? I...I..." I couldn't finish the sentence because I felt my throat was swelling. "You think you're smart and nobody else knows anything! You..."

"It's not what you think it is. Believe me I'm safe." He stared at me for a long time before he added, "Where did you hear this?"

"Did you think nobody knew it?"

"No," he said proudly. "Not at all. Everybody knows what the USC is and is capable of doing." He stood up from the bed and drew up another chair to sit beside me.

"And you think you're doing the right thing?"

"Of course." He smiled. Oh, that old man could smile at any time. I remembered how he smiled at the prison guard when he told us to speak loudly so we could be heard. I remembered how he smiled when he was released and we had no food at home. "We will outlive them," he would say smiling while his children starved. He never gave up.

"Why didn't you tell me about this?" I asked. I was not crying any more.

"About the USC?" He was still smiling. "Would you have listened to me?"

I gave no answer for I didn't have one.

"Anyway," he added, "I was planning to tell you."

"When?"

"Now," he said. "That was why I came to your room." He placed his towel on my bed. As little boys my brother Hassan and I used to fight about who would massage that very hairy chest. But today the sight of it made me feel sick. I couldn't have touched it. I hated Dad. "But since you found out from your friend Musa, let me tell you the reality of the USC and their position for the time being and for the near future." He watched me curiously while I waited fearfully. How did he know Musa was my informant? I wondered. Was it a lucky guess or did he really know everything that was going on? Besides, I kept wondering, what was he going to tell me? Was he going to tell me that they were starting the civil war tomorrow? Or was he telling me it would be after that? I hated myself for being there. And I hated my father for knowing all kinds of awesome things. In fact, that's my biggest secret, even though I wouldn't admit it to anyone, I trusted my father's knowledge and experience and I trusted his judgement, and I didn't like

21

that one bit. I knew that he knew what I was made off. He knew me inside out, and he could tell what I was thinking and what I was up to. I knew that he knew everything that's going on in this world, and I knew there was for sure going to be civil war because Dad had said so. I just didn't like the way things were going. Not one bit. He was uncovering the truth about the cruel world which surrounded me. He was letting me know things I really didn't want to know yet. I wanted to have a life, and he was refusing me that life by revealing how unreal was my little world. I wasn't ready for that. Not yet.

"Listen, Ali," he started. "There are certain things that people should live for, fight for, or even die for." He was still looking at me. "Freedom is only one of them. And..."

"Are you one of the USC founders?" I asked.

"Yes," he replied bravely. "But that doesn't matter. I am a member just like you are a member. It is for every Hawiya."

Member? This was the most dreadful of all the horrible bits of news I had been coming across that evening. I was not merely a spectator any more. I was a USC member! In my father's words – just like he was a member! I was filled with terror and suddenly the cool breeze from the window turned into hot and boiling air. I wished the floor would tear apart and swallow me up at once before I could become a member of his organization. To my disappointment, however, the floor wouldn't swallow me up.

"All Hawiyas are members whether they like it or not," he emphasized.

"But I don't want to be," I said feeling sick inside. I didn't know what to ask or what not to ask. I was afraid of the possibility of raising yet another horrifying subject. "I don't want to be," I repeated turning away my watering eyes.

"Do you prefer then," he continued, turning my wet face towards him so he could see me, "to live like a prisoner! Like a slave! Huh? Look at me!" His strong hand was hurting my cheeks. "Do you prefer that?"

"Free?" I burst. "Who said I'm not free?"

"If you were free you wouldn't be afraid tonight! You wouldn't be afraid that I might be killed! Would you?"

I made no reply.

"Would you?" he repeated. "That's not freedom! That's slavery!"

Silence.

"Freedom is being free in every way!" he started again. "Freedom is being able to say what you want to say. Choosing what you want. Refusing what you want." He stopped again. "Can you publicly criticise the government? Can you get education without knowing somebody in the government? Can you get a job? For God's sake I'm a criminal simply because I'm a Hawiya! Don't you see it?"

I was not crying any more. I was not as afraid as before either. I knew he was somehow right but I just wished things were not like that. I was trying to think but I failed.

"Do you want to live like that forever?" he asked.

"No, but..."

"Do you want your children to live like that?"

"No, but how do you think we can solve the problem?"

"We have to fight for our rights, as I said many times before."

Silence briefly took over once again.

"Better die than live like a dead man." He was not shouting any more.

I looked down and thought about it for a while. He waited.

"Against whom are we fighting?" I asked after a moment.

"The Government," he said, then added, "and possibly the Daroods."

I was about to say something when he interrupted me.

"I know you don't like it like that." He paused. "I don't either. It is not the intention of the USC But we don't have a choice if the Daroods defend the Marrehan government. We're going to fight them! We're going to fight anyone who tries to do that!"

"But if the USC doesn't intend to fight all the Daroods why is it that the USC is a Hawiya-only organization?"

"Because that's the only way we could make the organization"

"How is that?"

23

"Because we don't trust others and they don't trust us either."

"But it's impossible to fight a government when you are a tribe."

"Why do you think that?"

"Because we both know we can't fight the government – we don't have weapons and we don't have as many troops as the government. You remember how many smart guys tried that same thing. They all failed. Why the hell do you think they failed?"

"First of all this is not a government. It is a tribe who is ruling the country. Secondly, most of its troops are Hawiyas. And third, we are not following in the steps of those who tried and failed."

"How do you mean?"

"We have different strategies."

"Like what?"

"That is not what we are discussing here."

"But give me an example!"

"We're not going to fight only from the far regions of the country – we're also fighting right here in the capital."

"This capital?"

He smiled with deeply sad and honest eyes.

"When?" I asked in a tone of surrender.

"You'll find out." He stood up. "Now," he said grabbing his towel, "get some sleep."

"One more question! Do you know that the police are looking for you by now?" I wanted to scare him.

"Not yet." He said indifferently. "Good night." He touched me on the head and stepped out of the inside door. "Be a man!" he called back.

"I don't want to be a man," I mumbled.

# 3

We were a family of seven who lived scattered throughout the city, or I should rather say throughout the country. My father married and divorced many times. I use the term 'many times' simply because I don't know the exact number of marriages he went through; he said it was only about ten or twelve, but my grandmother claimed it was well over eighteen. The reason he married so many times, according to my father, was because his wives were either barren or bad-tempered. Whatever the reasons were, I wouldn't blame them because I knew what it was like living under the same roof with someone as stubborn, bossy, and poor as my father. Yet on the other hand, to everyone in the community my father was known as an honest, hard working, intelligent and entertaining figure. I think it must have been the reputation which attached to these last adjectives that enabled him to marry as many times as he did, in spite of the fact that in those good old days marriage was considered an expensive business, unlike today when there is no longer the obligation to pay a hundred head of livestock – camels, cattle, sheep or horses – for your bride. However, in spite of his extraordinarily successful efforts at winning his brides with a good heart and brain, and an empty hand, he only managed to beget four children, a matter remarked on by most of our community elders as being unfortunate. Dad had married first as early as sixteen, when his peers were struggling against the odds to get started, collecting a dozen or so livestock and raising them until they could multiply and number a couple of hundred; then, and only then, could they think of what Dad was thinking about at sixteen. Despite his early marriage, now at the age of sixty his oldest child was not even twenty. Compare this to his younger brother, Mahmood, who, despite the fact that he didn't marry until he was twenty-one and died in a tribal war at thirty-four, had nine children, the oldest being now above thirty years of age.

Anyway, we were four brothers and no sisters. Each and

every one of us had a different mother, and we didn't share any uncles or aunts from our father's side, since Dad and Uncle Mahmood – who died before we even saw him – were the only children who survived for his parents. There had been two older brothers who died mysteriously in their infancy. My grandparents, in light of the unexplained and sudden deaths of their offspring, had visited a doctor-magician to seek advice. He told them to shave the heads of any other children they bore from that time on if they wanted then to live. They followed the advice and the result was that the next two children, Dad and Uncle Mahmood, survived to reach adulthood.

Of the four of us, Ali, who is me, is the oldest. I am seventeen. I have just finished high school and, just like almost everybody else in my country, I didn't go to college. Hassan is the second oldest. He is not slim and tall like me but a strongly built and short guy. Dad says he took after his mother's family. He was only eight months younger than me because Dad had married Hassan's mother only a couple of months later than he married mine. So I and Hassan went to the same schools at the same time. Hassan's mother not only belonged to the Marrehan, the ruling tribe, but also had lots of relatives and friends in the government, which is why Hassan was now in Canada for studies. Universities were for those whose parents or relatives were bigshots in the government, and being a bigshot depended on your tribe. "Get yourself a Marrehan mother!" Dad loved to tell me, "and you'll get a place in the university, and even go to Europe for your education!"

The four main tribes of the country as far as I know are Isaaq, Darood, Hawiya, and Gadaburse, and then there are the Maay, and other groups, but I don't really know where they fit in. Don't take my word for it, but I think that's how it is. Anyhow, all the people from all the tribes are Somalis – not like the tribes of some other African countries where they seem to have different languages and things. We call all the Somalis taken together the *faradheer* which means 'longfingered' people, to distinguish them from other Africans.

The Isaaqs live mainly in the northern regions, and none of the presidents the country had since independence was from their group, even though I think they had most of the prime ministers. Either way, they felt badly treated, and they organized a rebel group, called the Somali National Movement – the SNM. Some people, including my father, said they were fighting to become an independent state and some said they simply wanted to have their turn to sit on the president's chair. Well, the result was a disaster. Thousands or maybe even hundreds of thousands of Isaaqs were massacred in their homes when they tried to fight the Government a few years ago.

The Darood tribe had the last two presidents, one murdered by themselves and the other still ruling. They lived partly in the central regions and in the eastern regions and they were very political. The Majeerteen branch of the Daroods were the first to establish a rebel group, according to my father, after some of their military officers tried and failed to make a *coup d'état*. Anyhow, they got treated by the Government the same way as the Isaaq rebels.

The Hawiyas had the first president of the country. He survived his term of office and might even still be alive. The Hawiyas occupied the central and the southern regions, including the capital city. They were never interested in politics. Or at least that is what it looked like. They were mostly business people. They owned almost every business in the city. But now it seems they've changed their minds about politics, and created the USC organisation.

The fourth tribe, the Gadaburse, live somewhere near the Isaaqs and on the border with the Djibouti Republic, and as far as my knowledge goes, they have little to do with the politics of my country. Djibouti is a little country that used to be called French Somaliland, in other words it's lived in by Somalis and belonged to France before independence. The Maay people live in the south, and the other minority group live around the two rivers of Jubba and Shabeelle.

It was not only in education that tribal things were important, as a matter of fact, in that country of mine, but it was the only way to get anything done, whether something legal or illegal. To get rich, to get education, to get a job, to put someone behind bars, to free him, to kill, to harass, to rob, to loot, to rape, to be a minister, you name it, good or bad, all one needed to achieve these things, as I have said and will keep on saying, because it bothers me so deeply, was to be in with the government or have somebody who was a 'yes man' for the government. If, on the other hand, you had a man or woman in government who was not a 'yes man' that didn't help at all, in fact it was rather devastating, and that was what was wrong in my family.

My father wasn't a 'yes man'. He had joined the colonial army when he first came to the city, on the threshold of his adulthood. Becoming a soldier was a means to survive in the city, and he proved to be, according to his own account, a very hard-working and intelligent soldier. These were later to cause my father's dismissal from the Italian-controlled Somali army, and he was charged with being an anti-Italian revolutionary and was jailed. Again according to my father's account, he had been among those who were active in bringing about the country's independence under which we were now supposed to be living; the very independence whose destruction the present regime was bringing about, the independence which according to my father he and his colleagues had fought so hard for only thirty years earlier. Going back to my father's career, he rejoined the army, now the Somali National Army, after independence, this time not as a mere soldier but as an officer, and was called to a position of honour in the army. According to my father's very words, that was the only time he felt his efforts were recognised by his country. He had loved being a soldier, but to his dismay the national government didn't last, and the present regime had succeeded through a *coup d'état*. Most uniformed officers who were felt to be loyal to the deposed civilian government were imprisoned, a few were even executed, I think, and some were simply dismissed. Dad belonged to the last category, but along with a few others he was released from prison after serving three years, and forced to rejoin the army. That was when he began to hate being a soldier, and his negative attitude, along with other things which he never told me about, had caused his dismissal and imprisonment once again. This time he served four years in jail, and ever since his release five years ago he had been more or less under government surveillance.

Ahmed and Nasir, who were twelve and seven, were always considered by me and Hassan to be luckier than us, because their mothers, Anab and Falis respectively, were the most recent wives of my father, and were present in the home as they were growing up. Anab, the senior wife, belonged to our tribe, Hawiya, whereas Falis, the junior, belonged to one of the Darood sub-tribes, though not the ruling one.

My stepmothers loved their children, of course, but not us two. I am not sure why, but it is very common – at least in my country – for stepmothers to dislike their stepchildren and vice-versa. There were and are a considerable number of sayings, proverbs, songs, short stories etc. that illustrate this strained relationship between the two above-mentioned parties, all of them throwing the blame on the stepmothers. These relationship are based on hatred, and I think that jealousy and envy are at the root of everything. Anab and Falis didn't like us to get near Dad, and we then did our best to. For example, we loved to eat with Dad while the women ate in the kitchen, and to join the men and listen to Dad telling stories – he was famous as a great talker and story-teller. We were disobedient and my stepmothers used all their power to try and tame us, but we were as untameable as flies. If they hit us we would run. If they tried to starve us we would steal food or money or whatever it took to survive. The only way they could ever win was when they plotted to complain to our father – usually with a lie, but they would testify for one another and we would be found guilty of all charges. When we couldn't defend ourselves against their sophisticated lies we took refuge in running away to our mothers, friends, or other relatives living in or outside the city.

# 4

Perhaps I should mention a funny little fact about these two stepmothers of mine. These women were absolute opposites on the surface yet underneath they were unanimous in every respect. Anab was tall, fair-skinned, long-haired, slim, and very sharp-tonged. She was in her mid-forties, and was often ill. I think it must have been that last defect that made Dad marry another woman, because Anab had miscarried the last three times she was pregnant. She also belonged to our tribe, Hawiya. Falis looked the total opposite. She was a short, dark as hell, and not-so-slim creature in her late twenties. She belonged to one of the Darood sub-clans. Although she was not a big-mouth like Anab, she was more cruel and devastating in her silent, secret plots. She could also negotiate about anything. Once she told me she wouldn't tell Dad that I broke a chair if I bought some things for her from downtown. The funny thing, though, was how perfectly these two women got along. They never had any trouble as far as I knew, and I knew a lot about these two women. Hassan and I even played tricks to make them fight, and to create animosity and jealousy between them, because the truth was we were sick and tired of them always winning over us when we took our grievances to Dad's court. The bad, sad news is that we failed in all of our attempts to separate them.

A week had passed since I had that conversation with my father. Nothing important had happened, except that that night a state of emergency had been declared over the whole city, starting at midnight. Nobody could leave or come into the city, and most businesses closed down, either out of fear or from lack of customers. I hadn't been out since then. I hadn't seen Musa since, either – I understood that he would have to obey his parents, which was exactly why I too had been keeping a low profile for the last six days myself. It was about eight o'clock in the evening and I was in my room listening to a foreign radio station and waiting for the dinner to be ready.

"Mona!" I called.

"Yeah!"

"What happened to the dinner?" I said getting up from the bed I was lying on. I was not wearing much clothing so I grabbed a towel from the floor near the bed and threw it round my shoulders and went out to the daash to see what was wrong with the girl. "Or is there no dinner tonight?" I was in the daash now. I could see the pot cooking on the portable charcoal-burning stove.

"Just be patient, Ali," she said as she uncovered the pot. "A couple of minutes more."

"Beans?" I said in a complaining tone. They cooked that stuff almost every night. My father thinks beans are very nutritious. I disagree. I think they are very boring and they stink.

"Yes, beans," she said twisting her mouth to imitate me.

"Get lost." I smiled and went back to my room.

The English transmission ended and a strange language started so I turned the radio off. I tried the local radio and it was worse. They were playing songs in praise of the President as usual. Liars! I thought and turned it off. I opened the outside door of my room and sat on the steps to entertain myself. I usually sat there when I had a date. By the way, a room like mine is called *irid-banaan* which means 'a room with an outside door'. It is convenient to have the boys live there so that they don't bother the family with their countless friends and lovers. Nobody notices what you are doing because you have your own door to come in or go out of. I sat on the steps and lit a cigarette. It was very dark, because the small sandy street in front of my home, had no public lights that night. Families had lights on top of their front doors or gates but that night most of them were off for some reason. Our house's front gate light was off too but that was because Dad always worried about the bills. There were people passing by every now and then, usually young lovers going to and from the main street for transportation; it was the street to which I would take my girlfriends to see them off as they took the buses to their homes.

"Ali!" Mona called from the house. "Dinner is ready! "

"Put it in my room!" I yelled back.

I blew the last puff of the cigarette into the dark, cool air and looked over at Musa's home to the left. The most beautiful house in the neighbourhood, two-storey, modern and white, with plenty of rooms and a big garden, even though there were not many people living there. But it didn't look as lively and as lit up as it usually did. In fact it looked very quiet and dark. Their front door light was not even lit, though they never worried about electricity bills like us. I wondered if Musa had been obliged to go to sleep already. Almost every evening we used to sit on my front steps and talk until late in the night. He usually used my room if he had a date. I would have rung their door bell if things had been normal. But…

I wondered where my father could be. I was sure he knew what he was doing but I would have felt easier if he had been home by now. I don't know how long I was sitting there when I sensed I had company.

"What's wrong with you?" asked my company.

"Hi," I said looking up at the girl standing beside me to see who she was. "Hey, Asha!" I said in recognition. "How long have you been here?"

"Just for a moment," she said and sat beside me. "I just spoke to you and you were away in your own thoughts." She held my arm tight. "Are you OK, lover boy?"

"Yes, yes."

"Are you sure?"

"Oh, yes," I shrugged. "What about you? Is everything OK with you?"

"Not bad." She pushed me away from her to get a better look at my face. "Are you sure you're all right?"

Asha was Musa's girlfriend and a good friend of mine. She was living a couple of blocks away. Her brother, Ali-yare, was also a good friend of mine. He was my brother Hassan's classmate and best friend, and I used to visit them sometimes.

"You were at Musa's?"

"Yeah," she shrugged.

"By the way, where is that guy? I mean I haven't seen him these days? Is anything wrong?"

"I was about to ask you the same question." She turned away. "I thought you might know something about his travels." For the first time I sensed that she was feeling upset.

"Wait a minute!" I turned her face towards me and looked into her eyes. "Did you just say the guy was travelling?"

She nodded.

"I don't understand! He didn't mention anything to me!" I was still looking at her. "How come?"

"He and his family travelled to Bay."

"I see," I relaxed because there was nothing unusual about that. He occasionally went to Bay to see his father and his other brothers.

"You scared me!" I started. " I thought he'd gone for good. I mean for a long time. To Europe or somewhere, you know?"

"He's not coming back, Ali," she gulped.

"What is that supposed to mean?"

"You don't understand." She was crying. "He and his family have moved to Bay. They…"

"Moved?" I sat back. "What do you mean by moved?"

"His father is wanted by something called the USC and they're afraid…"

I didn't listen to the rest. My heart sank. Maybe the damn civil war had started, I shuddered.

"The USC?" I repeated in an questioning tone.

"Yes," she answered.

"But why?"

"He's accused of killing civilians living in the Bay region. Mostly Hawiyas. The USC is murdering everyone who's accused of malpractice."

"How do you know?"

"Last night the USC killed three government officials at their homes in Boli-Qaran."

Boli-Qaran was right here in the Medina quarter. It was a rich neighbourhood, for high government officials. The name 'Boli-Qaran' was not allowed to be spoken publicly because it meant 'the funds looted from the people', and succinctly explained how somebody whose official monthly salary was not more than a couple of thousand could afford to live in a multi-million dollar house like those in Boli-Qaran.

"General Qasim was killed too, for his part in last week's Wardigley massacre," she continued.

"I heard that."

Silence. A very long one.

"Does your family have any plans?" She broke the silence.

"Plans?"

"I mean the country is not so safe any more, and I'm sure your father knows that more than anybody else."

"We don't have any plans," I said sadly. What else could I tell her? That my family had decided to stay and fight?

"What about your family?" I asked.

"We're leaving the country," she declared.

Before we said anything else a small Japanese-made car braked right in front of us, very fast. I couldn't see much dust for the car's engine was turned off as soon as it braked, but I could smell the dust. Six men jumped out just like in the movies. The driver stood by the car door which was open, while three of them stood at a distance of three yards from my face, like statues. The two approached us, one speaking very fast and commandingly.

"This is Mr. Farah's house, I assume?" said the man.

"That's right, sir," I replied slowly.

"Where is he?" said another. "Is he sleeping?"

"No, he's not." I stood up to see his face. He had a big moustache like a policeman. "Who are you?"

"We're friends," said the first man. "Are you his children?"

"Yes…No…I mean.."

"I recall that Mr. Farah had no daughters. Am I right?"

"That's right, sir."

Asha stood up, too.

"I'll see you later," she excused herself, probably feeling what I was feeling. Fear.

"Yeah. See you."

The first man, who also had a big moustache, watched the girl leave.

34

"Girlfriend?" he asked.

"Yes, but I'm his son."

"We know that," he said and smiled. "Ali or Hassan?"

"Hassan." I could tell the men knew my father very well but I was not so sure they were friends. Anyway there was nothing I could do – as if the stupid little lie I told about my name could be of any help!

"Are you sure you're not lying to us? I mean it is important we see your father." He was still smiling.

"Why should I?"

"Anyway, we'll see him later."

"If you want to leave any messages…"

"There's no need," said the second man. "I am sure we'll see him later." He waved to the three statues to indicate that their mission was over and it was time to go.

"Good night, Hassan," he said and went back to the car. The six of them rode off as fast as they had come. I could still see their red tail lights through the dust as they disappeared into the darkness. I looked around to see if anybody was there. Nobody. I sat down again and tried to figure them out. Could they be the police? I wondered. Or friends perhaps? Whatever they wanted, it was very important. I could see it in their sharp faces and eager eyes. Whatever it was they were doing, the khat they were chewing would keep them awake and lively, so that they could stay active all night long. For sure it was political. But the question was which side did they belong to? I wanted to see my father at once. There were many unanswered questions I wanted him to answer for me. I looked both ways along our little street every now and then hoping that he would show up. Nothing. No sign at all. I was startled by the muezzin in a nearby mosque. God! I said that must be the morning prayers. About four o'clock already? I stood up and went back to my room. I put a pair of jeans and a T-shirt on. I don't know why. I just felt that I should be ready for something. I tried to turn the radio on in case they said anything about anything. Nothing. The transmission had signed off. I opened the inside door to see if anybody else was awake. Nobody was in the daash and all the lights off. I closed the inside door and tried some other international radio wavelengths. I found the Voice of America. "President George Bush is expected to travel to Europe... ...Arafat is expected to fly to Cairo to meet the Egyptian President... ..."

I came back to my place and sat again on my doorstep. Everybody was travelling. Asha, Musa, Bush, and even Arafat. I was not particularly interested in food, so I drank the glass of milk which Mona had put there for me.

I couldn't wait to talk to my father about how he could get us out of this country. I couldn't wait for my father, to talk to him about many things. Yes, so many things that I'd never really wanted to talk about with him before.

## 5

I was awakened by a strange noise. I opened my eyes and tried to concentrate on the noise. It seemed like I had slept only a couple of hours, and I couldn't adjust to where I was at that moment. And then I realized that somebody was banging on my door. I lifted my head slightly and I had a terrible headache like a strong hangover. The noise persisted.

"Ali!" Somebody was shouting. "Ali, open the door! Open the door!" It was my stepmother, Anab. "Open the door!" I couldn't hear what else she was saying because there were other voices joining in. All of them very close. I thought she mentioned my father but I was not sure.

"Open the door for God's sake!" she went on.

I jumped out of the bed, stumbled over a chair and reached the door after what seemed an hour. I flung it open. My two stepmothers, and Mona and my two little brothers were there, all of them in a state of consternation. My brother Nasir was not weeping or screaming like the rest, but stood frozen and silent in a corner by himself. Mona was weeping quietly and

leaning on a wall for support. My stepmother, Falis, was jump-
ing up and down like somebody who has just received the news
of a child being stabbed. Anab was at my door screaming like
a wild animal in a fight. My other little brother, Ahmed, was
crying and clinging to the hem of his mother's dress.

Anab grabbed me by the T-shirt as soon as I appeared.

"Your father's been murdered!" she cried. "Oh my God!
They killed him last night!" Ahmed came nearer and clung to
my jeans. "They killed him last night!" she repeated.

"Shut up!" I shouted, because they were scaring me too.
Nothing changed.

"I said shut up!" I repeated.

Suddenly everybody was quiet.

"I don't want anybody screaming in this house! You hear
me?"

They said nothing and they did nothing, but their watery
eyes said it all.

"I want somebody to tell me, very quietly, what is going on,"
I instructed, rubbing my eyes with my hands, trying to adjust
to the sudden light. My head felt heavy.

"Your father is dead!" my two stepmothers shouted it together.

"I said quietly!"

They were all quiet again.

"Now," I said bending down to my two little brothers
who were both clinging to my jeans now. I dried their tears
with my hands. "Who brought that news and how dependable
is it?"

"One of the two men who were here last night came back
and said that your father is believed to be dead. He...." Anab
tried to continue the story.

"What makes him think he is dead?"

"He said that government troops shelled a home in which
the C.U.C was having a secret meeting! They killed seventy
Hawiyas!"

"You mean the USC?"

"I don't know what it's called and I don't care!" She wept.
"All I know is that Farah didn't come home last night!"

37

"Shut up!" I shook her by the shoulders. "My father's not dead! I know he's not dead!"

They all stared at me hoping that I was right.

"Dad is alive," I declared as though I knew his whereabouts.

"Did he tell you something?" asked Falis. "I know he was talking to you a lot lately."

"Yes," I lied. "So let's please act like grown-ups and respect the children around us."

"*Alhamd 'lillah!*" Anab thanked God. "Where is he? Why didn't he tell us what was going on?"

"It's secret!" I sounded like my father for the first time. "You are not supposed to know!"

"Please," pleaded everybody. "Where is he?"

"He is not in the country," I made it up.

"*Alhamd lillah*!" Everybody cheered again.

"He went abroad?" asked Ahmed.

"Yes," I assured him. He was still clinging to my jeans. "Now," I told Anab. "Give me the keys."

"Which keys?"

"The car keys."

"Can you drive?"

"For God's sake give me the silly keys!"

"I'm sorry," she apologized as she went to her room. "I was only concerned about your safety."

Since when did these women develop such passion? I wondered. If the truth were to be admitted, a deep dark place in me took some pleasure in that otherwise sad scene. I never dreamt such a day would come in my lifetime. It was beyond my imagination to see my stepmothers pleading with, begging, and obeying me. Life, my grandfather used to say, is just a series of odd experiences. Each new day brings its odd happenings, he used to say. I could see already the responsibility ahead of me, and I accepted it 'like a man' as my father would have put it.

Neither of my two stepmothers wanted me to touch the car – that I knew – let alone drive it. Dad had once suggested that I get a driving licence but Anab had convinced him to get one for her instead. She wanted to take over everything as though

I didn't exist. Falis was no better. She used to try and influence Dad into not letting me see my mother. Even though she had never seen my mother in her life she said she was an evil woman. If there were a law that a father could divorce his son like he could his wife, these stepmothers would have made sure my father divorced me. Wow, what a turn around! I thought. These two women now in front of me seeking refuge in me. I am their only hope of getting things done in this 'man's world' in which we live. To tell the truth, though, as one part of me enjoyed the new authority another was scared as hell.

"He can drive," declared Mona, who had seen me a thousand times stealing the car. She'd never mentioned it to anyone. It was one of our little secrets. In return for this I always took her to wherever she wanted to go. She loved to sit beside me and say 'hello' to her various boyfriends and girl-friends. I would take her to this house and she'd say hello to a guy and I'd take her to that house and she'd chat with a girl for a while.

"Here they are," Anab said as she handed me the car keys. Somehow I was feeling heavy-hearted.

"Where are you going?" Falis asked.

"I'm not sure. I'll try to find out something about the USC and their bloody campaign." I went back to my room.

"Be careful," said Anab.

I sat on my bed. I noticed my feet were trembling. I stood up and closed the door then came back to where I was sitting and started crying. I tried not to make any sound for that was not what a man was supposed to do. Crying was a woman's thing not a man's. I hated whoever made that rule, and cried as silently as possible. God! I prayed. Save my father's life. We just can't afford him dead now, in the middle of all this.

"Do you want breakfast?" somebody asked, I wasn't sure who.

"No!" I yelled and stood up again. Weeping is not going to do anything, I thought. I must accept the responsibility. I grabbed my diary and wrote the date. Friday, December 28, 1990, about 10:00 am.

# 6

It was only as hot as any other day but I was sweltering in the green Volkswagen. I was heading downtown but with little hope of finding whatever it was I was looking for, since I didn't exactly know where I was going. I was hoping that I might somehow come across something useful. A miracle or something, you know. I turned left in the direction of KM4, a major crossroads four kilometres from the city -- hence its name. I noticed that buses were only half full, not overcrowded as was usual. If only I knew some of my father's friends! I wished. Then I could easily have found out everything. Why had the government killed the seventy men? Did it mean the civil war had started? And most important of all, was my father one of the victims? I remembered how on countless occasions Dad had wanted me to meet some of his friends: politicians, businessmen, educators, everybody. God! I banged the steering wheel. If I had only listened to my father!

I turned right at the Benadir Hospital, passed the Equatore Cinema and kept straight on. Some youngsters were sitting in front of the teashops along the stree. Not many people though. There were usually dozens of young men in front of every teashop. They would be playing dominos, chess, cards or talking about politics. Just to reduce their frustrations.

The younger people were divided into two groups; one sat around teashops and talked about the political situation of the country, the other was interested in music, sports, dating and that kind of stuff, and knew little or nothing of their country's political, economical, and social situation. I belonged to the latter. There was no place for either of them in their own country. No jobs, no colleges, no newspapers, no radios, no TV, no nothing.

As I waited for the Shaqalaha traffic lights at the Workers Union building to turn green, I remembered a friend whose house was nearby, so I turned left at the light, down through the Hodan quarter and towards the middle-class neighbourhood of Casa Popolare. This friend of mine, Abdulkadir, was nicknamed 'Sette', from the Italian word for seven, because this was the position he played when it came to football. Abdulkadir and I, even though we had lost contact lately, had been very close friends during our school years. He became a member of the Ikhwan Muslim Brotherhood Movement after high school so now our lifestyles were very different. Unlike most of the religious men of his age, he was a very interesting and entertaining guy, open to ideas regardless of whether they were religious or not. I considered he was much more intelligent and mature than I was even though he was only a couple of years older. The only thing I didn't like about him was that he was always preaching at me to become religious like he was. Anyhow, along with religion he was particularly interested in politics and, I told myself, he was sure to know something if not all of what was going on in this country. I noticed that the Case Popolare traffic lights were red after I'd already passed them. I could see the young traffic policeman writing my registration number. To hell with your numbers! I shouted aloud and changed to another gear as I sped past the African Village buildings on my left.

African Village was an arrangement of about fifty small three-storey blocks of flats all looking alike. They had been built in the seventies when the Organization of African Unity was to hold a meeting in our capital city, and they were to house the visiting delegates and guests. The meeting was of course only a couple of weeks long, but afterwards the flats were given out to certain people – those who had a foot in government. Some of the recipients were too rich or felt themselves too big to live there, so they rented or sold them to others who needed them.

In a couple of minutes I was parked in front of Abdulkadir's home which was on the left just four or five blocks beyond African Village, a big ordinary house of many rooms. Three of the rooms were facing the street and were rented out for business; one was a photographic shop and two were bibitos – little kiosks selling soft drinks and cigarettes – one of which belonged to Abdulkadir's family. Round the corner was the house entrance. I locked the car and knocked on the gate, remembering the last time I had knocked on that very same gate. Quite a long time ago – I think about four or five months. The occasion was a very important *sharad* game, and we had come to beg him to play for us since he had stopped playing football when he became religious. He had been a very good striker and used to wear football T-shirts with the number seven on. I knocked again to make sure I had been heard, because the house was big and it had a big daash. Abdulkadir's father opened the gate.

"*Aslam aleikum*." The old man greeted me in the Islamic way. The old man was very religious, not an Ikhwan like his son, but a traditionalist. He thought the Ikhwan were exaggerating the whole thing.

"*Aleikum aslam*, Uncle Nur," I returned the greeting, shaking hands with him.

"A long time, my son," he said, looking at the car in front of his house. "I didn't know you had a car!"

"It's my father's." I smiled.

"Well," he sighed. "Come on in, my son." He stepped aside. "Come on in."

"Is Abdulkadir home?" I was inside now.

"Yes, yes," he pointed to Abdulkadir's room. "He's probably in his room."

"I'm on my way to the mosque," he declared stepping outside. "I expect I shall see you there with Abdulkadir?"

"Sure," I lied. "Sure."


# 7


I knew Abdulkadir's room so I wasted no time. I knocked on the door, which was ajar.

"Yes?" came his voice from inside.

I entered the room. The same old Abdulkadir was standing there. He was as short, thin and coal black as ever.

He was standing in the middle of the room holding a bottle of eau de cologne. He was wearing a white maawiis and a white shirt. The kind of stuff he wore when he was going to the mosque.

"Hey!" he said as soon as he saw me. "Look who's here!" He pointed towards me with the bottle he was holding. "What a pleasant surprise!" He put the bottle on a table and came towards me.

"Hi," I said. We shook hands.

"Have a seat."

"Thanks." I sat on the edge of his bed.

"Tea?"

"No, thanks."

He sat down beside me.

"Is everything all right?" he asked putting his arm around me.

"Yeah," I sighed.

He took a closer look at my face.

"What is it?" he asked looking me in the eyes. I couldn't contain myself any more. I had to tell someone.

"My father is..." I started but he interrupted me. I was glad he did that because I couldn't quite complete the sentence anyway. It was too painful for me to say that my father was dead.

"W...what about your father?" He made a face. "He's all right isn't he?"

"No," I admitted. "No, he's not."

"What's happened?"

"He's missing!" That sounded much better to me. "Yes, he's missing!" I repeated. I could already feel a little hope inside me.

"For how long?"

"Since last night." I looked at him. "You know about this seventy-men massacre...I mean...Dad is...I don't know, I'm not sure, but some people think he was one of them."

He didn't say anything. He stared at me instead. I felt lost. He was my hope of finding out as much information as possible about the men massacred. Obviously he didn't know anything about it.

"The government killed seventy men last night," I tried again.

"And you think your father is one of them?"

"Yes," I said at once.

"That's impossible!" he said standing up very very slowly. He placed his hands on his head, closed his eyes and looked at the ceiling. He squeezed his little head so tightly as though he wanted to bring his big eyes out of their sockets. He was acting like somebody forced to remember the day he was being born.

"That's impossible!" he repeated. "I don't believe it!" He looked at me. "I read it with my own two eyes!"

I didn't know what the guy was talking about.

"I'll be right back!" he said and rushed out of the room.

"Dad!" he called.

"He went to the mosque!" I yelled.

"Mum!" he called instead. "Where are…"

I tried to imagine what the guy was up to. He was obviously looking for something precious but the question was what? I had a strong feeling it was connected with my father. I hoped for the best and waited impatiently.

"Here!" he said as he came rushing again. This time with a pile of papers. He was reading and looking at me at the same time. "His name isn't here, man!" He laughed.

"What is this?" I asked. His sentence echoed in my brain.

"It's the list!" He threw the papers on my lap. "Read it yourself!"

I grabbed the papers without even understanding what list he was talking about. It was a bunch of typed papers.

"What list?" I asked even though I was already reading the list of names in front of me.

"It's the list of the names of the seventy-two shaheeds who were murdered last night!"

I don't remember what he said after that. I was already in the middle of the list. Mohamed Ibrahim Abdi…Sheikh Suleiman Sugulleh…Sheikh Abdi Nur Abdulle… I read the whole list again and again until I made sure my father's name was not there.

"Oh! Sette, thank you very much!" I stood up with happiness and hugged him. "Where did you get this from?"

"You see, I knew he wasn't there!" He was breathing as hard as I was. "You scared me, brother."

I finished reading the goddam list of the shaheeds. The term *shaheed* is a religious one. It means some one who died during a battle on active duty and usually, anyone who died during a jihad war. This term was used only by the very religious. For the mass of people you were a dead man whether you died in a jihad or in a plane crash or in your bed.

"Where did you get this from?" I repeated.

"I have my sources," he smiled cockily as he reached for the bottle he had put on the table. He sprayed some cologne on his shirt. "You want some?"

"No, thanks."

"Let's go and thank God," he said tapping my shoulder.

I looked at him in response. I knew that he meant we were going to the mosque. He had tried that before and only rarely had he succeeded. But he was the only one who could ever convince me to go to the mosque, because I enjoyed his company.

"Come on," he begged. "God deserves to be thanked at least."

"OK," I gave in. Besides God did deserve to be thanked for this, I thought.

"We should hurry," he said placing his white emma on his right shoulder. Emma is a piece of cloth, part of the dress the religious people wear to their religious meetings. "There's a big speech at the mosque today."

"You always say that," I said dismissively.

"No...no. This time there really is!" he said. "Let's go and you will see."

"Let's go, then."

# 8

Sheikh Ali-Sufi Mosque was just beside African Village so it took us no time at all to get there. It was one of the biggest mosques in the city. When I say BIG I am talking about its adherents, for there were other mosques that were twice as big physically, but which had only half the crowd. People came from all over the city to say Friday Prayers here, though not during the rest of the week. Anyway this particular Friday the mosque was as crowded as hell. We parked the car where we could, somewhere between African Village and the Mosque, because there were cars parked all over the place. Hundreds of people were sitting outside the mosque since it was already full inside. "Let's go inside," said my friend. "It's more blessed to be in the front line."

"But we…"

"You just follow me," he cut me short. He took off his shoes and held them in his hand, and I did the same and followed him. We walked through the crowd and headed for the entrance. It was less than a couple of hundred metres away but it seemed far when one had to manoeuvre through such a crowd, and barefoot on the hot paving slabs. There were no carpets outside the mosque, and everyone brought his own prayer mat. My friend excused himself, smiled or said something to everyone he pushed or stumbled over. I did the same and followed in his steps. After what seemed like an hour we were at the entrance, and when we stepped inside the first thing I noticed was the coolness and the cleanness of the floor under my feet. The second was the smell of the different perfumes mixed with sweat.

"This is near enough!" I whispered to my friend. It is not allowed to speak loudly in a mosque especially when the Koran is being read. He ignored me and kept walking. I continued to follow him.

"Here," he said at last pointing to a less crowded section somewhere in the fifth or sixth line. I was glad to sit at last.

Abdulkadir reached for a Koran nearby and started reading. I sat quietly and watched the people. All of them was sitting facing a Sheikh who was seated in front of the people reading the Koran loudly into a microphone. Most of them were listening but some were reading, some praying and others just sitting like me. But I was the only one watching the people, I suppose.

"*Aslam aleikum*," an old man who was sitting on my left greeted me.

"*Aleikum aslam*," I gave the reply.

"Who is the Imam today?"

I looked at him blankly.

"Is it Sheikh Abbas or…"

"I really don't know," I answered and smiled politely.

He smiled too and turned to another old man on his left. The Sheikh at the microphone stopped reading, and almost everybody stood up and started reciting the prayers. I prayed too. I don't know what the rest of the crowd were wishing in their prayers but I was begging God to stop whatever was happening or about to happen in this country of mine. As I was about to finish praying the microphone crackled and somebody started talking.

"*Aslam aleikum warahmat Allah wabrakatuh*," started the Imam, a tiny guy with the longest beard you'd ever seen. He was wearing a khamiis, a long white shirt-like robe, one of those things we'd inherited from the Arabs during Islamization I suppose. He was also wearing a small round, white hand-embroidered hat which only covered the very top of his tiny head. I couldn't see the details of his facial expressions, partly because of the distance and partly because of his great beard, but I could see his shining blinking eyes every now and then and the movements of his mouth as he spoke. He had a deep strong voice despite his appearances.

"I greet all Muslims here and everywhere." He cleared his throat. "Today, I am not going to talk for very long. As you might already know or will soon know…" he cleared his throat again, "I am forbidden to talk in this mosque." I could see the outline of his naked lower legs through the semi-transparent khamiis robe. "I'm not allowed to talk in the mosque. But I will do so, so long as I am not dead. The country is in a very serious state. Seventy-two innocent men were killed in cold blood last night because they had expressed their views on the military activities of this regime!" He looked around and raised his voice. "They were people of God, who were against this Government which is destroying our country! Politically, economically, socially, mentally and most of all religiously! They are going to get rid of each and every one of us who tries to fight for basic rights! These seventy-two *shaheeds* were some of our best in religion and politics!" He glanced outside the mosque through the open window then continued. "We cannot save their lives of course, but we can save their beliefs, and in consequence our lives. They are not dead if we continue their struggle. Let us continue the struggle! If we..."

Trrcckk!!! Trrrckk!!! Trrrckk!! Gunshots were heard nearby. Very close. It sounded as though it was inside the mosque.

Trrcck! Trrcckk! Everybody stood up to see what was going on. People started screaming. The shots got louder and louder. Some people started running out of the mosque. I started to push my way out like everybody else but it was not easy. Lots of people wanted to get out. Trrrck! Trrcck! Soldiers appeared in the mosque. More people screamed. It was hard to say who was screaming and who wasn't. I think I was one of those screaming. Men dressed in military uniform appeared everywhere in the mosque. Some were beating the people with their gun butts, some were firing their guns. Now I realized they were not the ordinary military, they were what we called the Red Berets, the specially recruited and trained private bodyguards of the regime. I was out now. I ran. Everybody was screaming. Most people were bleeding. Some lay on the hot ground, screaming and bleeding.

And then *"Allah akbar! Allah akbar!"* the crowd started. *"Allah akbar! Allah akbar!* God is Great!" Everybody was rallying to the religious call. People started to defend themselves. Some even wrestled the guns from the Red Berets. We suddenly grew fearless and bold.

There were Red Berets on the ground too, bleeding and

screaming in their turn. Everybody, including me, was chanting the slogan now. The Red Berets started to jump into their
jeeps and drive away as fast as possible. If a Red Beret stumbled
or fell the crowd beat him unconscious or even to death. After
what seemed like a couple of hours the gunfire stopped and the
Red Berets had disappeared. Some people, recounting the
events later, said the incident took place in just ten or so minutes. To this day I can't believe that. Anyway, the mob was still
mad. Some were screaming with fear, some weeping with agony, some shouting with horror. I didn't know which group I
belonged to, and then someone pushed me heavily and
knocked me off the road. "Help me put the wounded man in
the car or stay out of my way!" he shouted at me. He was a
strongly built middle-aged man with a big beard. I remembered
seeing him sitting in the front row when we were in the
mosque. Bunches of women were crying in the street. Children
running up and down. All of them screaming. Ambulances
came later and the wounded were put there. I came to my
senses about five o'clock on that bloody afternoon. I looked
around. I didn't know what I was looking for. My body and
my brain were both numb. After chasing up and down for a
while, I remembered what I was trying to do. My car. I had to
get my car. I ran to where I had parked it several hours before.
It was there. The front right wheel was flat. I opened the boot.
There was no extra wheel. I started pushing and steering the
car away. Some young guys helped me and in a moment the car
was on the street. The guys said that they couldn't help more
than that. I had to keep on pushing. I turned right in the
direction of Digfer Hospital and kept pushing on and on. I
realized the whole neighbourhood was on the alert. All the
way, women, children, and men were standing in front of their
homes with questioning and terrified eyes.

"What happened?" an old woman asked me.

"I don't know," I mumbled and kept pushing my car.

"There's blood all over his shirt!" said a child beside her. The
woman glanced at my shirt and stepped back in fear. The child
clung to the woman's skirt.

# 9

I was taking a shower when I heard my youngest brother screaming.

"Ali's been shot! Ali's been shot!" he cried.

I didn't say anything for I was too tired to yell from the shower. I tried to enjoy the running water instead.

"What?" asked his mother who was probably in her room.

"Ali's been shot!" he repeated. "Come and see his clothes!"

"I'm not shot!" I yelled this time. "Get out of my room, will you?"

"What's going on?" asked the woman again. I could feel she was going to see what the child was talking about.

"Nobody enters my room!" I insisted.

Silence.

In a couple of minutes I was out of the shower wearing a towel round my loins. Everybody was there waiting for some explanation. None of them spoke as they watched me go inside my room, dripping wet. I purposely hadn't dried myself so I could feel the coolness of the air – like Dad did when he had had a long day. I threw the towel on Hassan's bed and was standing in the middle of the room when I sensed that I was being watched. I turned around. The whole family was pushing each other trying to get a look into my room.

"What are you staring at?" I asked.

"Did you have an accident?" asked Falis pointing to my bloody clothes on the floor.

"No," I said slowly.

"Then where's the car?" asked Anab.

"It's in a garage. A front wheel is totally flat and Dad didn't have a spare one."

She was in my room now. "What happened then?"

"The Red Berets attacked us in the mosque."

"Attacked? Red Berets?" Falis asked sharply. "Where...I mean which mosque?"

"Sheikh Ali Sufi's."

"Oh my God!" everybody said. "Was anybody killed?" asked Falis then corrected herself as she remembered the bloody clothes on my floor. "I mean...how many people?"

"I don't know...I think many people got killed."

"But why?"

"I don't know why! OK?" I eyed everybody. "Now everybody leave me alone – OK?" I dismissed them and closed my door.

I lay on my bed flat on my back. I reached out for the radio and played some music. The picture of the incident appeared in my brain. It was the first chance I had had to recall what happened. The Imam speaking...the Red Berets shooting...the crowd screaming...everything. I tried to remember how I'd got blood on my shirt but I failed. I suddenly remembered my friend Abdulkadir. I wondered if he was alive. I stood up and got the cigarettes from my jeans pocket and lit one and tried to hope for the best. I wondered if *that* was the beginning of the civil war Dad had talked about. I opened the outside door and looked around for anything unusual. Everything looked normal, although some people were standing on their doorsteps talking. They had probably heard the news, I told myself and closed the door again. I sat on the bed and fiddled with the radio dial. This time I was looking for something that indicated whether the country was in danger or not. It was time for the eight o'clock news.

"The news headlines." said the newsreader. "The President has sent greetings to world leaders on the occasion of the New Year, and the President has received goodwill messages from many world leaders in return. In his speech to the nation, the President has promised that the country will reach the peak of her development by the year 2000. Two new schools have been built in the Hawlwadag quarter of...."

I threw the cigarette I had been smoking on the floor beside the bed and squeezed it slowly with my right foot, then stretched out on the bed. I looked up at the dirty ceiling for a while and wondered why the radio hadn't mentioned the bloody clash. Our national radio belonged to the regime, I told myself, echoing my father's oft repeated comment. 'They never tell the truth,' he would say. 'They don't even bother to lie about things. They just ignore the things they don't like as though nothing has happened.' I wondered if Dad was right. Maybe we should fight for our rights after all, I thought. But that means a civil war! No, no. I'm not going to take part in a civil war. Not just because I'm afraid of it, but also because I am against it. The news ended without mentioning the incident. A popular song followed. "Long live Siyad! Long live Siyad!" the song went on. "Our beloved one! Our blessed one!" I turned the radio off and smiled. I wondered if these singers meant what they were saying. I knew the man who wrote the lyrics did mean what he wrote because he himself was the President's cousin. A well-known general and lyricist. People used to say he bought all the stuff he claimed to have written. The poems, the praise songs, the love songs, and everything. A knock on the inside door interrupted my thoughts.

"Come in," I said without sitting up. Mona peeped in.

"Are you not having supper tonight?" she asked. "It's ten o'clock."

"Ten?" I repeated. This time I sat up from the bed.

"Yes, it's a quarter to ten." She smiled. "Should I bring it here?"

"No, thanks." I lay down again. "I have no appetite."

The girl shrugged and left the door ajar like it was before. I wished my friend Musa was with me. Together we could figure out everything. Or at least if we had a telephone in our home, I could have called up my friends. I was sure I would have found out everything. But I already found out something today, didn't I? I remembered. Yes. I found out that Dad was not among the seventy-two men. I got out of bed, then out of the door to park myself in the daash. None of my family ever sat in the daash at that hour. But tonight was different. They were all there – from my youngest brother to my eldest stepmother. They had placed a mattress in the daash somewhere between my room and the living room. I could see all of them clearly, even though most of the lights were off, because there was a full moon. Anab, Mona, and my two brothers were sitting on the mattress and Falis was sitting on the sand. My youngest brother was helping her bury her feet for fun. They all looked all right. Not sad at least. I felt happy for those innocent people who knew nothing about the country's political situation. Only a couple of days earlier I had been just like them. My grandfather must have been right about his description of life, I told myself.

"So," I started, feeling the cool sand under my thighs as I sat down to join them. "What's going on here?"

"Aunt Anab was telling us a story!" declared Nasir as he stood up. He sat down beside me.

"What story did she tell you?"

"The crocodile and the fox!" he said. "Do you know it?"

"Oh, yeah," I answered pulling him towards me. "Long time ago. When I was about your age."

"Will you tell us another story?" he asked rubbing his tiny head against my shirt. "Aunt Anab said you know many stories."

"That's right."

"Will you tell us one?"

"Get my cigarettes first."

"Right away," he said and ran into the room. In a moment he got my cigarettes and sat back in his place. I looked at him teasingly.

"Please," he begged. "You promised."

"No, I didn't."

He looked at me in great disappointment.

"But I'll tell you one anyway."

"Yeah!" Both of them cried.

"But…" I raised my hand.

"But we should be able to answer your questions about the story."

"That's right, Ahmed."

"Are you ready?" I asked.

"Yes," said Nasir holding my hand.

"Once upon a time there…" I started.

"Wait! Wait!" interrupted Ahmed running to sit near me. He sat at my feet.

"Now I'm ready."

"Once upon a time there w…"

"What's the story called first?" asked Ahmed.

"The stupid hyena."

"OK," he said now that he had made sure he hadn't heard it before.

"Once upon a time there was an old hyena. She was famous in the jungle for her age and wisdom. She loved children but sadly she didn't have any…."

"Why not?" asked Ahmed.

"Because her husband died and she refused to marry again."

He was satisfied.

"She wished to have children so she could teach them all the things she knew. One day, however, she got pregnant and she had her first child. He was a boy. She loved him and they had a perfect relationship. But things changed as the boy grew up. He didn't want to learn from his sophisticated mother. He didn't understand how important it was to learn from his mother. She was so sad when she saw the mistakes her son was making. But then one day she died. Anyway, the young hyena found himself all alone when his mother died. He also found himself hungry for he had always depended on his mother's hunting. He never wanted to hunt for himself nor even go with his mother when she went hunting, because he was so lazy. Anyway, the day came when he had to hunt for himself for he couldn't stay hungry forever. But the trouble was he didn't know how."

I noticed Anab chuckling.

"What's the matter?" I asked smiling and looking around to see what was funny. I saw nothing.

"What is it?"

She pointed at the children. I looked at them and realised they were sleeping.

"Take them inside," I said and stood up. "And good night."

"Good night."

"By the way," I remembered. "I saw the list of the USC men who were killed. Dad's not one of them. I knew it anyway, but I was only making sure."

"The list!" She jumped to her feet. "Where did you see it?"

"I have my sources," I answered.

"We can talk about it tomorrow," I smiled again. "Good night."

I went back to my room and lay down on the bed again. I was feeling very restless but I was not as worried as before. I remembered it was time to listen to the Voice of America, and turned the radio on as usual. I loved listening to the radio. I usually listened to either the BBC or the VOA since they were the only English transmissions I could receive. The Voice Of America, however, was my favourite because I was more familiar with American English than British English. The only thing I didn't like about the VOA was that it hardly mentioned the Mother Continent, Africa, unless it was Nigeria or South Africa. I don't know why. The BBC on the other hand talked about African affairs continuously in comparison.

"....and that is it for the hour," said the news woman. Anyone could tell she was enjoying her work. "News is next but if you've got to go this is Teresa Coleman and Michael Hess wishing you a very good Holiday Season and a Happy New Year."

Happy New Year? I remembered. God that's right! I felt alive once again as I remembered that in only a couple of days' time it would be the new year of 1991. "Nobody is going to stop me from having a good time," I told myself, "Yes! No one is going to ruin my celebration. I and my girlfriend are going to the Hotel Al-Uruba discothèque, and dance and eat all night long. We'll be there when the lights are turned off in the last minute of the old year. Yes. Everybody will count the last thirty seconds of the hour and I will be counting it with them in my loudest voice until the lights are turned on again to welcome the new year. It's going to be a new year and I will be having a new life. Yes! A better one!"

# 10

The small bus was not crowded. There were only six passengers on board, two men, two women, a young girl in her teens, and me. The two men were sitting in the back seat. One was old and wearing a maawiis and a blue and white striped shirt. I could tell he was from the countryside by the stick he was carrying and his dirty sandals. The other, short and in his early forties, was wearing an ugly pair of sunglasses, slacks and a casual shirt. The women and the girl were sitting together in the seat just in front of the two men. The other woman, who looked lost in her thoughts, was sitting alone in the front row. I sat behind her by the window. It seemed they had been talking earlier.

"Are you sure the incident took place inside the mosque?" asked the woman with the girl. "I thought it was only outside."

"I'm telling you, I was there!" snapped the younger man in the back seat. "The Red Berets came inside the mosque and fired their guns."

"*Inna Lillah!*" exclaimed the old man raising both his hands. "In a mosque!" His stick hit the ceiling. "It's obvious they know nothing about a mosque. It's supposed to be the House of God. And God's house should be safe." He shook his head in disbelief. "*Inna Lillah!*"

"How many people were killed?" asked the woman.

"The unofficial figure is sixty-eight."

"And what is the official?"

The woman in front of me gave a crooked smile as she turned around.

"The official figure?" she asked in a sarcastic way. "Where are we to get an official figure? Wake up brothers!"

"You're right," agreed the younger man. "We aren't told anything about what's going on in our own country."

"I bet some of you didn't even hear that this very morning forty politicians and religious leaders are being sentenced to death by the High Court?"

Silence. The driver even turned round to see who had said that. The younger man frowned. The old one turned away in hopelessness.

"Today?" I asked.

"Yes, now." She was still wearing that crooked sad smile of hers. "Driver!" she called. "Pull over here, will you?"

"You young guys," she said as she pointed at me and the other man, "are the hope of our country. Do something. Demonstrations, revolutions, something, you know." She stepped down from the bus.

Another forty men! I thought. Politicians again? I wondered if Dad was in the group this time. He hadn't called or written to us. Abdulkadir! I remembered. He must know something about this. A blast of air came through the open window. It washed my body with a new fear. Is Abdulkadir alive? I wondered. God! I prayed. I noticed that I had already reached where I was going.

"Driver!" I yelled. "Right here, please!" I got off as he braked right in front of the garage I was going to.

I entered the garage, paid for the wheel, and drove off. Now I was not very far from Abdulkadir's, near Digfer hospital. Memories of what happened in the mosque came flooding back. What if Abdulkadir had been killed that day? I wondered. Even though I was worried about Abdulkadir's life, I was deep down afraid for mine. What would I do if he was dead? I turned left to African Village passing by Sheikh Ali-Sufi Mosque. Everything looked normal except for the blood on the ground. I stepped hard on the accelerator. In a moment I was at Abdulkadir's. The gate was open so I didn't bother knocking. Hajia Halimo, Abdulkadir's mother, was washing clothes in the daash. She didn't look upset or anything. She was also religious, as her name suggested. The title Haji for men and Hajia for women can be used by people who've been to Mecca for the pilgrimage, and Halimo was her given name. She went to Mecca a couple of years ago and she brought me a maawiis back as a present. Unlike her son she was a traditionalist, just like her husband. All she did was pray five times a day, take care of her family and leave people alone. Everybody in the neighborhood liked her. She was a real down to earth and loving woman. She didn't notice me coming in because she was busy in washing clothes and had her back to me. As I got closer she turned around and gave her all-time kindly smile. She didn't look upset or anything.

"Hello," I said.

"Hello, Ali," she said cheerfully. "How are you? We were worried about you?"

So Abdulkadir had told her about the mosque, I guessed. He is alive then. "I'm fine," I said. "I'm fine. How's Abdulkadir?" I asked.

"He's as fine as a horse. He's ..."

"Hi, Ali!" said Abdulkadir who had probably heard me talking to his mother. "Come on in." He was not wearing a maawiis or an emma or anything of that sort. He was dressed normally, in a white long-sleeved shirt and black trousers. Just like he used to in the old days when we were dating girls together.

"I was worried about you," he said as we entered the room.

"So was I."

"God, it was horrible!" he said fearfully. "I thought I was going to die!"

"Yeah, tell me about it."

"How did you get out?"

"To tell you the truth, I don't know."

"Neither do I." He agreed shaking his head and blinking his big eyes. He looked more scared than I thought I was.

"You must be feeling good?" He said coming back to the present.

"Good?"

"Yes, I mean your father has called you or something?"

"Did I mention my father?"

"No, but I thought you knew he's in Kenya!"

"Kenya!" I exclaimed. "You mean my father is in Kenya?"

He nodded.

"Who told you this? I mean…are you sure? I hope it's not just a rumour", I looked at him.

"It is not a rumour. It's for sure."

"That's great! How did you find out? And don't tell me you have your sources!"

"Alasow called his family this morning."

"Aha!" I remembered the name but couldn't say more.

"You don't know him?" He asked as though I should know the man. "He is the USC chairman!"

"I see.." I sighed. If only that son-of-a-bitch hadn't seen my father that night they were having the meeting at our home. If only…

"He said your father and five other top USC officers were with him."

"Thank God!" I said at last. "I love you, brother."

I remember that he smiled and hugged me. I didn't know what I would have done without him. He was always helpful. He had always been someone I could depend on.

"So why are you dressed like this today?" I asked, noticing again his clothing. "Are you going back to the old Abdul-kadir?"

He laughed, a little embarrassed.

"He's forcing us, man."

"Who?"

"Who else!" He got serious again. "Afweyne – Big Mouth!" That was one of the names the President was known as. Abdul-kadir always called him by that name. "He said that everybody who's dressed like a religious person should be arrested."

"No kidding?"

"So here I am again acting like a teenager." To Abdulkadir dressing like a European meant dressing like a kid. He developed that theory after he joined the Ikhwan Brotherhood. "By the way," he added. "I'm going to the High Court."

"I'm coming with you."

He smiled before he said: "Do I detect a change of attitude?"

I didn't reply.

"That's good, brother," he said. "Wake up!"

Abdulkadir was right. I was never interested in what was

happening in the country. I just wasn't. It was too bothersome. One had to talk to different people all day and all night to collect the news and opinions, since the radio, the TV and the newspapers never mentioned anything. That kind of news chain was called Radio Yobson. Yobson was a well-known teashop in the downtown commercial area where the unemployed gathered, and where gossip was exchanged round the clock. The shops and teashops in this area were open twenty-four hours because khat was sold there. Chewing the narcotic khat leaf was practically a national pastime. Khat stimulated conversation and interfered with people's sleep so that they would talk all night. Anyhow, most of the news that came from Yobson was pretty unreliable, and so 'Yobson' became the word that people used to describe market gossip and news picked up in the teashops and khat-chewing sessions. It was too much for me to keep up to date with something like that. I didn't like eating khat and I didn't like sitting at the street cafes. That is why I was lost. Almost everybody of my age was the same. They would rather have fun.

"Do you have the car today?" he asked when he was ready to move.

"Yep."

"Let's go then."

Abdulkadir and I didn't say much until we got to the Shaqalaha traffic lights where the Workers' Union building is located, and I turned left in a downtown direction. The Shaqaalaha area was new, bright and shiny, with all kinds of cloth boutiques and shoe shops, restaurants and barbershops. The area was famous for its shopping, and was always abuzz, but on this particular day the Shaqaalaha was deserted. No pretty girls and handsome boys hanging around, hardly any place was open, and no vehicles were running up and down the street.

"So," I started "Tell me about these forty men? I mean…what did they do exactly? And what are their chances?"

"There are actually forty-seven," he said staring away at the closed bibitos along the Maka Al-Mukarama street. I noticed there were not as many cars as usual, nor were there many of

60

the buses which run up and down that main street. "They are the Manifesto Group," he added.

"Manifesto?"

"Yes," he explained. "The Manifesto is a group of citizens consisting of elders and intellectuals from every tribe."

"I see."

"They proposed that the regime resign before it was too late for all of us. They…"

"Ali! Ali!" Somebody called me from the street. I looked sideways to see who was calling me but I was going too fast. I looked at the rear mirror instead. Somebody was chasing me. I slowed down still looking to the rear. I saw that they were two young men. I recognized one as Rambo, one of my friends. He was waving his hand to get my attention. I pulled over.

"Hello, Rambo." I said as he came beside me.

"I've been waving at you since you turned at the Shaqaalaha traffic lights!" he complained. "Don't tell me you couldn't see me?" He smiled. Rambo was a strongly built guy as his nick-name suggested.

"I swear I didn't see you," I got out so that Rambo and his friend could slip into the back seat. "Besides how did you recognize me?"

"Recognize you?" he snapped as he squeezed in. His friend joined him. I got into my seat again and drove away.

"I mean with the car?" I explained.

"It looks like you forgot that when you were learning how to drive you stole this green bug every day?" He laughed. "You even once gave me a driving lesson in it. Did you forget all that?"

"And you crashed into a Koranic school hut!" I remembered. "You almost killed two of those little kids learning the Koran."

"It was your fault, asshole!"

"Damnit, it was yours!"

He was right. He knew me and the car very well. Rambo was a close friend of my brother Hassan. He lived in our neighbour-hood, and used to come over to our home almost every day when Hassan was in the country. .

"So where are you guys going to?" I asked. "Downtown as

usual?" Rambo had become one of those guys who sit at the teashops in the downtown area ever since Hassan had left the country. That's why we had lost contact.

"Downtown!" He said it as though it was unmentionable. "When was the last time you were downtown?"

"I don't know. Not lately. Why?"

"There's no place open today. It's because of this court thing. I don't know if you guys heard about it but that's where we're going."

"Yes, we did hear about it, indeed. We're also going there."

"God, it's horrible!" He pulled a pack of cigarettes out of his shirt pocket and offered me one.

"No, thanks."

"Have you got a light, then?"

"Sure." I handed him the matches.

"What about you guys? What were you doing in Hodan?"

I looked at him through the mirror. He was blowing smoke out.

"I mean, is your new babe living there?" he asked.

"Do you think everybody's like you, asshole?" joked his friend. "Looking for girls in the middle of this situation?"

"You don't know the guy!" he joked back. "He never gets tired of girls! No matter what!"

I could see Abdulkadir smiling. I smiled back. Abdulkadir wasn't very crazy about the idea of chasing girls, and all that.

# 11

I had seen the High Court building a thousand times but this was the first time I had ever been there. It was a big building on the main street. There were usually a dozen or so policemen in front of it and nobody else, but that day everything was very different. There were thousands of people – it looked like the whole country was there. Men, women, and children. Most of them standing, some sitting on the ground. All staring at the closed gate. Just like an audience waiting for a play to start. Half of the crowd was security. Not policemen, but the Red Berets, armed just like the other day. They were trying to disperse the angry crowd.

It was not easy to get to the front of the crowd so we just stood at the back. My heart pumped hard as I saw the Red Berets. I had the feeling that Abdulkadir was feeling the same way.

"Let's stay back here," suggested Abdulkadir.

"I think that's a good idea," I agreed.

"What happened so far?" I asked a man who was standing right in front of me. The man looked at me with angry eyes and ignored my question. He had a long mustache and looked like somebody who was not from the city.

"Excuse me?" I repeated as I touched him by the shoulder. I thought he misunderstood me. "I asked…"

"I know what you asked!" He was still angry. "You just wait and see what happens!" He turned away again.

I felt Abdulkadir nudging me. I looked at him. He pointed at the man's belly. I noticed he was wearing a gun just under his maawiis. I stepped back in fear. The man noticed my gesture.

"It's not for you," he said, this time very slowly and in a friendly voice. "It's for them!" He pointed to the Red Berets.

"Let's get out of here," whispered Abdulkadir. We all smiled at the man and moved away. We changed our place in the crowd.

"Don't talk to these people, man," said Abdulkadir as he looked around in case somebody was eavesdropping. "Half of what you think are ordinary citizens are in fact security men. You never know."

"It's strange," said a woman behind Abdulkadir. "Nothing's happened in there yet."

"What did she say?" asked Rambo who was beside Abdulkadir.

"Nothing. The court started sitting early in the morning and nothing has happened yet."

"That's a good sign," said a man beside the woman. "I don't think they'll be sentenced to death."

"Whatever they do," added another. "Something new is going to happen from today. I mean Afweyne never before hesitated to kill innocent people."

I looked at Abdulkadir when the man said Afweyne, as this was an uncomplimentary way of naming the President.

"I wish we'd all stuck together like this when Afweyne was murdering our people every day right in front of our eyes," continued the man.

Everybody near him felt uneasy.

"Don't be afraid!" he shouted so that everybody could hear him. "It's over! It's all over for the regime! I can tell it. From this day!"

I felt so good and so scared at the same time. I liked what the man had said but I didn't like where he had said it. In the middle of a crowd! God, this could become another nightmare. Hundreds of times citizens had been arrested just because they criticized the regime in public. I even remember one night I was in a bus. A drunken man said something about the regime and two of the passengers, obviously the regime's informers, dragged him out of the bus in handcuffs.

About five o'clock that afternoon the verdict was announced. A man dressed in military uniform spoke into a loudspeaker as he stood in front of the crowd. Somebody said he was the Chief of Police.

"Your attention, please," started the man. Everybody was as silent and as still as a stone. "The verdict has been reached. The Manifesto Group has not been convicted of crimes against the state!"

"Wooooohhhh!!" The crowd cheered.

The court's forecourt gates were opened. A crowd of elderly men appeared. They were smiling and waving to the crowd. It seemed like everybody wanted to touch them except me. I stood still as the crowd moved to greet the Group. Most of them had big beards. All of them were wearing maawiis and shirts. Some had emmas. I suddenly came across a familiar face amongst them. He was a thin man with a huge beard. Although the man looked familiar I couldn't remember from where. Abdulkadir suddenly appeared beside the man. He was shaking hands with him.

"That's the ex-Police Chief!" somebody said.

"And beside him is the millionaire!"

"That one there is the Imam of the Sheikh Ali Sufi Mosque!"

That's right! I remembered the man. That's where I had seen him. He was the man who was giving the Friday sermon when the Red Berets entered the Mosque the other day. That's him!

The Manifesto Group were free. Everybody and everything around seemed suddenly to smell of freedom and humanity. Anyway, the Manifesto Group were free at last. The crowd started to walk away peacefully. I looked around and found none of my companions. I looked for them. I couldn't find them. Abdulkadir had again disappeared into the crowd. I gave up and walked away to where my car was parked.


# 12


On my way home it seemed that people were looking happier. Bibitos and other businesses were open once again. Young men were crowded in front of the teashops talking as usual. This time I knew what they were talking about; how the people had stopped the regime's slaughter; how all Somalis were united against the regime. I too felt victory. For the first time in my life I felt that I had done something for my country. I also felt safe. My father was being proven wrong. Everybody was united against the government. The Daroods were not siding with the regime. I had seen with my own eyes. I reached KM4 in what seemed like no time at all. I parked the car in a garage near there for I didn't want to risk having Anab take the car from me. In my head I was once again preparing to celebrate the New Year. There was nothing to prevent that now, I thought. Buses were working normally, too. So I took a bus from KM4 to Medina. When I came home, everything was as usual. Actually my family looked happier.

"Dad is in Kenya," Anab greeted me as soon as I came in.

"I know," I said smiling. "Did he call?"

"Yes. He telephoned Haji Ismael's house!" She was grinning. "I talked to them. He and Haji Ismael."

"That's good." I unlocked my room. "Anything else new?"

"No. Nothing." She glanced outside to see if I had the car with me. "You didn't get the car yet?"

"I don't have any money. Will you pay?"

"No!" she said, just as I expected. She hated anyone who asked her for any money. "Where should I get the money from?"

"I'm expecting some money by Wednesday or Thursday. I'll take care of it."

"I can't wait until Thursday!"

"That's the only way out." I entered my room and locked the door. I noticed an envelope on the table beside the bed. I stood up and grabbed it. I tore it open and read. It was from my friend Musa.

"Dear Ali," I read, "I am doing fine. I hope you are, too. I am sorry I had to rush out of the capital. Believe me it was not my intention. My father planned the whole thing without even telling me. I am sure that, by now, you know why I had to leave my city, my friends, and my whole world behind me. Anyway, I am still here in Bay. My father has been missing since last night. Nobody really knows where he is. My family doesn't know I am writing to you. They wouldn't like it. But nothing is going to separate us ever. I promise. Your best friend – Musa A. Kenadid. P.S. Say Hi to everybody for me and HAPPY NEW YEAR TO YOU ALL!"

There was no return address. I grabbed my towel and came out of the room. On my way to the bathroom I passed Falis who was watering the daash. They did this every day so that the sand in the daash wouldn't blow about in the wind.

"Who brought the letter on my table?" I asked while trying to avoid getting wet from the water she was splashing about.

"Mohamed Ismael. He came here this morning and took the post office box key to collect some letters he was expecting." She was closing the tap now. It looked like she had finished the watering. "Why?" she added. Mohamed Ismael was Haji Ismael's eldest son. He used our PO box address since he didn't have one of his own. He didn't want to share with his family for reasons he didn't say.

"I don't know," I explained digging a little hole in the wet sand with my big toe. "My letter was from Musa, but I thought he had also sent a letter for somebody else."

"No, that was the only letter. Why?"

"Because he didn't give his address."

She shrugged before she said: "Did he say if everything was all right?"

"Yes, except that his father's missing." I said. "He wishes you a happy new year."

"Moallim Osman and his family went off this morning," she declared.

"Moallim Osman?" I had heard the name but I couldn't remember who it was. "Yes, Moallim Osman," she pointed to indicate where the guy was living. "Ali-Yare's father."

"Aha," I remembered. "Went off? Where to?"

"To Saudi Arabia!"

"Good for him," I said and entered the bathroom.

God! I said to myself standing under the shower. How lucky! It was only the other day that Asha, Ali-Yare's sister, had been talking to me and wishing that her father was rich enough to take them out of this unpredictable country! I stepped aside from the shower and looked at the blue sky. Our bathroom, like everybody else's, was not covered. I don't know why. Maybe it had something to do with the hot weather. I don't know. A flock of white birds appeared suddenly in the sky. It was noticeable the freedom these creatures were enjoying. They flew up and down at will. I wished I were a bird, then suddenly I changed my mind and thanked God I was a human being. I don't know what exactly made me change my mind,

67

but one of the reasons was that I once heard that birds had a very small brain compared to other creatures. I was feeling contented in my thoughts when somebody knocked lightly on the bathroom door.

"Who is it?" I asked.

"You don't own the bathroom!" said Anab. "Stop singing and come out so that other people can use it."

"I'm coming," I said and grabbed my towel from the hook where it was hanging. "I'm coming."

Later that evening I had supper with the family, something I hadn't done for ages. Everybody was there except Mona. We were sitting at the big table in the living room. Falis, Anab, Ahmed and I were sitting on the four chairs. Nasir was sitting on his mother's lap. We were all eating beans and rice cooked together.

"Where's Mona?" I asked looking at Anab who was sitting beside me.

"I don't know," she said. "I wasn't home when she left. "Maybe..."

"She had a date," Falis said from the opposite side.

"With the same guy?" I asked. Everybody knew I disliked the guy she was seeing. I thought he was too boring to be with.

"Yes, the same guy!" joked Falis. "What's wrong with the same guy? You think everybody's like you? This girl tonight, that girl tomorrow?"

"What's wrong with that?"

"Nothing," she said dismissively. She knew I could argue on that topic for hours. "I know you're a free man," she gave up. "Anyhow," she continued, "What's happened to your girl-friends these days? Did you tell them not to come, or don't they like you any more, or what?"

"They don't like me any more." I said to her playfully.

"All men are the same," she said. "They behave in one way to us women when there's nobody else around, pleading and all that, and then they act tough in front of other people."

Everybody laughed including me. Silence followed and everybody was once again busy with his spoon and plate.

"Isn't it pretty hard for you that all your friends have left?" asked Anab when we had finished supper.

"Yeah," I sighed. "Everybody's leaving the country. I wish Dad was rich like those people in the government."

"Not everybody in the government is rich," Falis said.

"Not all of them, of course," I stood up to leave. "But at least the Marrehans are rich."

"Some Hawiyas are rich, too."

"Yes, but we're not talking about Hawiyas and Daroods, are we?"

"No, but I know what you're trying to say."

"Listen. I know some Hawiyas are in the government and as corrupt as everybody else. Some Daroods, too. But almost all the Marrehans are in the government and rich." I stepped out of the room because I knew where the conversation would lead us. I had seen it all before.

Falis was like that. She was very sensitive about tribalism. Because she was a Darood, she sometimes acted differently than the rest of us. Whenever the regime was mentioned she jumped to defend her tribe, the Daroods. I don't know why. Nobody ever discriminated against her. Or at least not that I ever saw. Yet she put herself in another category when it came to tribalism or anything of that sort. Nevertheless, she was part of the family and she knew that.

Young people could make fun of each other's tribe without any hard feelings at all. Actually one of my friends was called Saeed and we gave him the nickname Saeed 'Marrehan' because he was the only one of our group who belonged to the Marrehan tribe. But to older people it was different. Very different. They could kill each other for less.

I was in my room once again. I thought of what I would do to make myself busy. I suddenly had an idea. I started to sort out my clothes. I chose the best I had and put them aside so they could be washed for the big night. I also decided on what I would wear tomorrow – yellow slacks and a free-size white T-shirt with the word AFRICA in black on it. In the morning, I thought, I would wake up early and buy black braces to go with the outfit I had chosen for celebrating the New Year.

Everything was set. The car, the money I had saved for the occasion, the girl. Everything. Nothing was missing. Nothing was wrong. I felt good and thought about what to do next. I grabbed one of the novels I had never finished. I had many novels in my room and I had a habit of reading all of them at the same time, so I never finished any one of them. I would choose a new one depending on my mood. This time I chose *Robinson Crusoe*, and retired to my bed.

# 13

At first I thought I was dreaming but I soon found that I wasn't. I opened my eyes slightly and tried to concentrate. Half awake and half asleep, I felt my pillow moving. Or at least that's what it seemed like. I held my head up and looked around the small room. The whole room was shaking; the bed, the walls, and even myself. I remembered a film I had once seen about an earthquake. It was like that, except that the things on my wall were not moving or falling down like in the film. I jumped to my feet. I heard a very powerful thump. I had no idea what it could be, it was a noise I'd never heard before. The noise went like hhhiiiggg! ggiiigggg! I heard voices in front of the house. I reached for the outside door and flung it open. Everybody was there; my family, the neighbours, and others too. They were all talking, and looked terrified.

"This is crazy!" a woman gasped.

"It's the best solution," a man said.

"It started about half an hour ago."

I rubbed the sleep from my eyes and approached the crowd. None of my family noticed my presence. They were, like every one else, looking up at the sky for something.

"What's going on?" I asked Mona who was pointing

skywards. My eyes followed where her hand was pointing. I saw black clouds.

"It's war!" she said not even looking at my face.

"War?"

"Yes!" She looked at me. "I'm scared, Ali!"

"Who's fighting?" I demanded.

"I don't know!" she held my hand tightly.

"The USC freedom fighters are fighting the government," a man said looking at me casually. My heart ached.

"No, it's not that," another disagreed. "It's the government's troops against the civilians."

"The civilians!" snapped a woman. "Which civilians?"

"I don't know, but you should have seen the other end of the city! The troops are shooting at people. At everybody!"

That was enough for me to hear. More than enough as a matter of fact. I looked at the sky and at the black clouds that seemed to be increasing. It looked like the whole city could be under fire. Civil war! the words came back to me. The civil war had started. I was worried more than afraid. I was worried about my family. My mother. She was living in Huriwaa on the other side of town, and only God knew what had happened to her. I had to do something. Anything.

"Get in the house!" I ordered Falis, Mona and my brothers who were standing silently at the gate. They gazed at me in response.

"I said get in the house! And nobody comes out!" I repeated, "Nobody! You hear?"

They obeyed me silently.

I went back to my room and changed. I had to see my mother. I took the first bus to KM4 where my car was.

My mother, a very pretty woman in her late forties, lived in one of the northern quarters of the city. She didn't marry again after she was divorced by my father, and so, since it was not the practise for women to stay by themselves, she worked in the family businesses and lived with one or other of her eleven brothers and their family. My maternal uncles were doing very well financially. They owned a restaurant, farms, and numerous heavy-duty transport lorries. I used to visit them when I had problems with my father or his two dreadful wives, my stepmothers, and would stay there until things cooled down. Whenever I visited them, though, except for my mother and her youngest brother they were always in meetings in one of their houses. They endlessly discussed politics and tribalism. Just as my father and his friends did at home. It was so boring to stay with them for very long, that I would come back as soon as everything was back to normal at home.

"They took my car!" said a man on the bus. I don't remember where he was sitting in the bus. "They told me to get out of the car. I agreed because they aimed their guns at me. They hit me and told me to get lost. I..."

"You were lucky!" said another. "They killed a man and a woman simply because they refused to get out of their car. They..."

I was lost in thought. I didn't know what to do. After considering the situation, I decided that instead of risking taking my car I would take a bus all the way. I got down at KM4 and waited for a downtown bus to connect me with another bus to Huriwaa.

The time was eight-thirty as I waited at KM4 bus station. Huge numbers of people were there, all waiting for buses to take them in different directions. I had never seen such a crowd there. The buses from Medina were working normally so they kept bringing people in, but there were no buses going to town. The only buses available were going back to Medina. There were not even any private cars around. We waited and waited but there was no sign of any change. Jeeps appeared. They were full of armed men and were rushing in a downtown direction. They didn't stop. Their occupants didn't talk to us. They didn't even look at us. People started to take the buses to Medina. Some walked away. I decided to go home.

I was back home by ten. I entered my room from the outside door without anybody noticing me. Filled with terror, I sat on the bed. I had a sort of intuition that things were really bad. I tried hard to think straight and failed. Two things dominated my thinking. My father, and my mother. The way I saw it, I needed my father more than at any other given time in my entire little life, and my mother needed me. That's what was going around in my head. Then my terror tripled as I heard Anab crying and screaming in the daash. I jumped to my feet again and opened the inside door. She was sitting on the ground and everybody else was watching her.

"What happened?" I asked.

"There's nobody left alive!" she wept. "Nobody!"

"What are you talking about?" I struggled to hold back tears.

"My people! Our people!"

"Don't cry for God's sake." I didn't know what else to say.

"Nobody in Wardigley is alive! They've all been killed! Oh my God! I…"

Almost everybody in Wardigley was from our Hawiya tribe. Wardigley was one of the oldest quarters in the city and the Hawiya were its original inhabitants, so almost everybody who lived there was a Hawiya. Most of my relatives lived there.

"Who told you?"

"I was there this morning….."

I noticed that Anab's brother, Mohamed, was sitting on a chair in the other corner of the daash. Silent and still. I greeted him.

"You've been in Wardigley this morning?" I asked Anab, surprised.

"Yes." She wiped the tears from her eyes. "It was about five o'clock. I got up for morning prayers. I heard the most terrible noise and went outside to look. The neighbours told me that it was Wardigley burning. I took the first bus. I was worried about my people. When I reached there I found the government troops shooting the people. Oh my God! You should…"

"First it was between the USC and the troops," interrupted Mohamed.

"How did the whole thing start?" I asked.

"Don't know exactly. I went to bed about four o'clock last night because the whole neighbourhood was tense and on the alert. They said there would be fighting in the morning and…"

73

"How did they know?"

"Don't know. Half the people were even armed with guns. Looked like they were ready."

"How did they get the guns?"

"They've been collecting them lately. The USC supplied them."

"Tell me about this USC thing first. Are they visible? I mean… what do they look like? Do they have uniforms?"

"No. It's difficult to know for sure. They live amongst us and yet we can't see them. Everybody claims he or she belongs to the USC We all have guns and…"

"We?"

"Yes. Anyone who wants a gun can easily get one." He held his shirt up to display the gun resting against his belly. "I've got mine. Self-defence, you know?"

Silence.

"Tell this woman and the children to stay away from places like Wardigley. Anab came to Wardigley because she was worried about me. I had to accompany her all the way here to Medina. I was scared to death myself but I didn't have a choice, did I?"


Mohamed stayed with us a couple of hours and then took off again to his place in Wardigley. From his conversation I gathered that the whole thing had started with USC fighters hunting the Darood Government officials whom they accused of murdering the Hawiyas. They broke into their houses and killed them. They planted explosives in their cars. Shot them whenever they had the chance. More people might have been enthusiastic about what the USC called 'eliminating the corrupt' if the USC had been killing all the corrupt. Not only the Darood corrupt. The regime, of course, had to retaliate against any group that threatened its stability. In consequence the USC should be eliminated. Their stronghold, Wardigley, must be destroyed. According to Mohamed, that was the reason Wardigley had been shelled this morning.

After lunch that day I took a short walk to the main street to look around at the general situation. In other words to assess the general safety. To my surprise, there were thousands of civilians on the streets. It looked as if they were all leaving the city. Thousands and thousands of people. Young and old, men and women. At first I couldn't comprehend the scene. But sure enough, people were leaving the city and heading towards Afgoye, the nearest town to the south of the capital city. It was clear they were leaving the city, because they were carrying all the things they could possibly carry: food, water, tents, clothes, pillows, mattresses, babies, you name it. Everything. Some were on foot, others on all kinds of transportation from donkeys to lorries. All going towards Afgoye. None were heading towards downtown Mogadishu. Almost as many as the refugees were the hoards of spectators standing along the street, as though to welcome a VIP delegation. (It reminded me of when Nicolai Ceausescu of Romania visited the city when I was in intermediate school. Then the whole population had been commanded to stand along the streets to welcome him.) I took my place with the spectators now. I could see the hot street disappearing under the feet of these refugees. The lucky ones – and it was only some of them – were wearing sandals. Some would stop every now and then to say a few words of explanation to the spectators.

"I'm not sure if you can trust those Hamaris!" Somebody said.

"You're right!" another agreed. "They're probably exaggerating things."

Some, but not all of the people fleeing the city, were indeed Hamaris. Hamaris were the people who lived in the very oldest stone-built part of the city called Hamarweyne. They were not involved in politics and were not known for their fighting spirit like the rest of the Somalis. They hated violence. Even when we were little kids I don't remember them fighting in football matches, or throwing stones at the roofs of their neighbours, or forming gangs to cause trouble like we always did. They were well-known for business, on the other hand. Most of them, if not all of them, were engaged in commercial activity. They owned most of the shoe shops, sweet shops, and tailoring businesses in the city. They were light-skinned and could easily be recognized, if not by their complexion, then by their dialect.

I had learned, after talking to some of the refugees, that the city centre was under heavy fire. The shelling was not confined to Wardigley any more, it had reached the city centre. People carrying guns could be seen roaming the streets, they said. There was some looting going on. When I asked who was doing it, they said that it was coming from the government. No other explanations. Just the government.

"I don't think all of these people are lying!" a woman suggested. "I think there's more to it than being a Hamari."

"Oh! Don't you believe it!" a man said dismissively. "For them lack of business means the end of life!"

I wanted to tell him that he was wrong about the Hamaris but I didn't. I just didn't utter a word, but by now I knew that we were all going to end up like that. It was almost five o'clock when I walked back home. I stopped and looked back to the main street every now and then. I don't know why. Maybe I was hoping for a miracle to happen. Maybe the Hamaris and the others would suddenly start coming back, yelling "We were wrong! We were wrong! Everything is under control! Nothing is wrong!" Even though I knew better than that, I kept looking back over my shoulders until I was home.

"What's happening!" exclaimed Anab, who was watching the scene from the gate. "Where're all these people going?"

"It's the Hamaris leaving the city," I murmured absently. I was so busy inside my head. I had to have a plan.

"Leaving!" Her eyes were rolling swiftly to right and left, trying to look at me and at the people in the street at the same time. "Has it started in the downtown areas, too?"

"Yes," I said. "And I think we should be leaving as well."

"We?"

I made no response and entered the house. She followed me

full of questions but gave up as I entered my room, having passed the rest of the family in the daash.

Flicking aside the things scattered on my bed, I sat down and thought carefully about my plan. I had to do something about my family. My two brothers were my main concern. I had to get them out of this city. Whatever it was called, something awful was happening here. Thousands of people don't just leave behind everything they worked for with no good reason. It was foolish to wait for the end. I had to get my brothers out of the city while I could. Or could I still?

Late in the evening I called everybody and put to them my plan.

"Where are we going?" asked Falis.

"Wherever you like."

"And what about you?" Anab inquired.

"I'm going to stay and wait until things change."

"No, you are not!"

"Yes, I am."

"We'll stay with you if…"

"If you guys don't want to go it's up to you, of course. But Ahmed and Nasir have to leave this city."

They all eyed me silently. I waited.

"OK," agreed Anab. "But where will they go?"

"They'll stay with my mother and uncles in Huriwaa until we know what is going on."

"If you say so."

"And if things get out of control they'll be taken out of the city to Jowhar and stay at our house there. What do you think?"

"Good idea," Anab agreed probably realizing the helplessness I was feeling.

# 15

I got up at six o'clock the next morning according to my plan.
The only time in my history I ever got up that early. Not even
in my school years. My stepmothers were awake already and
preparing the children to go. We washed ourselves, had anjeelo
pancakes for breakfast and were ready to take off by seven
o'clock. Ahmed had a small plastic bag in his hand, I supposed
with some clothes in it.

"Now," I addressed both of them at the gate. "Are you guys
ready?"

"Yes," they said in low clear voices. Their mothers must
have been lecturing them all last night because they didn't
ask many questions. I preferred it that way because I didn't
have any answers for their silly questions anyway. After standing half an hour at the main street for a bus we found out
that there were no buses running from Medina to anywhere,
and vice versa. We would have to walk. So we hit the road
in good spirits. I led them by the hand. I could feel their
tiny hands wet with sweat as we headed down the main street.
Even though it was early, people were in the streets in large
numbers, still leaving the city. All of them were going south
while we walked to the north. I asked a few questions of
the people we met, and was told that the situation was really
much worse than yesterday. They said looting and killing
were the norm in many places in the city. Luckily or unluckily
for us, Medina was on the outskirts of the city and that's why
Medina people hadn't seen what the people were talking
about, not unless they had gone to the other parts of the city.
Following the advice, we changed our route from the main
road and took some smaller streets. On the way we came across
worrying signs: very old people walking alone with sticks, children lost and crying helplessly, young guys carrying guns publicly and looking very threatening, and more. I held Ahmed's
hand tightly while carrying Nasir and kept walking, jogging, or
even sometimes running. Occasionally we hid behind houses.

By about ten o'clock we were at the Banadir Bus Station. Safe and sound.

Today, unlike any other day in my life, the Banadir Bus Station, the biggest and the busiest station in town, had almost no people. Or rather I should say had hardly any ordinary people. For every dozen civilians there were twice as many soldiers in uniform. Not the Red Berets but the national army. They stood in lines, their faces as hard and cruel as a rock in the ocean. They were lining up the civilians near one of the buildings.

"Why are they searching the people?" asked Ahmed.

"I don't know." I led them to the shade so that we were protected from the awfully hot mid-morning sun.

"Hey, you!" a soldier called to me as he saw us pass the line towards the shade. "Where the hell do you think you're going? Line up!"

I came back and joined the line. My hands hurt because of the way my two brothers had been gripping on to them. We waited our turn to be searched. The men in uniform performed their duties, searching the pockets of all the people, one after another, with no exception whatsoever. Old men and women, young guys and girls, and even children. We waited impatiently and watched. Most of the people left the spot immediately after being searched; few of them waited for the bus. Now I was number three in the line. A man and a child, probably his, were in front of me. The man smiled at the soldier all the time. I could see the gun he was hiding, tucked down the back of his trousers. He busied himself with the child as he was being searched. My heart was banging through my ears. What if they find out the man has a gun! I wondered. I couldn't bear to imagine the result so I prayed for him.

"Hands up!" ordered the soldier as my turn came. I could see the man looking back every step he made as if afraid the soldier would call him back for another search. He dragged the child by the hand and turned right at the cinema, almost running. His behaviour didn't stand out, since almost everybody else, with or without a gun hidden on them, was also running for his life.

"What is in here?" the soldier asked as he pointed at the small plastic bag in Ahmed's hand.

"I don't know...I...mean...I think it must be his clothes or something.."

He grabbed the bag from the boy and took a quick look.

"You'd better check everything in your possession next time."

"Yes, sir."

We stood at the other end of the shade with three other people.

"I don't think there are any buses working today," remarked a very old lady beside me. It looked like she was hungry for conversation. "I've been here waiting for a bus for more than two hours," she continued. "I wish I were as young as you people. You can walk. But me..." she shook her veiled head from side to side in regret at her age. "This sun...to Yaqshid...I can't make it."

I left her before she could start on the story of what she could or couldn't do, and maybe her life history. We walked away undecided about what to do next. A man pulling a big cart of fruit appeared about five hundred metres down the street. People rushed to him from all sides with cash in their hands, and we, too, walked towards him. After buying an armful of mangoes we resigned ourselves to sitting on the steps of a closed shop to eat, and to plan the next move. We ate two mangoes each, kept the rest, four or five of them, in the plastic bag, and hit the road which would take us to town. Every now and then a dead body or two could be seen in a corner of a doorway. I would cross the street so the children wouldn't see them, though actually I had never seen a corpse before either. I felt like vomiting whenever the corpses appeared but I had to contain myself because of the children.

"You'd better not take the main street," advised two men who were coming in the opposite direction. They were the first people we'd seen for a while. I nodded gratefully and kept walking.

"Are there any signs of buses back there?" one of them asked as they passed us. "To Medina?" he continued as he looked back.

I shook my head in negative response. None of us stopped as we talked. Neither the passers-by nor us. We turned from the main road once again and used a sand road parallel to the main road. It was more busy than the main street. Not a minor road any more. The people, even though not many, preferred it to the main road. After the rest we had had we were able to get back to our earlier pace. We started jogging on the hot sand. After what seemed an age, even though it was only an hour or so, we came to the roundabout marked by the famous Sayidka statue. Exhausted, dehydrated, and starving.

We joined about ten people who were hiding behind the nearby buildings. The reason was that we were now near the area of the Presidential Palace, which was just beyond the statue. The President lived there, so we used to believe, although some said he didn't. Either way, everybody shuddedred when passing by the goddam palace. The mention of the place alone brought fear. Normally there were a dozen or so guards with machine guns who would harass the passers-by with their threats and silly questions. Where are you going? Where did you come from? Why are you not asleep? etc. Today, however, was worse. Instead of a dozen men, there were a dozen jeeps guarding the street. Obviously none of the people huddling against the wall wanted to go along that street today, but we had to get past it, and we were scared about what could happen to us as we passed in front of them. We crowded behind the building, and two or three of us at a time would take a chance and cross over to the road beyond the traffic lights. I was standing behind a wall with some other people when somebody touched me on the shoulder.

"Aren't you one of the Awalehs?" asked the stranger. Awaleh was my mother's father.

"Yes," I answered guessing that the man had seen me some time at my uncles' place. I didn't have the slightest idea of what the man wanted. Was he just saying hello? Or was he about to give me a piece of good advice? Or was he...? "That's right. My mother is Awaleh's only daughter."

"How is your uncle?" the man asked easily. "Bile Awaleh."

"What about Bile Awaleh?"

"Has he recovered from the shots?"

"Shots?"

"I heard he was…"

An army of jeeps came rushing down from the Presidential Palace on the other side of the street. The people around me, including my informant, ran wildly in any direction that suited their escape. I wanted to run too but couldn't. I felt my feet stick to the ground. The dark green jeeps drove wildly after the fleeing people then turned off in the direction away from us as the crowd was dispersed. The people, however, didn't stop running nor even looked back. They ran like hungry cats chasing mice. I could see the jeep drivers laughing, as though laughing at acts of cowardice. Don't panic! I told myself. Just get the hell out of this trap. More crowds appeared from behind the buildings around, running more wildly than the group before. As we sprinted down the hill away from the area, I realized I was dragging Nasir on the ground. I looked back for the first time, and stopped when I saw no sign of Red Berets.

"My knee hurts," the boy started to complain pointing to his grazed knee.

"Shut up!" I cut him short. "Just run!"

"I can't."

I scooped him up and kept on running, at a slower pace, towards the National Theatre. I realized we had company. A young man, a little bit older than me, was running beside me. We nodded to each other in greeting and kept running. We stopped at the National Theatre to rest a while.

"Stop! Stop!" A jeep full of soldiers braked near us. "Don't move!" a soldier inside called out. We stood still. This time my brothers must have felt I was as afraid as they were, if not more so. I was shaking so much that I was afraid I would collapse.

"Who are you?" Two of them were aiming their guns at us now.

We made no response.

"Speak up!" The voice repeated. "Who the hell are you?"

The question Who are you? meant To which tribe do you belong?. That was the way the question was put since the government was supposed to be against the use of tribes and tribalism.

"We are people!" my companion shouted back in a voice which was almost as authoritative as the enquirer's. "What else do we look like?" He understood the question just like I did but, still applying the government rule, he avoided giving a direct answer. I could tell, though, that he was an Isaaq from his dialect and courage. Those people from the north would never be afraid to speak up.

"Now we know who you are," said the soldier as he recognized the dialect. "And who the hell are you guys?" This time he was addressing me and my brothers.

"We are all brothers!" I yelled, just like my companion, using his dialect and courage. "Don't you see that!"

"Do you have any guns?" asked another man.

"No."

"Go away," he ordered. "Where are you going anyway?"

What a funny question, I thought.

"Home," my companion answered as the jeep moved off in the direction we had come from.

"Are you Isaaqs?" asked the young man when we were alone.

"No," I smiled. "Do I sound like one?"

"Now you don't," he smiled back. "But back then I could swear you were."

"Thanks to my friends."

"Are you Hawiyas?" he asked.

"Yes."

"Then that was very wise of you to do what you did," he said, "They're looking for you."

"I know. That's why I pretended to be an Isaaq."

He smiled again and held out his hand.

"Thank you for letting me be your brother for a moment." We shook hands.

"Sure." He looked around to make sure we were safe. "Where are you going?"

"Huriwaa."

"That's a long way to walk with these children."

"I know."

"Good luck."

"You too."

We split.

He turned right heading for the Hamarweyne quarter as we turned left towards Bondere. We continued to avoid the main street, taking one or other of the numerous unpaved streets running parallel. We hid behind a building whenever we saw anything suspicious. Once we had been hiding behind a building when we heard the following words:

"Stop! Don't move if you want to stay alive!"

The order echoed as if it was given by a number of people together. We turned around slowly, I with my hands on my head, to see who gave the order. There was no sign of people. "Don't move if you want to stay alive!" This time I realised that the voice came from a window of a high building behind us. I looked up at the window of the building which had some of its roof missing. There was something going on inside there, but the order had not been addressed to us. I held my two brothers' hands. We didn't wait. We ran. All I could hear were bullets being fired back there and the cries of my brothers either side of me. Neither noise stopped us. We just kept on running.

In ten minutes we were at Bondere Market. Just like you would expect, the Market was full of people. Not the usual kind of people who carried on their buying and selling, but another kind. A kind of people who did not buy, sell, scream, shout or steal, but a kind who lay still and silent as stones. There had been a massacre. It seemed none of them was left alive whether it be children, young men and women, or elderly people. Bagsful of fruit and vegetables were scattered upside down all around. The place was a wreck, devastated, looted, and lacking any signs of life. We seemed the only living beings in the place. I took the two boys away and hid them behind a burned-out lorry and told them to wait for me there. Then I don't know what came over me. I couldn't stop myself from going back to take a closer look at what we had just come across. I was mesmerised. As I started looking at each and every corpse's face was it to see if there were any people there that I knew? One after another I looked at them. Some vomited blood and some didn't. Some had their eyes shut and others looked fully awake as they gazed with frozen terror. I came across the corpse of a young woman lying almost naked across a table. She'd probably been selling bananas for there were smashed bananas all over the table and even on her body. The girl's 'face' could best be described as a hole. This was the one face that frightened me. Brought me back to consciousness. That was the last look I took at those people's faces. I joined the two boys who were both of them on their bellies and looking at me from under the lorry as I had inspected the corpses.

"Let's go," I told them and we hit the road again. Going through Yaqshid and Kaaraan we were home at last at three o'clock in the afternoon on that unbearable Monday; we had reached one of the houses my uncles owned. I knocked on the closed gate after first listening to see if there were any signs of a disturbance. My youngest uncle, Hassan Awaleh, opened the gate. Without any introduction he burst out crying at the sight of me. The children and I didn't cry. We might have been crying inside, but it is my firm recollection that none of us shed even one tear. Maybe we didn't find anything worth crying about after what we had been through, or maybe we were too tired to. I noticed that there were two other men with him, but I recognized neither of them. Hassan came forward and covered us with kisses and tears.

"Come on in," he said joyfully. "Come on in. We were dead worried about you and your family."

"We're fine," I said. "What happened to Bile Awaleh? Where's my mother?"

"Just cool down, Ali," he tried to comfort me. "I'll explain everything in a minute. Your mother is really fine."

"What about Bile?"

"I said I'll tell you all about it in a minute!" he yelled. I couldn't believe my ears. It was the first time I had ever heard him shout like that. At least at me. I was his favourite and he was mine. No matter what happened he never got angry with me. Even though he was ten years older than me, we were more like brothers than uncle and nephew. That's why I never called him uncle. Already I could tell that something was bothering him. Something big. We went inside without saying any more and flopped down on the ground. After drinking water and resting a while Nasir fell asleep. I noticed that something was being cooked but I couldn't recognise what it was.

"What's this you're cooking?" I inquired.

"Flour."

"Flour?" People in my country never cooked flour as a dish. "Why flour?"

"It sounds as though everything is normal up there in Medina," one of the other men explained, "But we didn't have anything else to survive on since last week. Only flour. As a matter of fact we consider ourselves lucky because most people in Kaaraan don't even have flour. People are starving here."

"Wardigley is out of the question of course," added the other as he stirred the boiling white liquid in the pot.

"We haven't eaten anything since yesterday," said Hassan.

"Thank God they haven't yet cut the electricity!" exclaimed the third man.

"We had our breakfast," I interrupted. For the first time I considered anjeelo pancakes a blessing. "Anjeelo of course," I added.

"We have some mangoes," I said and opened the bag. We had five left.

I gave two mangoes to the three men and I and Ahmed had one each while we kept one for the sleeping little Nasir. Silence took over as the fruit was being eaten. The only noise was of sharp teeth crashing into the mangoes like knives. In a matter of minutes mango stones were being licked clean by the hungry tongues. I watched Hassan as we ate. His face looked shadowed with grief. I waited impatiently.

"Take the kid inside," Hassan suggested pointing to Nasir. I carried the little boy into a bedroom and laid him on a bed. Ahmed followed me to the bedroom complaining of exhaustion and hunger. He said he didn't want to eat the flour that was being cooked so I told him to sleep.

"Are you people not eating the flour with us?" asked Hassan as I came back from the bedroom.

"Nasir's asleep and Ahmed refused."

"What about you?" he asked serving the white mixture. It was as sticky as good chewing gum. It looked disgusting.

"I can try," I answered.

During the flour meal my uncle Hassan asked about my family and told me all about his. He told me how Uncle Bile had been wounded.

It had happened the day before, and the place was the main family house where the oldest of my uncles lived – a very big building containing the residence of Uncle Mohamed, a big restaurant, and a big workshop for repairing and garaging all kinds of vehicles. The incident had taken place in the garage, where a good number of people happened to be at the time – mechanics, labourers, waiters, friends, customers, and most importantly, family members including my mother. It was an army of military jeeps and lorries that forced their way in, reported Hassan. Mohamed, the oldest of my uncles, as I said earlier, and the head of the family, was the first to see the army coming. Thinking that the force belonged to the USC fighters, he hurriedly ordered all gates, doors, and windows to be closed. He did so not because he was afraid of the USC (after all, the USC was the fighting force of his own Hawiya tribe) but because he knew they would bother him. They would expect to eat lunch without paying the bills, have their vehicles repaired at the same price, ask for a little cash for cigarettes, and things of the sort. Uncle Mohamed, however, was wrong. Deadly wrong. The armed vehicles were not the USC's. They were the government's. Or to be more accurate, since there was rapidly becoming no government any more, only people divided by tribes, the troops were from the President's tribe. They stopped in front of the garage and knocked on the gate. No one opened it of course. The people inside hid themselves behind the countless vehicles. The people in the restaurant, of whom Uncle Mohamed was one, applied the same tactic, creeping under the chairs and tables or hiding in the kitchen. The colonel in charge of the force, however, hadn't come accidentally. The whole thing, according to Hassan, had been planned. It was common knowledge that the place was one of the USC's hide-outs. Most of my uncles were loyal to the USC, and USC meetings were sometimes held in that very garage. It was widely rumoured that a big cache of weapons and ammunition was kept there for the USC. The people in the garage had at the time, though, only two rifles. Any arms cache was safely locked up, and the key was in Uncle Mohamed's pocket. The colonel had three armed vehicles, including a Bagaze lorry mounted with a huge 37-gun, and two jeeps full of armed soldiers. They broke into the garage and fired automatic machine-guns at random, shouting all the time: "We can see you!...You'd better come out now before we burn the whole place down! You won't get hurt if you come out of hiding!"

Seven men, including two of my uncles, Bile and Botan, who were wounded in the first random shots, came out of their hiding-places. The seven were herded into one corner and were told in a loud voice that they would be pardoned but that anyone else still in hiding would be burnt alive. The threat flushed out eight others but no more, even though there were twice as many more, including Hassan himself, who had not come out. The troops lined up the fifteen men, four of them my uncles, and shot them. Twelve died on the spot. Two of them, even though not even wounded, pretended to be dead and survived, and the fifteenth victim was Bile Awaleh. Bile had been wounded in the first round. He was bleeding badly and lay on the ground. As a parting shot a soldier aimed his gun at the first two fingers of my uncle Bile's right hand. Not a deadly shot, its purpose was to torture him.

My mother came out of her hiding place when she couldn't stand it any more. She pleaded with them to leave Bile alone. She even knelt down to beg the colonel. She knew Bile wouldn't survive the bullet wounds, but she begged the son-of-a-bitch anyway.

"Get out of here, bitch!" was the colonel's answer. He hit her in the mouth with the butt of his gun. Her four front teeth were knocked out on to the ground. He aimed his gun at her but changed his mind. Killing women was not something to be proud of. Not yet at least.

"Let's get out of here," the colonel commanded his soldiers.

On their way out they found a ten-year-old child hiding near the restaurant door.

"Where are the people!" he yelled at the kid.

"I don't know, sir," the boy lied.

The soldier noticed one of the restaurant doors ajar and ordered the child to lead him to where the money was kept.

"I don't know, sir."

The soldier, pulling the kid by the collar, entered the restaurant. Uncle Mohamed, as he told Hassan later, waited impatiently under a table with a machine-gun in his hands. He had heard the shots from the garage, and even though he couldn't know who exactly were the unlucky victims, he guessed a lot of people were dead. He held back from shooting the one soldier, hoping and praying that more fools would come in. The soldier looked around the dark empty place.

"Hey, guys!" he called to his companions and let go of the little boy. "The restaurant's empty!"

Two more soldiers appeared at the door. Now Uncle Mohamed fired his machine-gun wildly and killed the three of them on the spot. Everybody hiding in the restaurant took this chance to escape through the kitchen and out of the back way. More soldiers came rushing but it was too late. Their companions were dead and everybody had escaped. They proceeded to destroy the place completely, took all the money and went back to the garage. In the interval our people in the garage were given a chance to escape and they didn't waste it. Even uncle Bile, even though he died later that evening, was not there any more. Hassan carried him away instantly. In fury the soldiers destroyed the garage, took two Toyota Landcruisers and left.

"So four of them are dead now?"

"Yes," Hassan recounted, swallowing back his anger. "Bile, Botan, Hersi and Ashkir."

"Where's my mother now? Where's everybody else?" I asked.

"They're in the house in Waharaadde."

Hearing that story, it was as though something snapped in me. Some unknown thing inside of me snapped. Both my body and my brain were shaking with anger and violence. I never knew I carried so much violence inside me. I felt sick enough to vomit or faint. I think I must have felt every human feeling possible except for sadness and crying. I even felt like laughing, and I did. For a few seconds I actually laughed, can you believe it. Right in front of Hassan I actually laughed for a few seconds. The sickness in his eyes made me stop the laughter, I guess, for I stopped as suddenly as I started. I didn't know what to do or to say. It's as though my soul flew away into the sky right before my eyes. It's as though another personality was actually taking me over. I could even hear my own laughter as though it was something separate from me. Hassan later told me that all the while big teardrops were running down my cheeks. I don't recall that.

## 16

On our way to the house we saw some untidy-looking soldiers in very plain uniforms. They seemed to be hiding behind the buildings and trees. They were carrying small pistols and hand-guns, and grenades. Hassan saw my surprise.

"They're the USC fighters," he explained. "They're on guard against the moment that the Daroods come to loot and kill the people."

"All the Daroods or only the Marrehan-Daroods?"

"Since last night people are divided into Hawiyas and Daroods."

"And they're killing each other?"

"No," he said. "We don't have much weaponry. They are the government and we are the civilians. They kill and we die."

"I've seen dead bodies all the way from home."

"You haven't seen anything yet."

Remembering all the dead bodies I had seen in the streets, at Bondere Market, and the story of my uncles, I found myself developing negative feelings towards Daroods. I couldn't help it. For the first time I began to think that perhaps Dad wasn't mistaken in his attitude to Daroods. Dad was right. The Daroods were defending the Marrehans. And if Dad was completely right the worst was yet to come. I might kill somebody with my own hands. I prayed to God to lead me in the right way. I couldn't decide it for myself.

My mother and the rest of my uncles, who numbered six excluding Hassan, their wives and children and Haji Awaleh, my grandfather, were there in the house. Their faces were all swollen. Grief was written all over their faces, and their eyes showed that they had shed litres of hot tears. My mother covered my head with kisses and sobbed almost noiselessly. She looked as if she was drained of all energy. She kissed my two brothers with equal passion. I realized that I too was crying when my mother wiped my wet eyes with the hem of her shawl. I cried more. This time, for the first time in my life, I cried without shame. They were all sitting on chairs in the daash and we took our places after mother brought us some chairs. We sat there silently. None of us said anything apart from the traditional greetings. I didn't ask about the loss and they didn't mention anything. We sat there and stared at each another silently. Then Uncle Mohamed grabbed the gun which had been lying on the ground beside him and stood up determinedly.

"Where are you going, my son?" asked his father.

"I'll just take a look outside then come back," he answered heading for the door.

"Put the gun down."

"I'm not doing anything wrong!" he shouted.

"I said put the damn thing down!" The old man almost fell as he tried to get to his feet.

Uncle Mohamed put the gun on the ground and sat in his place once again. His hands were shaking and he was biting his lip nervously. Grandfather asked me at last about my family. I told him the things he wanted to know. I also told him why I had brought the children and the plan I had for them.

"Good idea," he said. " A very good plan indeed." He looked around at the four women and children behind him. "We were just discussing taking the children and women to Jowhar."

He looked at the clear sky for a while then called his oldest son.

"Mohamed!" he called. "Go and get the bus to take these children and women to Jowhar."

"Yes, father," answered Uncle Mohamed. He grabbed his gun again and went straight through the door.

"Be careful with that gun," called out Grandfather.

He was going to get the bus from the garage in which my uncles had been shot dead. It was not that far, but it was dangerous. During the couple of hours he was away, the rest of us didn't do anything in particular. We had tea every now and then and sipped it silently. Grandfather prayed his prayers. I had a little conversation with my mother privately.

"You're coming to Jowhar with us, aren't you?" she asked.

I didn't answer.

"You should come."

"I'll see what they need me to do," I answered, and kept up a conversation with anyone else that I could in order to avoid any argument with my mother, since it was not in my plan to go with them to another town ninety kilometres away. Besides I was supposed to be the only man of my family. Uncle Mohamed brought the bus at last. We all went outside when we heard it stop in front of the house. Grandfather collapsed as soon as he saw it. He fainted. I think it was because the bus reminded him especially of Bile, who had been the official driver, because it was a passenger bus used in the city as public transport. We splashed cold water on the old man's frail body to get him back to consciousness, which we eventually did.

After discussing all possibilities we decided not to make the journey until the next day. The children had already slept and since there was nothing to offer them for dinner we thought it better not to wake them up. We decided we should all get some sleep. The house had five bedrooms so we didn't have trouble finding places to lie down. All my uncles except Mohamed, who knew he would be driving in the morning, and Grandfather, lay down in the daash. The women and children shared two bedrooms leaving the rest for the men. After lying in the daash with the men I decided to go into a room and listen to some radio stations, since I was the only one who could speak English well enough to understand English transmissions. I undressed myself, borrowed a maawiis and found a radio for myself before I lay down on one of the two beds in the room.

"Listening to your strange languages as usual?" my mother asked from the daash.

"Yes."

I turned and turned the dial searching for an English-speaking station. I found the VOA at last.

"Good morning and a Happy New Year. This is the news on VOA read by Ros Williamson. The news headlines: The President is having talks with Japanese officials...Two men and a child were killed in a Chicago residential area after a mad gunman fired a machine-gun...A twenty-year-old woman was raped in her apartment last night...The organisation Amnesty International is investigating human rights abuses in Chinese prisons as one of its campaigns in Third World Countries... And now the news in detail. The talks between American and Japanese officials on the balance of trade have intensified following..."

Two men were killed? I wondered sarcastically. A girl raped? Humph? "To hell with Amnesty International. To hell with human rights. To hell with..."

"Are you talking to us, Ali?" somebody asked from the daash.

"I said fuck human rights!" I yelled from the bed. "I'm not talking to you! I'm talking to Amnesty International and their damned human rights abuse investigations! Fuck it! Fuck the whole world!"

The person didn't ask any more questions, and I didn't say more either. We all slept eventually. But I had a terrible stomach ache caused by the awful thing I had eaten earlier in the day.

Most of that night I thought about Dad and God. I was mad as hell at both of them for putting me in this situation. I hated that neither of them was around and visible. I later recited some Koranic verses that I knew by heart, and prayed silently to God.

# 17

All of us were in the bus by seven o'clock in the morning.

"We'll pass by my house to check if everything's all right," said Uncle Mohamed as he started the engine. In less than a quarter of an hour the bus braked in front of the garage. The place was busier than ever. Young men armed with all kinds of guns filled the place, and many approached the bus to shake hands with my uncle.

"I'll be right down," he told them.

"Everybody who can carry a gun should get off here and get a gun," he ordered, looking back at his passengers. "Come on. Get a move on."

He turned the engine off leaving the music on and stepped down to talk to the men. All of us except the women and children got out too, and then my mother followed us. The first thing I noticed was that the garage had no gate at all. The second thing was that each and every wall of the place was either pocked with holes, cracked, red with blood, or blackened by bullets. The restaurant was closed since there was no reason to open it. The garage, on the other hand, was open and full of people busy with some sort of activity. Most were working on vehicles either repairing them or painting slogans on them such as: Viva USC! Down Siyad. Down! Darood Killer! USC Rules this Country! and so on. Other men were involved with guns, either cleaning them and firing into the sky occasionally or simply enjoying letting the guns hang from their shoulders as they proudly walked up and down in the garage. I found my way through the crowd and stopped on the spot where Hassan said my four uncles had been shot dead. It looked like it was already forgotten. Blood was still there on the ground mixed with all kinds of vehicle oil. I felt a hand on my shoulder. It was my mother.

"Come and have breakfast," she said drying my tears with the palms of her hands. We went to the house adjacent to the garage and had the same white sticky liquid thing that had kept me awake last night. Mother told me that the children had been given milk instead.

"You should come with us to Jowhar," my mother started.

I made no reply.

"It's too dangerous to stay here."

"He's old enough to carry a gun," Uncle Mohamed snapped. "If he isn't fighting, who is fighting then?"

"He's not old enough!" she snapped back. "I'm his mother and I know more than anybody else what my son is capable of doing. He cannot carry a gun!"

"I don't want to go, mother. I want to stay and fight."

"Listen to your mother, son," Grandfather enjoined, and that was the last word. Nobody was supposed to talk back to Grandpa.

The bus took off for Jowhar at nine. All except four of us were women and children. Uncle Mohamed was the driver, Grandpa was an old man, Hassan accompanied his nine-months pregnant wife to make sure she was safe, and I was mama's sweet little boy. Nothing worth mentioning happened during that trip except that we saw burned-out cars and lorries along the road. Everybody was either sleeping or too tired to talk. After half an hour we were at Balad, the only town between the capital city and Jowhar. Balad seemed to be like heaven. They still had food, and at the roadside restaurant we didn't miss the chance. All of us ate as much as our bellies could stand before taking off again. We reached Jowhar peacefully after little more than another half an hour.

Jowhar was not new to me. I had been there many times before, mostly when I had run away from home. It was blessed with very fertile land and so its inhabitants depended on farming all kinds of fruit and vegetables, corn, cotton, but most importantly bananas and sugar-cane for which it was famous. The bus stopped in the parking lot just after the Sugar Factory. A dozen or so farmers circled the bus and asked countless questions about what was going on in the capital. We were not very helpful though. We were dead tired.

"Are you coming with us, Ali?" asked Grandpa. "Or do you prefer to go to your father's house?"

"I'll take the kids to my father's place and come back."

"Do you know the house where we'll be staying?" asked Uncle Mohamed. My uncles owned three houses in Jowhar and my father had one.

"The big one, I suppose."

"That's right."

# 18

On the way to my father's house, dragging my two exhausted little brothers, I noticed that the town was close to its normal self. There was electricity and all the businesses were open. People were going about their daily chores as usual. Kids were playing in the street. Anyway, within five minutes we were at our destination.

The house was made of sticks and mud and it had three bedrooms. The big grassy daash was all fenced by sticks. The place was as peaceful as ever. The old couple, Jimaale and his wife Haleemo, whom my father allowed to live at the place free of charge in return for keeping it in order, were working on the small plot of land attached to the house when I pushed open the daash door.

"Anyone there?" I called.

"Who is it?" asked the old man putting his hoe on the ground.

"It's me, Uncle Jimaale," I replied closing the door behind me.

"Who are you?" he asked, shading his eyes with his muddy hand.

"Farah's children."

"It's Farah's children!" he cried to his half-deaf wife who was watering some plants. "They're safe!"

"Look!" he said pointing at us so she could see us. She had better eyes than his, while he had the better ears. They made the perfect couple. "Farah's children are here!"

"There they are!" she cried as soon as she saw us. "My children!"

They welcomed us as cheerfully and generously as always. After we had told them our story they insisted that we take a rest. The three of us shared a vacant bedroom.

The children woke up before me for I didn't open my eyes again until eight o'clock in the evening. The old couple had prepared an enormous amount of food for us, and after enjoying the meal I left the children there and took off to see the other part of my family. Lighting my first cigarette for two days I felt joyful and dizzy and took my time to reach my destination. Looking around the shops to cheer myself even more, I bought a cold coke for myself and in ten minutes' time I was at the big house of my uncle's.

Everybody was now feeling better physically. Hassan said he was going out for a walk and invited me to go with him. I accepted the invitation and I was once again wandering about the town's streets, which Hassan knew well. All my uncles had lots of contacts everywhere, probably because they owned transport lorries and buses and travelled regularly. Anyway we visited one of the people he knew in the town and then spent time at a coffee shop where we played dominoes and chess. We left the place after a couple of hours and parted. We agreed that we should meet in the morning and decide from there what to do next.

By eight o'clock the following morning I was at his place and we had breakfast together. Hassan suggested we go to the main bus station and find out from the bus and lorry drivers who came to and from the capital round the clock, how the situation was developing. On the way he told me that Uncle Mohamed had taken the bus back to the capital in case the vehicle was needed, whatever that meant.

"Hey, Awaleh!" somebody called us from behind. We turned around and a man who looked like a driver appeared.

"Hi, Warsame," answered Hassan. "How are you? When did you arrive?"

"Last night." He stretched out his hand to shake hands. "I've heard about the family loss. My condolences. It must have been very difficult for the family to lose four men in one day."

Hassan didn't say anything. Neither did I.

After these exchanges the man told us that his bus was leaving for the capital in a matter of hours and that we were welcome to ride with him free if we wanted to go. Hassan and I thought it over and accepted the offer. We had to be ready in an hour so I visited both houses and bade everybody good-bye. Thank God I had saved some money for the New Year's Eve outing, and I gave most of it to the old couple. At first they refused to accept it but I insisted, as I didn't want my two little brothers to be a trouble to them. I didn't tell anybody my plans beyond the next few days for I myself had none.

# BOOK TWO

## 19

About midday on that Wednesday morning the light blue Borsani bus, which was carrying only one-fifth of its ordinary capacity of fifty passengers, reached Huriwaa. It had to terminate there, in the middle of Huriwaa quarter, instead of going to the regular bus station downtown. We began by going to the main family house. The restaurant was open again but lacked many customers. With the women and children gone the house too lacked life. The garage, on the other hand, was overcrowded, not by the usual set of youngsters who hang around car workshops doing the dirty work or learning the job, but by all kinds of men of all ages from sixteen to sixty. Some of the older men, I was told later, were former Hawiya high-ranking officers in the army. All of them, except the ones who were taking a break for tea or cigarettes, were as busy as bees. As well as the ordinary tasks of vehicle maintenance, they were involved in quite different work. Some of them were cutting the roofs off vehicles, especially from the four-wheel-drives like Landcruisers and Landrovers, while others were unloading all kinds of food and weapons from lorries and buses parked in front of the garage, and putting them in the stores. I noticed that the bus which my uncle Mohamed had been driving was one of those stuffed with food. I didn't ask any questions but, instead, as ordered, took part in the work without understanding. I carried some cartons full of spaghetti into the stores, stood by to help the mechanics and handed them the tools they asked for, brought tea and food from the restaurant for the busy men, and so on. About five o'clock in the afternoon the day's work was finished. The three big stores had been filled with food and ammunition. About twenty Toyota Landcruisers had had their roofs cut off and heavy guns, whatever their marks were, had been mounted on them. These vehicles explained everything. We were, as Dad had predicted, at the beginning of a civil war. The converted Landcruisers were our replacement for the military jeeps which we didn't have.

After the work had been done, a man came up with a piece of paper and a pencil. He said that anyone of us who wanted to register for what he called the 'liberation' war had to write his name down on the paper. I could have refused to register like my uncle Hassan did but I chose to liberate my people. After the registration was finished we were divided into groups. Even though I was almost sure that the so-called liberation would involve bullets and that sort of thing, I was not at all clear about what the liberation meant or how it was going to be implemented. Nor did I know who exactly were our oppressors. All I knew was that it would be happening on the following day. They didn't tell me and I didn't bother to ask. As a matter of fact they told nothing to the young men who registered for the liberation. We had a good dinner and were told to sleep in order to be fresh for the big day ahead of us.

The following morning I met the others in my group. We were five, and our car was a black Toyota Landcruiser with two fierce-looking guns welded on it, one on top of the main chassis and the other on the front. All the seats had been ripped out of the car except for the two in the front for the driver and his mate. The five of us had our jobs defined. One was to be the driver. Another sat on the seat beside him with one of the guns in front of him. His job was to fire that gun, and he was also the one in charge. Three of us sat where the other gun stood in the back. This was the bigger gun, and it was huge. It had three legs all welded to the floor. One of us had to aim the gun at the right spot, another of us had to fire, and my job was to keep reloading it with these long chains of bullets. Small machine-guns were also given out for people to carry on the shoulder for use in case of emergency. I didn't get a gun for I didn't know how to use it. I was there to learn from experience!

About seven o'clock that morning our convoy of about fifteen vehicles departed and headed downtown. On the way we met up with other groups. Each was more or less armed like we were. We might have been different in the kinds of vehicles we had but we were all similar in that each vehicle carried five or six men, heavy guns and ammunition to match. After about three kilometres we came to a halt as we met up with other

USC fighters. They were in groups like ours, and there must have been hundreds of them. I had never seen anybody as armed as those men. Very few of them, however, were trained soldiers. Most were just like me. The assembled groups, which seemed to have come from all over the city, were once again divided and despatched to different places. Our group along with many others were sent to the Aymiska where rich Darood military officers lived. Aymiska was one of the Darood hide-outs, I was told, and our job was to drive them out. Other groups were sent to the Presidential Palace or other important Darood concentrations.

In a matter of minutes, because we drove like hell, we arrived at the rich neighbourhood of the Aymiska buildings. To my surprise the fight had already started and there were more than twenty USC armed vehicles at the spot. The first shock was to my hearing which was suddenly shattered. The place was as noisy as hell. Not only were the people shouting with anger and crying with pain but there was the endless noise made by these strange guns whose existence I had not been aware of before. If the USC were armed, the Daroods were still more heavily armed, for they were the government and had direct access to the nation's weaponry. I crouched on my seat and put my hands on my ears. My companions, whose names I don't know to this day, took up the fight and did their part.

"Fill the chain!" one of them yelled at me.

I sat upright and filled the long chain with bullets then placed it in a small box from where it fed directly into the gun. I didn't look at the scene and I was really glad my job could be done from a sitting position. The fighting went on and on without any mercy, though so far nobody had been hurt from my group of five. In time I found myself watching the fight whenever I was between reloadings. We kept fighting and they kept fight-ing, so bravely, too. I could see men falling hard on the ground. Some were screaming with pain, others lay still. They were all red. I didn't feel sorry for them. I had no feelings at all. It was as if my heart had been removed from inside me. The tragedy, however, was that nobody was enjoying the occasion, yet eve-rybody was participating in it. I wondered why. The battle continued without change, except for the increase in dead bodies, until about five o'clock, when the Daroods started to withdraw. They didn't immediately leave the place but they moved a couple of metres backwards every now and then. And at about sunset we started to collect the few sophisticated guns we had been able to capture, then we left. I don't know how many people got killed but the five of us on the car were safe and sound. We went back to our headquarters, and when we arrived at the garage it was as busy as ever.

"How was your day?" Uncle Mohamed asked me.

"Horrible," I said. "I need a gun."

"You will get one when we've got enough guns."

That night we did nothing. What I mean is there was no fighting. Some of us, including me, just stayed at the garage. Some others went off for a time, then came back loaded with food, bottles of whisky, cartons of medicine, piles of clothes and a few guns. They had been away looting shops, pharmacies, and whatever they could think of, and even killed whoever tried to stop them.

"You didn't have to do that," I said to one of the guys who'd been in the raiding party.

"You're just a stupid kid!" he shouted. "Do you know where we got these things from?"

"No," I said. "Where?"

"From the government stores! It's the food they kept there while the Hawiyas were starving! We did the growing and they did the storing! That's not fair, is it?"

"No."

I asked no more questions after that. I didn't sleep much either that night. I begged a man to teach me how to use a gun and in a couple of hours I was shooting like a soldier. I felt so good that I could at last fire a gun. I told my uncles about my little accomplishment. They simply looked at me and said nothing. Uncle Mohamed patted my shoulder proudly. I could tell from Hassan's eyes that he wanted to say something but I knew he couldn't. He had to respect his older brother's point of view. We have a proverb: He who's one year older than you, is also one year wiser than you.

The following morning I was given a different job. I was not sent to fight like yesterday. New jobs came up all the time. Apparently there had been some unexplained explosions the other night and it was believed that there had been Darood spies with radio contact in the area. We had to find them. and I was told along with other young men that that was our job. We had to search everybody we saw. Again I was the only one who had no war experience. The rest, it seemed, had done it all before. I don't know where. Anyway we started our search patrol as soon as the fighters departed. It seemed as if almost everybody we searched was carrying a radio. Their radios were confiscated and they usually received summary executions at the hands of my colleagues. All kinds of people it seemed were working for the Daroods as spies. Old people, women, and even children. After two weeks of killings we received new orders. The main headquarters in Huriwaa had heard that we killed each spy we captured. We were commanded not to kill them right away any more. From now on we should bring them to the authorities. One day our group of three captured an old man with a radio. I was told to hand him over, so I led him to the garage at gun-point.

"Please don't turn me in," he begged when we were half-way to the garage. We were only the two of us.

"Just walk, you old bastard," I told him and pushed him with the gun.

"Please," he repeated. "I was forced to spy. I'm not even a Darood."

I decided to let him talk. He told me that he belonged to one of those small tribes who were not even supposed to be fighting. I somehow believed him, and let him go.

A few days later we again captured an old man whom I was instructed to turn in. When he had made sure it was only the two of us he tried to run away.

"Stop!" I shouted running after him. He ignored me. He kept running. "Stop, or I'll kill you!" I repeated. He wouldn't listen. I fired my gun a couple of times and he was suddenly on the ground. I reached him. He was bleeding like hell in his back, and his body moved slowly every now and then. I laid my gun on the ground beside the man and bent down to peer more closely at him. Even though I had been seeing human beings killed every day for the last fifteen days this man's death was different to me. I took a deep breath and closed my eyes. If only he'd obeyed my orders! I wished. He wouldn't have been dead. I could even have freed him if he really wanted. I don't know how long I had my eyes closed but when I opened them again the man was lying quite still. None of his limbs was moving. He was completely dead. I knew he was dead. The funny thing was, I felt such remorse and at the same time pride about that old man's death. I experienced joy at having killed the enemy with my own gun for the first time, yet it filled me with horror that I'd killed a fellow human being. For a moment I hated myself for not having spared his poor life. After taking another long deep breath, I stood up slowly and told myself not to weep for an enemy who was leading artillery towards us. I pushed the memory of him away after that. If I did remember it was only for a very short time afterwards, maybe for the few days following the incident. I didn't have time to remember him. I had better things to do than to think of one dead man. And anyway, was he any better than my beloved and loving uncles?

In the following days the USC troops fought every day but I didn't take part in those battles, partly perhaps because I was not sure I was ready to do more killing, but mainly because I was not told to. They sometimes won and sometimes lost, they told us, but I never understood what the terms 'winning' or 'losing' meant. I think victory, to them, was when you lose a brother and kill three other people's brothers. But as far I was concerned there had been no victory by anybody on the day I was there to fight.

However, something changed on the day of January the twentieth. My group changed for a start. I was grouped with another four men armed just like before, on the same kind of vehicle except that this time the colour was grey. The fighting front had also changed, and we were told we had to go to the residence of the President's wife, Kadijo, or Kadijo Hide-outs as it was known. We were also told that it would be more challenging, and more dangerous too. The place, I was told,

106

was also much bigger than the Aymiska and more strongly defended. In comparison, Aymiska was child's play.

"Do we have to go there?" I asked as we started the engine.

"Are you afraid?" asked the driver sarcastically.

"Oh, no," I defended myself. "No, I'm not afraid. I was only wondering why we had to change fronts."

"Aymiska is already done, boy," said the other man beside him.

"Done?"

"Yes. Last night. We overran the place and it's all ours," added another one, all pride and self-confidence.

"And now we'll conquer this other place?"

"Yep."

In a short while we arrived at the Kadijo Hide-outs. The place turned out to be horrific beyond my imagination. I have no words to describe it. It was as big, crowded, noisy and bloody as hell. The sights were unspeakable. The noise was intolerable. There was the sound of guns which never stopped firing, the roars of the crazy mob which never diminished, and the cries and the screams of the wounded were unbearable. Vehicles were being driven rapidly backwards and forwards, crashing against walls to try and breach them. We joined in the mayhem and fought like cats. Two men filled the bullet chains, two fired, and one was at the driving wheel. I think the two heavy guns on our vehicle were referred to as Dashica and SK 43 or something of that sort.

This time, unlike before, I had my own gun. I knew mine was called an AK. I kept firing and firing so no one could get near me. It was hard to tell if you were killing or not. Everywhere you looked people seemed to be falling down. Then one of my colleagues fell off the vehicle, suddenly, as if the wind had taken him. He was the one firing the gun on the back. His partner quickly replaced him, while another jumped down to get him back on the car. I suddenly found myself watching the two men. The one who jumped was trying to help his friend when they were both shot from behind. The first one fell to the ground and didn't make any more movements. The other who had obviously received a leg injury tried his best to creep on his belly towards the vehicles.

"Get the man!" the driver shouted at me, "or replace him!"

The gunner broke off and hauled our wounded colleague back onto the vehicle. I took his place immediately, and took the damned machine in my two hands and kept pushing the two small buttons to fire. I held the buttons down and I saw the long chain of bullets beside me being swallowed up. This time I could see what my gun was doing to people.

"We have to get out of this place!" the driver said as he reversed at great speed, smashing over anything that was in the vehicle's path.

"Good idea," agreed another of our group.

We left the awful place at about four o'clock on that bloody afternoon. But when we arrived at the garage we were told to go back, after getting two more men and more ammunition and leaving the wounded one there. We were not in a position to argue. It was an order. We got back to the Kadijo Hide-outs at seven that evening. It was just like before if not worse. We fought tooth and nail. By nine o'clock we managed to force our way inside the palace. That meant there were no more enemy soldiers left. Since neither side kept any prisoners and since there did not appear to be any other way out of the palace except where we had been fighting, it must mean that almost all of us and each and every one of them had been killed. The palace provided us with plenty of booty: gold, a huge amount of hard currency, weapons, sports cars, armed vehicles and much more. We took everything. We even searched the dead bodies. Each of us got something. My share was a good tape-recorder and two-thousand dollars in US dollar bills.

We went back to the garage in what was called 'victory'.

# 20

A week passed. Neither I nor my group fought during that week. We simply stayed around and helped the other men go to war. We nursed the wounded, cleaned the guns, and put the things we had looted away in the stores. (But not the two thousand dollars. I had given that to my uncle Mohamed to keep. That was for me.) Nobody talked about the dead ones. On one of these days which all seemed the same, we were storing things when a man pulled over in a car and cried, "The President is out! We won! The President is gone! The Presidential Palace is cleared!"

We all stopped whatever we were doing and looked at the man in complete disbelief. To me that really was a victory for it meant that the war was over and the regime overthrown.

"All the Daroods have left the city!" he went on.

The news was soon confirmed by another man who'd just arrived. There was great excitement at the garage. We jumped on to all available vehicles and headed for the Presidential Palace. Everybody had his own reason for going there. My reason was just to see it. I had always been curious about what they had kept inside that they didn't want other people to see. Whenever you came close to it they would chase you away as though you were a criminal. My curiosity would soon be satisfied. As we drove off we chanted cheerfully, and continued chanting all the way.

The Palace didn't look like a palace any more. Some of the buildings were on fire. We made our entry into the huge grounds without any interference. The Red Berets were all over the place as usual, but this time dead. The people were chanting freedom songs and looting the palace when we arrived. Some of us joined in the looting but most of us were told to chase the President's party which was on the run.

The Daroods, we were told, divided themselves into two groups and took everything they could carry. Weapons and billions of dollars in cash and gold. They took two different routes out of the city to cause confusion over their president's whereabouts. Both groups headed for Afgoye, thirty kilometres to the south. We also divided into two groups, to make sure we didn't miss the President, and each hoped it was chasing the one with the big man in it. Most people, including me, wanted to see the President's dead body more than anything else, and we were elated to think that we were pursuing the group which he was with.

It was a while since I last thought of Dad, but I thought of him now. I wished that he was there to see me. I wanted him to know that I was a man. Yes, a brave one, too. I wanted him to be proud of me. I wanted him to know that I was not only fighting to liberate my people, but that I was actually chasing the President of Somalia. Yes, the very man who put Dad behind bars for years, and killed and tortured many of his friends and colleagues. But he was not there for me. He was not there when I really needed him to see me and say, "That's my boy."

It turned out the President was not with the group we were chasing, but the other group. Anyway, it didn't make much difference since we had a band of our guys chasing them, too. We pushed on, and in no time we caught up with the government people. They were not only running but also fighting back as they fled. We kept chasing them on. An uncountable number of human lives, from both sides, were left behind as we fought. Some just died from falling off their cars and then being crushed on the ground by the ever-moving convoy of vehicles. Nobody cared and nobody was afraid. We all lost any kind of feeling. Anyway, in a couple of hours the four groups met up in Afgoye, and the President, wherever he was, was still not declared dead. To our dismay, however, the Daroods got stronger at Afgoye. It was later explained why that was so. There were other USC fighters in Afgoye whose job was to fight in the south. Those fighters, however, were USC sympathizers from the Daroods who were against the regime, but who changed their minds when they saw it was Daroods against Hawiyas. That complicated the war and made it more bitter. The Daroods had more weapons than they needed; all they wanted were more people and now they got them. I can never forget what happened that day. Suddenly our troops started to topple like statues. More than a dozen people I personally knew died that day. We were about to withdraw when we were saved by other Hawiya groups who must have heard the news. They came both from the far south and from the capital. The Daroods started to evacuate the area, but we didn't let them; we followed them. Thousands of people were killed that horrible day. Anyway after two weeks of that bloody war, the Daroods were driven as far away as the town of Kismayo which borders Kenya. We were able to do that not because we were better fighters but because we outnumbered them. In the southern regions the Hawiyas outnumbered the Daroods and so we got help all the way. Fighters joined us from almost every town and village until we reached Kismayo.

The story had another face, however, in Kismayo. All the other Daroods who'd run away were there, since Kismayo was near the border, and they couldn't cross the border into Kenya. They had been forced to stop running and to fight. They also developed new tactics. They stopped using the military uniforms they had been wearing earlier. They were plain-clothed like us. Some of them even sprayed USC on their vehicles. The thing was, they were not recognisable any more, and they were fighting back. This time they really fought. I mean they really did. I could see that our army was taking a step back every now and then. The Daroods were really tough this time. That is the time our vehicle was burned out. I was on the ground to help a man I knew when the bazooka hit our car. The whole car was soon in flames. My six-man group was history. I could hardly even recognize their faces. They melted like ice cubes on a hot pan. I was not happy about it of course, but thinking back, I was not very sad about it either. Maybe because I was stoned. I don't know. Those days everybody was high. Some drank liquor, others chewed khat non-stop, or smoked hash, marijuana or even heroin. Those who were not using things were also high. The flames, the smoke, the smell of the bullets fired, the smell of the bodies were all making the people drunk. I can't remember anybody who was in his complete senses so long as he was in that war. Anyway, after I lost my colleagues and my car I joined the infantry. This, however, was not a piece of cake like before. It was a job for a professional, I found out. Almost everyone in the infantry was a former soldier. Few were like me. Infantry fighting, unlike on the car, was more dangerous and at the same time easier. Let me explain. Being on a car armed with such a big gun was a very risky business. The enemy aimed their guns at you because you kill more people than those on the ground. Being in the infantry, on the other hand, meant fighting man to man. I knew I was not yet ripe for this kind of thing, so all that afternoon I hung back, and made sure I stayed behind the front lines and didn't come face to face with anybody. I watched the men fight. They dug each other's insides out with the bayonets of their guns, because people were very close to each other, and so it was often very difficult to fire a gun. Suddenly something big exploded right in the middle of us. I couldn't see what happened. I don't think anyone did. We were covered with huge clouds of dust and smoke. I staggered further to the rear in the hope of not getting killed. Suddenly there was a pause and both sides were backing off after hours of bloody fighting. In the confused withdrawal I didn't know where I was standing until I heard the people around me speaking in very clear Darood accents.

"Let's not run away again!" one said.

"The sons of bitches are almost in our hands!" another yelled. I looked around and saw a man approaching me.

"Who the hell are you?" he asked me. He probably asked this question because I was skulking in a corner. Luckily he was dead drunk. Even though he was drunk and I had my machine gun, I was nevertheless surrounded by Daroods. I had a small idea and I prayed to God it would work. Oh, God!

"What do you mean who am I?" I asked, straightening up and looking insulted.

"I thought you were one of the son-of-a-bitch others," he said and walked away swinging his gun. I had to get myself out of this mess, I told myself. I knew sooner or later they would discover I was not a Darood. Fortunately, for me at least, the fighting started up again. That gave me the opportunity of not being focused on. I started to take a couple of steps away from them when I thought no one was looking. I was trying to reach the outer edge of their army. I fired my gun towards my people every now and then, and after half an hour or so I reached my objective, then I ran as fast as the wind.

"Hey, you!" I heard someone shouting behind me.

"I told you that the son of…" another was saying but I was already in the bush. I looked over my shoulder and saw there were two men hot on my heels, but I kept running and didn't slow my speed.

Unlike most of the rest of the country, which is semi-desert and savannah-like, where anyone can see you for miles around, the bush in these southern parts of the country had more tall trees and lots of knee high grass. If I had the guts, I could really hide anywhere in these tall grasses and let the assholes behind me get lost. But I didn't. I didn't have those guts. There was this bit of extra energy in me though, so that the only thing I really trusted was my own feet. Not because I was naturally fast or anything, because I wasn't. I knew that from football. I was a defender and a damn good one too. Even though I had very good defensive techniques I hated any fast asshole who'd send the goddam ball far from me and then run past me like the wind. I really did hate these sorts. What I'd do was not give such types the chance to run with the ball in the first place. Anyway, now I ran and ran.

I kept looking over my shoulder, and the two men were still coming.

I zigzagged my steps so they wouldn't shoot me dead. After what seemed a long time I came to a large swamp-like water-hole. I stood on the bank and looked down. It was deep and dark. I crouched on the bank and looked back through the bush. One of the two men was racing in my direction. I could see his dusty bare feet jump over small clumps of vegetation as he made his way through the bush. I looked down at the huge empty dark hole again, and after having calculated that the hole was less risky, slowly immersed my body in the murky water. My feet found a rock to rest on. My right hand was clinging to the sandy bank while my left held the trigger of my gun as the butt of the gun rested against my neck. After a minute or so the rock, or whatever it was I was standing on, began to settle under my weight, and then broke and fell away. I gathered all my strength to hold myself up with my hands which were already busy. I strained to keep my feet steady in the mud, and I could feel my whole body tremble either with fear or because I was running out of energy. The man was now only a few hundred yards away, and had slowed down. He looked like he was in his late forties, and he had a beard. He was looking around him very cautiously. He held his gun in both hands and his finger was ready to pull the trigger at any moment. I prayed that he would either come nearer or give up and leave the place. I couldn't hold myself up much longer. Lucky me! The man decided to investigate the the huge pond in front of him. He moved carefully in my direction. I drew my head down hoping he wouldn't see it and blow it off. He kept coming and coming and coming and.... Not more than thirty yards away he stopped. I knew he would come closer if only I could be patient. But could I. I was running out of breath and I could feel the sand under my hands move. I tilted my gun into position with my shoulder, and pulled the trigger and fired non-stop like a mad man. The man was on the ground. I gathered the last energy in me and pulled myself up on to the bank. I was about to thank God and sigh in relief when I saw the man attempt to reach out for his gun which lay about two yards from him. I fired again, and this time his whole body rocked as I steadily fired my automatic. He was dead. I took a deep breath, took his gun and walked away to find my folks. After ten minutes or so I started jogging then running. I didn't want to think, I just wanted to reach the safety of my folks. I don't know how long it took me to do so, because time had no meaning, but it was still daylight when I got there.

Back at the battle-ground nothing much had changed. They wouldn't move and we wouldn't. Later that evening, however, things did change. Our fighting fortunes began to be reversed. They started to push us back and back and back.

After several days of heated battles our side was once again back to where we had started. Back to Afgoye. Only thirty kilometres away from the capital. By this time I was again on a car. Not in the infantry any more. I had replaced a wounded driver.

At Afgoye I was told to take wounded in my vehicle to the capital. I was more than delighted. And in less than an hour I was heading for the city with a load of wounded men.

Once there we headed for the SOS centre, which was a compound of good buildings belonging to an aid agency and which was run as some kind of orphanage before the war, but now it was operating as a hospital, and a a damn good one too. It was where we nursed the wounded. I don't know what we would have done without the SOS. We handed the wounded over to them, and found that three of the injured had already died on the way. In the SOS compound a volunteer driver came up to me and offered his services. He wanted to replace me. It was the opportunity of a lifetime. It was now or never. I gave him the car and headed for my uncles' garage. It was on the same side of town and not far from the SOS centre. I walked there.

# 21

When I got back to the garage I learned that the rest of my uncles except for Hassan had been killed. Hassan had survived because he was the only one who had never grabbed a gun during all this mess. He sometimes worked at the SOS compound where we took our wounded, and other times stayed home. I hardly reacted to the news of my uncles' deaths. I don't know why. Maybe because death wasn't such a big deal to me any more. Maybe because they were fighting and killing Daroods, and therefore weren't any better than those Daroods they killed. Whatever the reason might be I didn't inspect my thoughts too closely. Hassan, on the other hand, was stricken with grief. We didn't talk much about their deaths for neither of us knew the details of how they died and who killed them. They had all been fighting in the south just like me.

I stayed with Hassan for two days. I spent most of the time sleeping because I had hardly slept for the last three months. While I'd been away in the south the USC had formed a new government. No voting, no elections, no talks, nothing. Now they were calling upon the people to register in the army to fight and defend their victory. The response was positive. Men, women and children – anyone who could carry a gun was joining up. All were excited. It looked like everybody except me was joining the army this time.

On my third day back, while people were registering their names as volunteer fighters I was going to the Medina quarter to check on my other family. Uncle Hassan watched me silently as I got ready to go.

"How will you go to Medina?" he broke the silence.

"What do you mean?" I asked.

"There are no buses, no cars, nothing," he said. "Only military vehicles roaming the streets."

"Who cares," was my response.

"Maybe you should use one of those stolen cars that the garage is full of. I don't know why they're there anyway."

I nodded and we went to look around the garage together. There were all kinds of vehicles, military lorries and other strange-looking armoured cars which had been captured from the National Army, expensive luxury cars which had belonged to the regime's top officials – people who by now were probably dead – and there were also normal everyday cars. I passed over a smashed blue Mercedes and went for another white one just next to it. I opened the door to find blood all over the seats. I slammed the door shut and looked for another. I passed the next row which was mostly Fiats. "How about this Honda Accord?" asked Hassan pointing to a beautiful machine on my right. "No Japanese car," I said and kept walking, behaving like a millionaire who'd decided to buy the best car available for his mistress.

"It's a good car," said Hassan.

My eyes meanwhile focused on a black BMW parked alone

in a corner. I said nothing but instead walked over and opened the door of the BMW. I placed myself in the driver's seat and said, "I'll take this one."

"Suit yourself."

I started the engine.

"I'll bring it back when I'm finished," I said.

"Here," said Hassan handing me a white envelope.

"What is it?" I asked.

"It's your money," he said. "Your uncle Mohamed told me to give it to you if he didn't come back from the war"

We were silent for a moment then I took the envelope and opened it. My two thousand dollars were there.

"Thanks," I said as I stretched out my right hand to shake hands with him.

"You're not taking your gun?" he asked me smiling sickeningly.

"No," I answered. "No."

"Take care of yourself and say hello to your stepmothers from me."

"Good-bye."

## 22

The car was really something. I hardly did anything other than sit there in my seat. The doors closed themselves, the gear stick changed itself, the steering wheel was light as air. Everything was fast and easy. I stepped on the gas pedal and enjoyed seeing the world around me move away fast, as if I was in a space ship. I pressed a button every now and then to have the windows go up and down just for the fun of it. I went along 26th June street on my way to KM4. I opened the glove compartment of the passenger seat out of curiosity. There were different items inside: cassettes, house keys, a small book, cigarettes... I started

117

with the Benson & Hedges cigarettes and lit one for myself. Then the cassettes. I tried one after another and liked none of them. I reached for the small book and found it was written in a strange language. The only thing I could recognise was the picture of Lenin on the inside front page so I tossed it back to where it had been. I was already turning left at KM4 when I realised that the glove compartment door was still down. I reached to close it but suddenly my eyes glimpsed a man's face in the compartment. I reached in to find that it was an ID card with a picture. I held it in front of my face to read it whilst continuing to drive. The ID was one of the standard red IDs issued by the Ministry of Defense to its staff. I stared at the small passport-size photo. It was of a strong man with piercing eyes and a big moustache. He was not smiling at all. He could have won first prize in a competition for 'The Ugliest of God's Creation'.

"Son-of-a-bitch!" I shouted at the picture. "You're dead, do you hear? Dead! There's nothing you can do any more!"

I read the ID to see what his rank was. I was sure he must be a general but I just wanted to confirm it for myself. To my surprise the ID said the man was only an inspector.

"How can you afford a car like this when you're not even a general?" I asked the picture, this time almost in a whisper. "How can you?"

I placed the ID just above the steering wheel and kept talking to him. "I don't even think the generals in the Soviet Union have cars like this. How can you afford it?" I lit another cigarette. "These are your cigarettes and there's absolutely nothing you can do to stop me from smoking them, because you're dead! A dead bastard! You started this civil war from the day you bought yourself a car like this which is twenty times more expensive than your salary for the next twenty years! And now look at yourself. You are dead and probably sitting on a good chair in Hell, and here I am driving your fucking car!" I threw the cigarette butt down inside the car behind my legs and stepped on it as hard as I could. "And maybe I'm even wearing your clothes!" I touched the clothes I was wearing, all of them robbed from somewhere. "This is what the civil war is about, asshole! Corruption and greed!" I added. "And this is your payback!" I turned into the sand road towards my home. As I turned left I looked into the rear view mirror to see if there were any cars close behind, but I suddenly discovered another face in the mirror. I took another look to make sure I wasn't dreaming. The face was mine. It must have been a long time since I had last seen myself in a mirror. My face was almost not recognisable. Not even to me! It was a thousand times blacker and thinner than normal. It must have been due to the constant sun, the hunger and the sleeplessness which I had endured lately. My eyes were as red as blood and my teeth were discoloured because of the khat I chewed constantly, the liquor I drank steadily and the other drugs I smoked continuously for the last month or two. I turned away in despair and kept driving. Soon I was home.

# 23

My house looked different, too. The first thing I noticed was that the gate was not hanging on its hinges but lying on the ground. The wall was also damaged and I could see that there was debris all over the place. I turned the engine off and contemplated the scene from my comfortable seat. I knew from what I saw that my stepmothers were dead. I looked behind me and saw a kind of hill. The hill was what had once been a beautiful house – the house in which my friend Musa had lived. Looking around I could see that half of the neighbourhood had been destroyed and reduced to rubble. I didn't know what to do. I didn't know whether to get out of the car and look into the house, keep seated and watch, drive off and forget the whole thing, or simply laugh or cry. A woman suddenly appeared from the house. I watched her. The woman somehow resembled Anab, but I knew it was not her.

She was taller, more sunbaked, and a lot skinnier. She stood right in front of the house and looked at the car in which I was sitting. She ran her hand through her hair and kept watching the car.

"What do you want?" the woman asked.

I made no response. She went back into house and reappeared with a gun.

"What the hell do you want?" she shouted holding the gun without actually aiming at me.

Before I said anything another woman appeared from inside the house. I recognized the second woman – she was my stepmother, Falis. I smiled to myself, with some small gratitude to God. The first woman was indeed Anab. Then the two women, with four curious eyes swollen with sadness came closer.

"Ali!" both women screeched hysterically as they recognised me. They threw down the gun and raced towards me. "Oh my God, it's Ali!"

I opened the door but immediately the two women were on top of me screaming and shouting and crying.

"How are you?" I asked trying to get out of the car, and which I succeeded in doing after a furious struggle.

"Are you OK?" they asked instead, and started to inspect my body. "Are the children OK?"

"Yes, we're all fine." I looked around the now devastated house. "What happened?" I asked.

The two women stared at one another.

I waited.

"First one side attacked us," Falis started as she dried her tears. "They smashed the gate with a tank."

Suddenly Mona, our maid, came into my mind but as I formed my lips to pronounce the first letter of her name Anab added:

"Mona is dead."

I said nothing.

"They raped and killed her."

"How did you survive?" I asked.

"Thanks to God and many thanks to Falis," Anab answered, trying to swallow the tears that welled up in her big black eyes.

"She saved my life." She added and the tears rolled down on her cheeks.

"And now you're saving mine, too," said Falis blinking her tiny shining eyes so the tears would go away. Then Anab hugged her, and they both sobbed loudly.

And both were right; they had saved each other. Because the two women were from the two main tribes that were fighting, they had each pretended that the other belonged to her tribe whenever the situation demanded. They too had been through hell. They had witnessed the savagery of both sides. Had seen friends and neighbours killed. To cover up the lies about their identity they had been forced to journey with one group to Afgoye and with another group back again. I listened patiently as the two women told me their story. They had used all their wit to stay alive and to get out of danger.

"Isn't it a miracle?" Anab asked at last.

"Yes, it is," I agreed.

We sat down in the daash and had tea and biscuits. I noticed they had rather a lot of biscuits. More even than what we usually had on special feast days

"What are all these biscuits for?" I asked.

"We've been saving them up for the journey," said Anab.

"Journey?"

"Yes, we're going away," Falis added. "It's too dangerous to stay here."

"Especially when you are a Darood," Anab said.

"Yes," agreed Falis. "Some Daroods who were living with their Hawiya friends or families were still killed by other Hawiyas."

"So where are you going?" I asked changing the subject.

"Djibouti."

"Djibouti?" I repeated. "Why Djibouti?"

"Because that's the nearest place where we have some relatives," explained Anab.

"Relatives?"

"Yes," she said. "My brother lives there, remember?"

"Oh, yes," I remembered.

Anab's older brother, Erik, was a businessman in the small neighbouring country of Djibouti. Despite the fact that he was originally from Mogadishu he had Djibouti residency because his wife was from there. Even though I saw the man only once when he visited us some years ago, I knew almost everything about him. Anab talked about him all the time. I poured another cup of tea for myself.

"Does your brother know about this decision?"

"He's the one who suggested it when he called us some weeks ago."

"When?" I asked.

"When did he call?"

"No, when are you leaving?"

"As soon as we get space on a vehicle and some money," Anab answered.

"And how long will that take?"

"We're not sure," answered Falis. "Days perhaps."

I said nothing.

"Do you want to come with us?" asked Anab. "Or you'd rather stay in this bloody country and keep on killing other Muslims in this Holy Month of Ramadan?"

Ramadan? I remembered. That was right – we were in the middle of the month of Ramadan! Killing people should have been out of the question. Having sex or even eating before sunset was forbidden. It was supposed to be the month all people were equal. Rich and poor had to starve all day and share the food at night. It was the month when people helped one another. It was supposed to be the month of love and happiness!

"Is that what you want?" asked Falis. "To stay in this bloody country where human life has no value?"

"No," I mumbled guiltily. "No."

"Then you're coming with us?" added Anab.

"Yes."

# 24

I was in my room wondering what to do about my future when there was a light knock on the inside door, which was only ajar as usual.

"Come in," I said standing up from the chair by the window where I was sitting. It was Falis.

"You look pretty down," she observed as she sat on the bed and put the plastic bag she was carrying beside her on the bed. "I brought you some batteries for your radio," she continued. "I know the radio mean a lot to you." She pulled three pairs of Eveready batteries out of the plastic bag. She held them out to me.

"Thank you very much," I said. It was as if a part of me came alive once again. "Where did you get them?"

"From the lorry in the highway," she snapped for no apparent reason.

"Which lorry?"

"Didn't you see there's a lorry broken down in the highway?"

"And it was full of batteries?"

"Not only," she said. "Lots of other things as well. The whole neighbourhood's been looting it since yesterday. We got rice and sugar as well."

"I see," I said pulling my radio from under the bed. It looked so dusty. It was ages since I'd used it last. I blew some of the dust away and placed the batteries inside. "Thank you, Falis."

"You're welcome."

I tuned and tuned until I found an English-speaking station.

"Heavy fighting in the Somali capital of Mogadishu is reported to be continuing," said the speaker, "... although the number of casualties is not known, it is estimated that hundreds have died since the fighting began... That is the end of the news from London. You have been listening to the BBC World Service," she concluded.

"Liar!" I shouted at the radio. "Hundreds of *thousands* have died!" I looked around the room and found both my stepmothers staring at me as though I was crazy. "Liar!" I repeated. "I alone killed hundreds!" The women tried to make a move to put their arms around me and hug me but I raised my hand to reject them. They froze in their steps and made no further attempts.

"By the way," started Anab, in an effort to change the subject and break the tension in the room, "How's your family? I mean your mother and uncles?"

"Mum is in Jowhar," I said and put the radio back under the bed.

"And?"

I looked at her questioning eyes.

"Mum is in Jowhar," I repeated, "And Hassan is fine."

"And?" she put an arm round my shoulder and squeezed me.

I looked at her questioning eyes. I was trying to say the minimum, goddammit, but they didn't get the hint. She was still looking at me for a proper answer.

"The rest are dead," I added, cold as ice. I couldn't keep it any longer. And worse, I wasn't allowed to cry, for men didn't cry in my country. Some stupid bigshot probably made that silly rule.

I could see both women swallow back their shock. I could see that they didn't know whether to cry, scream, or run away. The room felt unbearably small, and the ceiling seemed to be coming down on top of me, making breathing impossible.

"When are we leaving this country?" I asked taking a deep noisy breath.

"Soon."

"How soon?" I almost shouted.

"We've found a vehicle that's going, and some of the money," said Falis.

"And we're trying our best to raise the rest of the money needed," added Anab. "Just make sure you're ready to leave any day from now."

"I'm ready."

Falis sat beside me and smiled.

"That's good," she said.

I hate women. I really do. They always want to go into details. She was trying to start something. I was sure she was about to tell me that I'd made a good choice in deciding to leave with them, and then she'd go on from there. What do they know about a good choice and a bad one anyway?

"That's really good, Ali," she repeated as though intentionally torturing me. But somehow, her smile was not the kind of phoney smile she generally gave when she's cooking up some fabulous plot. It was a genuine one, it was really genuine.

"Look," I said instead, and reached for my loaded envelope. "I've got some money, so maybe I can also contribute something."

"Oh, you keep your bit of change for your cigarettes," said Anab who was now also smiling. "We'll manage."

I tore the goddam envelope open and pulled the stupid wad of notes out.

"Here," I said and handed Falis half of it. About one thousand US dollars or so.

"What's this?" they asked.

"It's money," I told them. "It's American dollars."

"How much is that worth?" Falis asked.

"I don't know." I put the rest back in the envelope. "Enough to take us through the country, I guess."

# 25

The BMW kept me company in these days. I could drive around in it like a madman, listen to music in it, just go anywhere without much difficulty, and I could manage to get gas from the garage. It was also of benefit to my stepmothers. I took them places in the city and brought them back again. They thought it was the most wonderful machine they had ever seen. Falis even commented that she would have married a Marrehan if she had known how comfortable those cars were, and Anab's response was that she wished she had so that she could have had Dad all to herself. I joined in the friendly banter and said that the best thing would have been for Dad himself to be a Marrehan then we would all have had big cars. We all burst into laughter. But the laughter was superficial, and hid our real fears. We were anxious to leave the city. During these days which I used to call the days of "Me & My Car", things were going badly in the country. The former President was still hiding somewhere to the south where he was born. I wondered why he was still there in the country. Was it because he was now forgiven? Was it because our leaders didn't want him out of the country after all for some mysterious reason? Yet it was he who was the boss of the Mafia that had led the country into this chaos. It was all too political for me to figure out. Anyway, the so-called victory wasn't much of a victory. The city was as dead as stone and the people were close to starving. All government buildings, all the hotels and public facilities had been destroyed. It hadn't all happened only during the fighting, but also afterwards. It was as if people didn't want anything the government had built. The city was without electricity, except for a few people, looters and the tribal chiefs mainly, who had small electric generators – they boasted that the victory had brought them freedom. People were allowed to say what they wished and at least a dozen new newspapers came out. Everybody was allowed to do whatever he liked. But this wasn't freedom, it was anarchy. And if you were not living amongst people of your own tribe you were hardly even free to exist.

# BOOK THREE

## 26

There were people in front of our house when I arrived, driving very fast, that midday. Some of them were our neighbours but others I had never set eyes on before. Women, men and children. You could have thought it was a funeral since the people didn't look very happy and there was not much noise coming from them. As I got closer I could see they were saying their good-byes, my stepmothers being the focus of the farewells.

"I really wish you a safe trip," a woman was saying.

"There he is!" exclaimed Falis as soon as she saw me coming towards them. "We were beginning to worry about you, Ali."

"Worry?" I asked.

"Yes," she explained. "We're leaving today. Everything's all set at last. Pack and get ready!"

"When are we leaving?"

"Today. At two o'clock."

"Are you sure? I mean..."

"Absolutely," Anab cut me short. "There's a car leaving at two o'clock this afternoon." She looked at her watch. "That's less than three hours from now."

"Actually we're a bunch of cars and lorries," added Falis.

"Bunch of cars and lorries?"

"Yes, you see...we're not the only ones who're leaving this country. Besides it's too dangerous, they say, to travel in a small group."

"Oh!" I said. "So we'll be part of a convoy travelling together?"

"Exactly."

"You're the one who should know more about these things," a woman said in an accusing tone as I went to my room to pack. As I stood in my room I remembered I had to return the car before leaving the country so I grabbed one of my favourite tapes, hurried out of the room, passed the people in front of the house who had now grown in number, and hopped into the car.

"I'll be back in time," I shouted to my stepmothers who were half listening to the people and half watching me. I drove off as fast as I had come. I also fastened the seat belt for the first time in my entire life.

## 27

The invisible loud speakers in the car were going full blast as the deep strong voice sang. "Through these misty eyes – I see lonely skies – Lonely road – to Babylon…"

I came to the KM4 crossroads and instead of turning right to Maka El-Mukarrama street I decided to take the longer way so I kept going straight on, to the street that went past the Tribune edifice. The song kept blasting from those wonderful loudspeakers: "Seagull carry me – over land and sea – to my own folks –that's where I wanna beeee…."

Soon I passed the Milk Factory and turned right to Soddonka street, the biggest highway in the whole capital. I stepped hard on the gas and soon was like a flying carpet. In what seemed like a minute I braked right in front of the group of people who were sitting on the ground in front of the garage work-bays. Dust and other particles blew into the air and clouded the people to invisibility. I unfastened the seat belt and waited a moment until the dust cleared away. Just like a good actor, which was what I had in mind to be at the moment, I wound down the window at the press of a button and was faced with expressions of wild bewilderment looking back at me. Some were clearly admiring of me, others seemed unmoved, and simply waited to see who the mad driver could be. All the faces seemed more or less familiar, faces I had encountered during the war, I supposed, though I couldn't quite remember where and under what circumstances. Hassan, my uncle, was there and not many others who I really knew. All were having tea.

"You almost killed us, you USC driver!" a man shouted.

"You almost killed yourself," said Hassan.

"You're one hell of a driver," said another.

"Have you been watching an action movie?" somebody asked.

"All USC drivers are crazy one way or another," another observed. "They are either very good or very bad drivers."

All I did was smile while still standing by the open door of the car, as though posing to be photographed for a racing car magazine. I took my tape out of the player before I slammed the car door shut and took my place on the ground with everybody else.

"Help yourself to tea," said Hassan at last.

As I poured a cup of tea for myself from the thermos flask I noticed that one of the men, in his late thirties and probably crippled because there were walking sticks beside him, was watching me very intently. I ignored him.

"Who is this boy anyway?" he asked after a while.

"He's the only son of my only sister and closest surviving kin," answered Hassan.

"He's the son of your sister?" repeated the man as though it was a riddle, then looked at me with eyes smiling.

"Do you know me?" he asked me.

"Do I know you?" I asked. "No, I don't. Should I?"

"Not really," said the man still with the same expression. "The doer of an action forgets," he said, "but the receiver..." He paused. "The receiver doesn't."

I didn't know whether to agree with him or not for I didn't know what the man was talking about. Could it be one of those I shot and almost killed, I wondered?

"The receiver of an action doesn't forget," he repeated. "Never. The receiver doesn't forget it regardless of whether that action was good or bad."

I was almost scared as I noticed that there were not only walking sticks beside him but also a machine gun. Still talking to me and with his eyes focused on me he reached to his side, seemingly for the gun but grabbed the walking sticks instead.

"You see these things," he said raising the sticks. "I can't walk without them, and don't take it as a complaint because it isn't, and I wouldn't have them without you. I'd be dead by now without you! Hear me? I'm very grateful to you, young man. You saved my life."

He kept on telling me stories of things that certainly I'd experienced, and said how I had rescued him deadly wounded and put him on a car back to where he was taken care of. But I couldn't remember his face. I could remember the tales he told but not his face. I had no choice but to take the credit. The men resumed their previous conversation after this episode.

"So you think we should stop the war?" asked one of the man.

"Yes," was the reply from a man who was the oldest of all, a thin man with a small neat beard, who seemed in his fifties. "Nothing was ever achieved by war," he added.

"That's not true," another disagreed. "We liberated ourselves from the Daroods! We wouldn't be this free if we hadn't fought!"

"Maybe," agreed the first man. "But what did we exactly achieve in this war so far?" He eyed the men slowly. "More food? Peace? Happiness? or ... did we achieve ..."

"We achieved power!" exclaimed another.

"Power?" The first man shook his head in despair. "True we have the presidency and all, but what power does he have? The people won't even listen to him. They're too excited from the war, like you are. The Daroods are out of the country and yet we don't have peace. What kind of power is that? Besides you hear all the rumours like I do. Some of the Hawiya sub-tribes don't even want him, simply because he doesn't belong to their particular sub-tribe. What kind of power and achievement are we talking about here, eh?"

The men were silent for a while thinking about what he had said. "Even the Hawiyas are going to divide," he continued. "Mark my words. Wait – God forbid – for the day even Hawiyas become enemies! Then I want to hear from you, if you are alive still, whether you want the war to continue or not!"

"Then what are we supposed to do, eh?"

He thought about the question for a while before he said, "Anything but war."

I liked the thin man. He was not only sharp with his comments but he also sounded self-confident and all that. I wanted to say something. Actually, I wanted to ask the thin man something. I knew I wouldn't see Dad for a while, if at all, so I thought I should perhaps ask a few questions of this man instead. I remembered the comment of the other thin man with the glasses who was with Dad in our living room. He'd said that my country needed true tribalism. Full stop. And he didn't explain himself. I wondered if this other thin man could be any more help in clearing my troubled thoughts. It's a silly question, but I needed to ask it anyway. I really did. I cleared my throat to catch the men's attention. The thin man and Hassan turned my way. "I say," I started. I was speaking to the thin man, and looked straight at him. "Why do you think the Hawiyas might divide?" I asked. "Aren't they all Hawiyas together? I mean ... what kind of a tribe are they anyway, if they do that?"

"My boy," he said, "this is not about Hawiya or Darood or anything of the sort. This is about power. It's nothing to do with tribes and tribalism."

"How do you mean?" asked the man who was against him at the beginning.

"Most of you might not be old enough to remember it, but I was a young man in the sixties when we were forming our first government."

I never liked it when old men told you that you're too young or something to remember what happened a century ago, but this time I didn't mind too much. Although the thin man was bragging a bit and all, I didn't really mind it this time. After all it was me who raised the question.

"The beginning of the 1960s," he continued, "was when we succeeded in driving the white man out of our country. It was up to us to form our own government for the first time, after eighty years or so of European domination. The people were trusting, but our newly elected rulers started corruption right from the beginning."

133

"Why d'you think that happened, then?" I asked.

"Well," he answered in a bragging sort of way. "In a few words, we started to do things we didn't know anything about and we abandoned what we knew."

"What's it we started doing?" I asked.

"We started what they call democracy."

"And what did we abandon?"

"We abandoned tribalism."

I liked the neat answer but, to tell you the truth, I was a bit lost for a meaning.

"You mean tribalism is better than democracy?" I asked him

"No," he said right away. "I'm not comparing them, even though they might be quite similar in some ways. I'm only saying that we knew tribalism but didn't know democracy."

"So?"

"So we chose to eat with some one else's hands instead of our own."

"But our own hands were dirty, weren't they?" asked Hassan.

"Well, yes, in a way," he poured himself another cup of tea. "But hands are supposed to get dirty every now and then, aren't they?" He put three spoonfuls of suger in his tea. "Besides, we could've cleaned them by ourselves."

That guy could really talk. He's a typical old Somali. A walking encyclopaedia of advice, you could say. I really admired him by now, I must admit.

"You said," I started again, "that tribalism and democracy were the same or something?"

"I said they might be the same in some ways," he corrected me. "Democracy, in principle, is a system of government imported from Europe. They say it's a government by the people and for the people." He took a hot gulp of the tea. I could tell he was really enjoying his tea . "But so is tribalism. Or so *was* tribalism, I should say," he added.

No one said anything. Everyone, it seemed, was digesting the explanation.

"You said democracy is government by the people and for the people, just like the real old tribalism. That doesn't sound very bad, does it? But, I mean … we don't look much like democrats, do we?" I asked and lit a cigarette. I offered my pack around. A few guys took cigarettes, but the thin man shook his head as though I was interrupting his lecture. I didn't like that, to tell the truth. It upset me.

"No, we don't look much like democrats," he said, shaking his bald head. "Democracy is not bad. In fact it's as good as old tribalism and even more adaptable to the modern world. The thing is, we lost what we knew best and at the same time we didn't learn the new system. We're like the fox that didn't like the way she walked. She started walking like someone else and ended up looking ridiculous."

I liked this guy's talking ability. He really knew his lines. It was very obvious that he was enjoying everybody's attention on him. You could tell. You really could. He went on and on reminiscing about how things had been in the past and how they should have been, how democracy was this and tribalism was that, and all the time throwing in proverbs and things, like 'borrowed clothes never keep you warm because you're always worrying about when you'll have to return them'.

Actually, the guy was beginning to irritate me a bit with these sophisticated words of his. Not because I didn't like it, because in a way I did, but I also wished he'd use everyday words and phrases and all, if you know what I mean. I just did't like him being so superior.

"…the only obvious way," he was saying now, "is to go back to our system…tribalism is just as good…all we've to do is modernize it…write it down and teach it in schools …"

Teach tribalism at school? Now *that* was a really fascinating idea. I mean, talking about tribes in schools instead of hiding it? That'd certainly be cool, I thought.

"…we've to change it to fit the world's politics…we've to make a parliament representing all tribes on an equal basis and numbers, then *they* have to elect the president."

I looked at the man's watch as he said these last words. It's time I was going, I thought. I cleared my throat to catch my uncle's attention.

"I've got to be going soon, Hassan," I said, "and I'd like to have a word with you before I go."

"Why don't you stay a while?" Hassan asked.

The thin man stopped his speech.

"Yes, you should," said the thin man. "After all, I was actually talking to *you*."

Everybody looked at me as though I'd suddenly become important. "I can't," I said, "I'd really love to, but I can't. I really can't. I'm leaving the country in an hour or so."

He looked at me with a curious, knowing sort of smile in his eyes. "Son," he said, "you made the best decision in your life when you decided to leave this country. Go and don't come back until the war is over and you have a university degree with you," he added.

They all stared at me and talked about how dangerous it was to travel, and how brutal were the gangs on the roads between the regions, but in general they agreed with me about leaving. They also said it was a good idea to be a group of people together so we can also defend ourselves if the need arises. They wished me the best of luck and I thanked them, then Hassan and I entered the house.

"Who the hell is this guy, anyway?" I asked. "He's really something, isn't he?"

"Yes," said Hassan. "He used to be a professor at the university."

"No kidding?"

"He taught political science or something," he added. "He's really not a bad guy, but the government didn't like him."

I didn't ask why because I knew why. It happened to many people I knew, my Dad being one example. Hassan changed the subject.

"So you're going away?" he repeated as soon as we were inside. "When?"

"At two o'clock this afternoon."

"How?"

"By truck."

"That's too dangerous."

"Not as dangerous as living in this country."

"You're right." He was silent for a moment then added: "Nothing is more dangerous."

"Why don't you come with us?" I asked.

"No," he said. "Not me. I'll wait until the war is over. Or I'll die here in my country. I don't want to go to any other place. I shall wait for whatever the future holds for me right here in my garage."

Silence.

"Where are you going, then?" he asked after a while.

"Djibouti."

"Alone?"

"No, my stepmothers are also going. And we're going to pick up the kids from Jowhar on the way. They're coming with us, too."

"That's good."

Soon we had changed the subject again and were remembering all the good times we had had together as a family. At the height of our remembrance of happy times we also for the first time talked openly about the dead members of the family, most especially of my uncles. We both cried shamelessly and our shirts were wet with tears. We concluded with bidding each other good-bye.

"Let me give you a lift home," he suggested, "you'll be late otherwise. It's almost half past one."

I accepted.

"This time we'll take one of our own Fiat cars," he suggested. "No more stolen cars, OK?"

I nodded.

"What will you do with all those stolen cars by the way?" I asked after a while.

"Don't know," he said. "Maybe give them back to their owners if they ever show up. Or sell them one of these days, and make a lot of money perhaps. Who knows?"

During our drive home Hassan explained to me that it was in fact very risky to journey through the country in the present state of affairs. People taking advantage of an unstable situation were everywhere. There were gangs of looters who, out of the blue, became everybody's enemy without any tribal exception or affiliation. They were their own tribe, Hassan said. Gangsters. Bandits. I also learned that even though many people were leaving the capital most of those who were fleeing were either Isaaqs or Gadaburses. These two tribes were not taking part in the civil war, at least not officially, since they were neither Hawiyas nor Daroods, and in any case their land was far away to the north and northwest of the capital. Among the other people who were leaving the country were a few Hawiyas, who either didn't like the idea of civil war or couldn't stand the sound of the bullets. But most of those fleeing were Daroods, for they had been defeated and were running away from hell. However different, all had one thing in common: they didn't want to die!

"I think they're all ready and waiting for you," remarked Hassan who saw some women standing in front of my house.

"Yeah," I said.

Hassan dropped me off and, since he really didn't know my stepmothers, he drove off immediately. Before leaving he told me that Grandpa was ill in Jowhar, though the rest of the family were fine as far as he knew, and he handed me three hundred thousand shillings to give to them. That sum of money was worth more than 20,000 US dollars ten years or so ago, but now it was only worth a few hundred.

There were seven of us waiting in front of our house for the car to come, as arranged. Three young men and four women. There was an unmarried woman in her late thirties, who was not only a close friend of my stepmother Anab but who also had her name – Anab. She worked in a local bank, one of those few women who knew their way around. Zeinab, Anab's younger sister, was a very beautiful nineteen-year- old who was a professional basketball player in one of the First Division teams in the country. The other two women were my step-mothers Anab and Falis. I was one of the three young men. Of the other two, one seemed two or three years older than me and was Zeinab's boyfriend. His name was John. He had a beard which probably made him look a little older than his age. Saeed, who was even more darkly sunbaked than me and whose face was expressionless, was the other man. Even though he was about my age or maybe only a year or two older, he was Anab and Zeinab's uncle. We all had bags and cases and impatiently awaited the car which was to take us out of the country and which was due to come any moment. My bag was a small brown one and inside it were some of my best clothes, a black walkman and my Rod Stewart album, my thousand dollars and a red diary for 1991. The other two young men also had one small bag each whereas all the women had two or three huge cases and bags each. I wondered if they had left anything at all behind. My stepmothers brought everything valuable with them: clothes, radios, cassette tapes and re-corder. They even brought the typewriter Dad said he had bought in Germany but which I now found was made in Italy.

Anyway after an hour or so in conversation about how dangerous and scary it was to do what we were about to embark on, the awaited vehicle arrived. It was three o'clock. A gigantic white and blue striped four-wheel-drive Toyota Landcruiser pick-up, which according to my experiences during the war would prove reliable in any circumstances, already full of people and their possessions, braked in front of us. There were fourteen people already on board: eight children, four young men and two women. The four men were on the ground as soon as the car stopped, while the rest stayed in their places. In the front seat was a slim woman in her early fifties called Shukri. She was, I learned, a rich lady who lived both in Djibouti and Mogadishu. She was the owner of the car. Beside her were her thirteen-year-old girl, Heersare, and a little boy who was her nephew. In the back there were two long parallel benches joined by a shorter one across the back of the driver's compartment and facing the rear doors. On the bench to the left sat Arabo, the oldest and the fattest of all the passengers who seemed in her early sixties, and six children who were all hers. Among the four young men who were at this moment on the ground and helping us come aboard was a twenty-year-old fancily dressed fat character called Farouk who was the driver and the son of Shukri. Then there was Mohamed, who was a colonel and lawyer in the army, though he didn't look like one because he wasn't more than forty years old, and seemed too young and fat as well as having a big beard. He was a friend of Farouk's. The third man was Bustale, who was about my age except that his beard made him look older, and was Farouk's cousin. The last man was an eighteen-year-old boy nicknamed Tuke, who was the mechanic. He was the only one, except for me, who didn't have a beard. Everybody in my country who could, seemed to have been growing beards lately, as though it was the fashion. For one reason or another, people weren't shaving these days. We all got aboard. My stepmother Anab sat in the front seat with Shukri and her two children, while the rest of us found places in the back benches of the car. There was enough space for all of us, for not only were there two benches available but the floor between the benches was also very comfortable to sit or even sleep on. On the floor there were pillows, blankets, mattresses and other materials that the women had brought along.

After ten minutes of lifting, carrying, pushing and pulling heavy stuff under the mid-day heat of the sun, we were ready to take off. Since the canvas roof of the car was missing, the sun beat directly down on everybody's skin. Everything got better, though, when the car started moving, for the wind cooled us off. After a little while, still in the Medina quarter, we stopped in front of the house of the people who owned the car. A fat man was already waiting at the gate. He was Barqad, the head of the house, father of Farouk the driver and husband of Shukri. Farouk and his mother got down from the vehicle while the rest of us waited. After a short exchange of words the three disappeared into the house. All of the younger men and women also stepped out of the car to stretch their legs. Most of the young men smoked, while the children played. After a quarter of an hour Farouk and Shukri came out again.

"We're going to Casa Popolare," instructed Shukri, "to pick up some more people."

We drove off.


# 30


We were sitting in, around, and near the car talking about the war when Farouk appeared from inside the house in Casa Popolare where we'd been stopped for ten minutes or so.

"Well," he started, "I think it's a good idea to spend the night here because it's already almost six o'clock and I'm sure all of you are aware of the dangers of travelling at night. The rest of the group are already in Balaad but they'll spend the night there. They'll leave Balaad tomorrow around midday. I'm sure we'll make it there before they leave Balaad."

"The rest of the group?" asked somebody.

"Yes, we're about fifty vehicles travelling together. In a convoy. There's safety in numbers!"

"Welcome, folks," said another voice. We looked in the direction of the voice and found it came from a huge, very tall man who had just appeared from the house. It wasn't difficult to guess that he was the father of that house; he had an air of authority. "Make yourselves at home," he added, as we approached the entrance to the house. "We don't have much space but we can certainly provide you with a place to spend the night." Before he went inside he repeated, "Welcome."

By now there was nobody in the car. We were all inside the house. It was an ordinary house not very much different from mine in style. The main difference was that the daash was concreted, not sandy. The men carted the pillows, blankets and mattresses from the car and the women arranged them in the daash, until it looked like one big bed. But it was just enough for half of us – who now numbered twenty. All the women and children were already making their choice of sleeping spots when we, men, offered the whole place to them. They didn't turn the offer down. "But where are you going to spend the night?" they asked us.

"Don't worry about us," was our answer. "We can sleep anywhere as long as we are tired."

We went outside. Some of us sat on stone benches in front of the house, and some on the cool sandy ground. Some simply stood around the place. We were all talking and smoking. We were not talking about anything in particular since we hardly knew each other. We talked about how women and children were so innocent, and worried about where to sleep in the middle of war, while a man could make love in front of his friend who had been shot dead a second before; how some of us had sometimes not slept for ages, while others slept through the noise of explosives. We found out that the only one among us who hadn't fought was Farouk, the driver. We made fun of him for a while and then dropped the subject. Anyway, about seven-thirty that evening the girls brought us some tea from inside the house. They stayed with us for a while and then went back inside. Over tea we decided on a plan, having remembered that we were starving. We would eat out. We didn't want to bother the family since it was difficult to feed twenty people from one house. We decided to find a restaurant. Some looting continued here and there but otherwise things were getting back to normal. The capital was not a slaughter-house any more. The war was officially ended. We decided not to tell the others about our plan though, because we knew that the family of the house would feel insulted. They would not wish to be known as the family that couldn't feed their guests.

After a quarter of an hour of wandering in the neighbourhood and visiting three restaurants which were either closed or destroyed, we found one called the Red Sea Restaurant. The owners were of course Hawiyas since there were hardly any more Daroods in the city. One half of the restaurant was destroyed and the walls that remained were full of holes and scars made by bullets. Just near the entrance was a hole, itself big enough to be an entrance, but in respect for the owner's obvious preference we used the old entrance. We sat inside and everybody ordered what he wished. After eating huge amounts of meat, rice or spaghetti, and milk, we ordered as much food again for the other people we had left behind. Farouk paid the whole bill and we left. On our way home we took a short cut through a small, dark back street. After a while we heard music coming from one of the houses. It was somebody playing the lute and singing. The voice sounded familiar even though we couldn't place it immediately, but the song he was singing wasn't. We stopped in the dark and listened. The words went:

Oh, my country. Oh! – Oh, my land. Oh!
I can see you're bleeding – I can feel your sadness. Oh!
But what can I do – except cry for you. Oh!
Oh, my country. Oh! – Oh, my land. Oh!

"Let's get closer!" somebody exclaimed from the darkness. We walked towards the tune, and we came upon a man singing, alone on a bench in front of a house. He looked at us but was otherwise unmoved. He simply continued his song in the same touching voice.

"Beddel!" somebody screamed. "That's Beddel!"

And so it was. Beddel was one of the most popular musicians in the country. As we sat beside him we noticed a half full bottle of whisky standing beside him. There were also cartons full of cigarettes all over the bench. No words were exchanged between us and him, and he continued singing, one song after another. We kept on listening and he kept on singing, until one of us remembered: "Hey the food!"

"Let's wait for a while."

"But the food is getting cold."

"Never mind."

"The women and the children are hungry."

"Let them be."

"That's not fair. Let's go."

"You must go if you are carrying food for children and women," said the drunk man as he stopped playing the lute.

"Just one more song," someone begged.

He sang one more song then he said, "Go now."

We stood up in the darkness.

"Remember," he said as we turned on our heels. "This country is waiting for you and for Almighty God."

We paused to listen some more.

"You are the future of this country," he continued, "We are too old."

He lit a cigarette. "Perhaps you can put right our errors and learn from them."

He was silent for a while as he slowly smoked a cigarette. We waited.

"Here," he said pointing to the bottle and the cigarettes beside him. "Take them. Take them before they kill me." He stood up, grabbed his lute and, swaying as he walked, entered the house behind him. We could hear him stumbling over the furniture as he disappeared into the dark room. We took the half-full bottle of whisky and the five cartons of Embassy cigarettes and departed without uttering another word. None of us said anything until we were home. We gave the food we had brought to the women and the children, half of whom were asleep already, but all of whom were awakened when the food was served.

The women and children went back to sleep right away, and we spent most of the night singing, drinking and smoking. And we talked about how politics and tribalism were ruining our lives and our country.

## 31

We started to get ready at six o'clock the next morning. After we had had tea we put our luggage back in the car. Three more people were added to the list, a woman called Jamila and her two daughters, Faduma and Iftin. Faduma was eighteen and Iftin seventeen, and they were both pretty. Everybody took his place in the car. Mrs. Shukri and her nephew, my stepmother Anab, and Farouk the driver, were in the front. Falis, Faduma, Iftin and I sat on the right hand bench, John, Zeinab, Saeed, Mohamed and Bustale sat on the middle bench leaning back to back with the driver's compartment, and Arabo, Jamila, Anab, and Heersare sat on the left hand bench. Most of the children, except for those who sat on somebody's lap, were, along with the luggage, on the mattresses and pillows on the floor. Tuke, the mechanic, stood on the metal plate at the back which formed the step into the car. We hit the road at seven o'clock heading for the Djibouti Republic.

The twenty-four of us on board belonged to different tribes. My stepmother Anab and I, and Arabo's six children were Hawiyas. Saeed was the only Isaaq on board. My stepmother Falis, and Mohamed (whom I had only just found out about) were Daroods. The remaining thirteen people were all Gadaburses.

Nothing particular happened during the first twenty-five kilometres except that we had a flat front tyre. We looked at the landscape as Tuke fixed the wheel. There were farms of all kinds all along the highway. Just before nine we reached Balaad, which was the first town after the capital when going north, thirty kilometres from the capital. It was a small agricultural place on the banks of the Shebelle River and it was famous for its good cotton. All the school uniforms in the country were made in the cotton factory there. Only a few houses were made of stone or brick, most being of wood, palm thatch, and sticks, or mud and sticks. Most of the inhabitants there were Hawiyas, though there were some Daroods – government officials and functionaries.

We decided to have a quick breakfast and parked our car in front of a small restaurant on the right of the main road. We all had anjeelo with tea, coffee and milk. I usually disliked anjeelo but was surprised to find myself emptying my plate that morning. I was the first to finish so I paid everybody's bill. In fact, for the first time in my life I paid in US dollars! These days all kinds of money was being used, so long as it was known. I mean … you couldn't change money from Scandinavia, China or somewhere, only the kind of money known to Somalis, things like US dollars, Saudi riyals or something of that sort. The funny thing was, whatever money you paid in, you got Somali Shillings as change. I liked that. I really did. It was kind of crazy, like so many other things at the time, I admit, but I liked it anyway. It was sort of like getting something for nothing, if you know what I mean. Anyway, where was I? Yes. I paid the bill. I paid for everyone in the goddam restaurant. I mean all those who were travelling. That was the tradition. The first person to pay his bill must pay up for everyone. If you don't want to pay for all, then make sure you are not the first one to pay.

I remember when I was a school boy. In the bus I would see that some of my friends or classmates and I were broke. "The bus fare!" the conductor would shout. We'd eye one another and everybody would reach into his pocket. If I couldn't afford to pay for all of us I'd fumble with the coins but not bring them out. If the other guys were also broke they would do the same, and linger as much as possible. Then we'd know that each of us was broke and we would exchange shy little smiles. (The most embarrassing thing, though, was when your friend in this situation happened to be from the other sex.) "I said the fare!" the conductor would repeat. I would pay up for myself and they would do the same. If we were not broke we would jump up and flash a big denomination note and proudly pay for all. That was the tradition.

Farouk was the second one to finish breakfast. We stood in front of the restaurant to wait for the rest of the crowd. The

146

town of Balaad had changed a bit since the last time I was there. First of all some of its buildings had been badly shell scarred. The second change was that some people, mostly young men, were carrying guns.

We were watching two women arguing about something or other and we didn't really hear a tall man approached us.

"Look at you!" exclaimed the man reaching for Farouk's shoulder. "Is this Farouk Barqad or am I day-dreaming!" the man continued. What the hell are you doing here in Balaad?"

The two men embraced and shook hands.

"We're going to Djibouti," declared Farouk at last.

"Djibouti!" exclaimed the man. "Are you nuts?"

"Why?"

"Going to Djibouti all by yourself?"

"No. We're more than fifty vehicles."

"I see. I heard there were sixty vehicles which spent the night here in Balaad. Are you part of those guys?"

"Yes."

The man looked at me.

"This is Ali," Farouk said. "Ali, this is my old friend, Mowleed." We shook hands.

"Ali's not only a Hawiya," he continued, "but he also happens to belong to your own sub-tribe."

"I'm really glad to meet you, Ali," said Mowleed as he shook hands with me once more. "Times have changed. Tribes are more valuable these days."

I nodded.

"But I would never choose an asshole over Farouk simply because he happened to belong to my tribe," he said sarcastically.

"I can understand," I said.

"You know, Farouk and I spent four hard, unforgettable years together."

"High school years, eh?"

"Not high school," said Farouk. "The military academy."

"Military academy?"

"Yes."

"I see."

Now everybody had finished breakfast but we had to wait to find out when we would be leaving. Most of the women and the children went direct to the car and took their places while the rest of us stood around smoking.

Farouk called Tuke, who was smoking nearby and talking to some of the other men. "Would you mend the tyre which got punctured this morning, and check the other tyres as well?"

"Right away," said Tuke, and disappeared.

Farouk and his friend walked away and I joined the others who were standing nearby. Tuke reported that it would take some time to mend the tyre and also to replace another one which he found to be almost flat. There would be some hanging about to do whilst waiting for Tuke to get his jobs done. We talked to the women and children in the car and told them about the delay. Arabo and her six children said they'd wait under a small tree beside the restaurant where we were parked. The rest of us walked off behind the main street and found a big tree with wide spreading shade. We sat there enjoying the cool sand where the grass had been worn away from use. Some women declared that they needed a toilet badly, so Mohamed went to a nearby thatched house and asked if we could use their toilet. The family welcomed us, and we used the toilet one after another because we were not sure of the next time we would find toilets. Some of us wandered around. Others waited in the shade. After a while Farouk came and joined us. His friend was not with him. We talked about nothing in particular. We ran out of matches so I volunteered to get some from the nearest shop. I walked back to the high street and into a bibito. I had bought matches and was drinking a pepsi when somebody tapped me on the shoulder. I turned around to see a familiar face.

"Hello, Oofeey!" I exclaimed. "What are you doing in Balaad?"

"What are YOU doing in Balaad?" he answered straightening his machine gun. "Don't tell me you are one of the USC's men in Balaad."

"No, man," I shook my head. "I'm on my way to Djibouti."

"So you're with these sixty vehicles which are taking the Isaaqs and the Gadaburses to their lands, eh?"

"Yes." I offered him some of the pepsi that I was drinking. He shook his head in response before I added: "What about you? Are you travelling around as usual or are you in Balaad for other reasons?"

"No, I'm still travelling here and there. The only thing new is that now I drive my own bus instead of other people's."

"Your own bus? How come?"

He smiled.

"A stolen one?" I asked.

"If you want to call it that. Yes."

I lit a cigarette and offered him one. He accepted it.

"It's not worth more than my wife and the house the Daroods burned down, is it?"

"No."

We stared at one another silently. Oofeey was a very hard working, honest man. In spite of his huge size, he was also a very unaggressive man. I first knew him more than six years ago when he worked for my uncles as a mechanic in the garage. Later he'd collected enough money to build himself a house so he could get married. Unfortunately the war started when he'd been married for only a week. The government burned his house and killed his wife who happened to be inside the house at the time.

"I haven't killed any Darood yet," he added, "but I took their bus. In any case it was bought with the people's money, and the owner is dead anyway."

"I've got to be going, man," I said at last. "There are people waiting for me."

He nodded.

"So when are you leaving?" he asked.

"I don't know," I replied. "Some time today, I suppose."

"Well, if you need me I'll be around. Everybody knows me in this small town so you won't have difficulty finding me. Just ask for me, OK?"

"OK."

"*Ciao.*"

"*Ciao*," he said before he added: "And by the way…I heard about your uncles. May God give you courage!"

"Thank you."


# 32


About two hours later Tuke came and reported that he had had some problems but that everything was ready at last.

"I think you should drive the car to the garage where the rest of the group's vehicles are parked," he told Farouk. "I saw some of them and they thought it was a good idea."

"I'll do that," said Farouk as he stood up to go.

Five minutes or so later we heard a couple of gunshots and people shouting. We stood up and ran in the direction of the commotion which sounded as though it was in the high street. What we saw happening in front of the pharmacy behind which we had been sitting terrified us. We saw two men struggling with a gun. One, a young fat man was looking horrified and trying to get hold of the machine gun and aim it towards the sky, while the other, an older, stronger and taller man, was very upset and trying to regain control of the gun.

"I'm gonna kill you, you son-of-a-bitch!" the stronger man was saying.

"Believe me, I'm not a Darood!" the fat one was begging in a desperate voice. "I said I'm not a Darood!"

We saw the fat man was Farouk. We ran to the spot immediately to prevent disaster.

"He's not a Darood! He's not a Darood!" We all shouted and threw both men on the ground. Farouk ran into the pharmacy as soon as he could scramble to his feet. The other man who had been temporarily disarmed grabbed the gun before anyone of us could reach out for it. We stood in a line in front

150

of this mad fellow with the gun in his hand and his right fore-finger on the trigger.

The people in the pharmacy pushed Farouk back on to the street shouting: "Kill the son of a bitch! Kill him before he gets away!"

We stood as a barrier between Farouk and the man, who were sweating and shaking, one from fear and the other from anger. Farouk could only repeat continuously, "I'm not a Darood. Why don't you believe me? I swear I'm not a Darood!" as he hid behind us, weeping.

"Get out of my way!" the man shouted at us as he flailed the gun and fired it at the sky every now and then. Farouk's mother, Mrs. Shukri, and his cousins, Tuke and Bustale, were also weeping beside the pharmacy door. Mohamed the colonel, and Falis my stepmother, who were the only Daroods on board, were standing silently beside a nearby car. The rest of us surrounded Farouk. Anab, my other stepmother, begged the gunman to wait and listen before he did anything stupid. The man refused to listen to reason. He said he couldn't trust us because he didn't know who we were, either, and threatened to kill all of us if we didn't get out of his way. I saw Mohamed and Falis take to their heels. "I swear I'm not going to leave that Darood alive," the man yelled, "They killed my seven brothers."

While all this was going on an idea hit me. I ran towards the restaurant where we had had breakfast that morning, looking for the man we had met there who'd been so glad to see Farouk. I was sure he would find a way out of that mess. I didn't know where he lived, but I ran from one bibito to another, into shops and restaurants, looking for him. At last I approached some men who were playing cards in one of the teashops, and Mowleed was one of them.

"Mowleed!" I cried, "We met this morning. Do you remember me…?"

"Sure I remember you," he said resuming his game. "What can I do for you, now?"

"We need you, Mowleed," I started. "Your friend Farouk's in trouble. They're going to kill him!"

He stood up quickly, grabbed me by the shoulders and said, "Who? Why?"

"They think he's a Darood. Please, we don't have much time. Come."

We ran back to the scene. The only thing that had changed was that the crowd had grown, and there were now many people shouting "Kill the bastard!" and looking very pleased to be part of the show. The man was still waving his gun threateningly, and Farouk was still cowering behind our group of men, unable to speak any more. His mouth merely opened and closed but no sound passed his lips. Mowleed ran to the scene and stood in front of the crazy gunman. He said loudly, "My name's Mowleed Hassan," and continued by reciting his family names and clan lineage. As soon he mentioned the name of his sub-clan my stepmother Anab picked it up and shouted it out repeatedly. That is the way to call relatives when one is in need. She cried out the name, like a market seller might shout out what he was selling, so that everybody in Balaad could hear. The idea was to bring out any family members who happened to be in the neighbourhood. It was very shameful if you heard your family name being called and you didn't come to the rescue, especially when the person calling it was a woman. Two of the men who were standing in the crowd came over to her.

"What can we do for you, lady?" they began by asking. The mood at the incident began to change and the tension was subsiding.

"All I want is to save that young man," answered my stepmother. "I know him – I've known his parents for years. He's not a Darood, he's a Gadaburse!"

"OK. OK," said the men. "Just stop crying for God's sake, and we'll do what we can!"

My stepmother became silent.

Mowleed continued to speak for Farouk. "We were classmates for four years. I know everything about him. His family, his job, his hobbies, everything."

Suddenly a man in his late forties appeared from the crowd and approached Farouk who was now hanging on to Mowleed's arm.

152

"Isn't your name Ibrahim Soudi, young man?" the man asked Farouk. "Are you not a captain in the army? Did you not graduate four years ago from the State Military Academy? Was I not your teacher? Are you not a Darood? Or to be more specific a Marrehan?"

A huge silence prevailed over the place. Some were desperately upset at what they knew to be the man's lies. Others were happy to find somebody at last who seemed not only to know the guy but had also been his teacher.

"Listen to me, my friend," Mowleed broke the silence. "Do you know me?"

"No," answered the man. "Should I?"

"Yes, you should, you son-of-a-bitch! If you were his teacher you were mine too! And since you don't know me and I don't know you, everything you said is pure lies! I happened to be this man's classmate for the four years he spent in the Military Academy."

"But that's impossible," said that man. "I remember his face and his name."

"Let me tell you one more thing!" shouted Mowleed. "First of all this man's not called Ibrahim Soudi, so that also discounts your second claim of remembering his face. This man is called Farouk Barqad and he's a Gadaburse. Not even a Darood. Forget about a Marrehan!"

The man was silent.

"Listen" continued Mowleed, too angry to stop. "if you don't get out of our way now, I'll have to kill you myself!" Mowleed was so furious, and people were hanging on to him and begging him not to do anything violent.

"I need good proof!" yelled the man with the gun. "I don't want to leave a Darood alive!"

"Why don't you look at my ID if you think I'm lying," pleaded Farouk, who had now got his voice back.

I noticed that the man who had just lied had disappeared from the crowd. The two who had come at my stepmother's call stood quietly watching and listening. Mowleed stood right in front of Farouk while we surrounded them. The two men came forward. They were both tall and strongly built.

"OK, OK," said one of them in a loud and authoritative voice to the man with the gun. "That's enough. Put the gun down, Qoorgaab."

Qoorgaab wouldn't put the gun down or even drop the angle at which he was holding it.

"I said put that gun down!" the man shouted again.

He just kept pointing it at us all. The second man reached over with his large frame and put a hand on the gun, pointing it to the sky. He simultaneously pulled a pistol from his belly, pressed it to Qoorgaab's stomach and said: "Put this thing down or I'll blow your goddam guts out!"

Qoorgaab looked at the man then at the pistol pressed against him. "I mean it," the man added. Qoorgaab surrendered. The man now turned to address Mowleed. "You, Mowleed. You said you know this young man?"

"Yes," Mowleed answered, "take my word for it."

"We don't take anybody's word here, Mowleed," said the other large man. "We simply deal with facts. How many times has it happened that Daroods passed this way under cover, because they happened to have some Hawiya friends who swore that they were Hawiyas. I'm sure you know what the Daroods did to us, don't you? We don't want that to happen any more."

"Yes, but that's not the issue here. This man isn't a Darood. Not because he's my friend but because he is truly a Gadaburse."

"OK," the man said, seeming to relent. "We will soon find out if that's really the truth or not. How about a fair trial?"

"OK," said Mowleed. "Whatever satisfies you is fine with us."

"Yes, it's fine with all of us," the rest of us agreed.

"Fine," said the man. "let's go then. We'll take you to an old man who's the oldest Gadaburse in this town. He will surely know your parents and grand parents. Don't you think so?" he addressed Farouk who still seemed to be too shocked to speak.

"Yes, yes," we once again said in chorus on his behalf.

We were confident about this solution for many reasons. First we knew that every old man of a tribe certainly knew his people by name. We also knew that Farouk's uncle was a very well-known general in the army and married to a close relative of the President, and therefore would be known to every Gadaburse, let alone to an old man. (Having an uncle so placed was the reason Farouk himself had reached the rank of major in the army in only a few years while his classmates, like Mowleed, never even made it past lieutenant.)

"If that old man doesn't recognize your claims," said the man calmly, "you're dead, my friend." He turned to us. "Anyone of you who attempts any stupid move to save him will be dead too, do you hear?"

"OK."

He led us to the old man's house which was not very far. Our whole travelling group, except for Mohamed and Falis, trailed behind him. Most of the crowd also came, eager to see the event's conclusion. The old man's house was one of the better ones in the town, made of bricks and with a small gate. The man when he came out seemed very healthy. He wore a maawiis and a shirt and walked very briskly. He talked to Farouk and asked him to count his ancestors and give their names, like we could all do by heart. That process of reciting your lineage was called 'abtirsiimo'. Farouk did it very successfully. The old man asked a few other questions to which Farouk again replied successfully with the names of his uncles.

"Your mother's name is Shukri, isn't it?" the old man grinned, finally.

"Yes!" we all cheered. Of course old Mrs. Shukri, who was weeping and clinging to her boy and all, couldn't contain herself with joy.

"That's me!" she cried like a little girl. "That's me!"

The old man got a little closer to her face. He gave a genuine little smile, showed his rotten teeth and said, "It *is* you, isn't it?" He touched her face. "It's really you! You grew up a little bit – but so what – who didn't."

Oh, old men are funny. Grew up a little? She grew the hell old, what did he mean by *a little bit*? I could see he also grew to be the oldest wizard around, and for Heaven's sake, the woman *grew* a *lot*. Not a little bit but *a lot*.

155

"Yes, that's her!" cried the rest of us, altogether.

The old man now turned to Farouk.

"I remember when your father wanted first to marry her and how he was refused," the old man said proudly at last.

Good old Shukri gave a shy smile. I almost believed she was a little girl after all.

"I was one of the people who went to petition her parents."

Farouk's fat sweaty face gave a sickly smile at last.

"Are you sure this man is a Gadaburse?" asked one of the men who'd brought us.

"Yes," was the old man's reply. "I'm sure he is the son of Barqad Awale."

The men of Balaad stared at one another silently.

"Look," said the old man. "If you want to kill that young man go ahead and kill him. But if you do, know that you killed a Gadaburse and that his people will hear about it." The old man turned and walked away as briskly as he had come. The two huge men who had taken charge back there looked at us and smiled and said: "Well, Farouk. I think we made a terrible mistake. We're ready to apologize by all means. We're very sorry for what happened to you."

"I'm awfully sorry, Farouk," added Qoorgaab. "I was given the wrong information. Tell us what we can do to make it up to you?"

We could hardly believe our ears. Farouk said nothing. He only bit his lips and smiled nervously. We told the men it was all right and that words were enough. They offered us money as compensation, but we refused. They repeated their apologies and asked us if they could do anything for us. We told them that they should leave us in peace. It was already evening when the day's events were over at last.

## 33

Farouk was in shock of course. He was still not back to normal. We talked to him and told him he should be glad to be alive after being at that crazy man's gunpoint. We tried to console him by reminding him that we were in the middle of a civil war and that such things were happening all over the place. We told him that they were only angry village people and that their lives depended on tribal solidarity. We went to a nearby bibito and said all that we could think of that would help him to feel better. It helped a little. It was completely dark by the time we were on our way to the garage where Tuke had taken the car and where he had told the rest of the cars to wait for us until the incident was resolved. Tuke led us towards the garage and we trailed behind him with heads down.

The garage was on the outskirts of the town, big, with huge entrance and exit gates. Inside there were all kinds of vehicles – buses, lorries, and cars belonging to our group. There were more than sixty of them. Behind them were all kinds of other vehicles, abandoned vehicles, all of which had printed on them the words MINISTRY OF AGRICULTURE. The garage had obviously been a depot of that ministry before the war. But now every car that could be driven had been taken. Only the wrecks were left. There was also a bibito inside the garage compound, originally for the workers but now a source of food and drink for our party of travellers. There were people all over the place, lying in and under vehicles and on the ground in between. There were women, children and men, some sleeping and others simply lying down and talking or smoking or maybe thinking about their unknown destiny.

We looked for our Toyota and found it where Tuke had parked it somewhere in the middle. We took some of our possessions from the car for sleeping, but I had nothing to sleep on so I just took my small bag, from which I took out a cotton t-shirt and my walkman. I changed into the cotton shirt and put on my walkman, then found a spare patch of grass and lay down using my bag as a pillow. Everybody was making his own arrangement for sleeping but all of us had one thing in common, we were all pretty quiet. I stared at the shining stars and wondered why God had given me such a lousy life. I wondered whether He was testing me like people used to say or whether He was torturing me for doing wrong. My stomach hurt with emptiness and my body shivered with cold and hunger. I opened my bag again and pulled my small diary out. I made a few sad notes then put it back into the bag. The memory of the man with the gun who had threatened us all day flashed through my mind. God how I hated the man. I sat up and lit a cigarette. I belched with hunger as I blew the smoke out of my lungs. As a matter of fact one thing was going around my head now. That's the odd thing about my head. I can only think of one thing at a time. One single thing can actually occupy my whole head sometimes. That one single thing can even be irrelevant sometimes. Like the time in Mr. Dheere's physics class, when I was in the first year of secondary school. I suddenly thought of something funny. I can't even remember now what the funny thing was, but I remember the occassion because it was so embarassing. I started to laugh and couldn't stop. The physics teacher was really tough and people were scared of him, 'cause he always used a long broomstick to hit pupils. No one dared to speak in his class. No one dared to cause a distraction. Anyway, I remembered something to do with this guy, Gureey, who sat beside me in class. Good old Gureey was really the funniest clown in the class. He's dead now, though. Some guy who was high on drugs or somthing shot him dead on a bus at the beginning of the war. What I did was I first chuckled and then began laughing out loud, right there in the class and with the teacher writing something on the blackboard and all. The whole class stared at me as though I was crazy, but I only continued laughing. I couldn't stop. The teacher looked at me with his fierce eyes, but I couldn't contain myself. I really couldn't. He threw his chalk at me and told me to shut up, but I continued laughing. I laughed till I had tears running down my cheeks. The teacher had to come all the way over to the back row where I and Gureey liked to sit. By this time the whole class was laughing too, and I could see that even Mr. Dheere was trying to stop himself from laughing. Anyway, where was I? Yes, my head could sometimes get taken over by one single thing, and I was thinking of one single thing this time too, but not something funny. I was thinking of my gun. My gun. Yes. I regretted I'd left my gun in the capital. You don't beg for your rights when you have a gun, you know. That's what I had learned during the war. You either kill or get killed. No asshole threatens you as if he were made of steel. Suddenly an idea came to me out of the blue. I stood up and approached my stepmothers who were both lying silently on the carpet that had been removed from the car. They saw me coming. Anab sat up.

"I'm going back," I declared.

They both sat bolt upright on hearing me say that.

"Are you crazy, Ali?" they asked together, as though they shared one brain. "After all we've been through? No way, Ali. You are not going back. You're not going anywhere. You'll stay with us right here and go to Djibouti first thing in the morning."

"I'm going back," I repeated stubbornly.

"Are you afraid?" Falis asked.

"No, I just want to get my gun."

"So you're afraid, eh? You're a man and afraid, eh? What kind of a man are you anyway?"

I was silent.

"Besides what do you need that gun for? You want to kill or get killed, eh?"

"No, I just don't like the idea of an asshole threatening us simply because he has a gun!"

"Look, Ali," Anab took over. "The idea behind this journey was to avoid killing or getting killed, right?"

I nodded and sat down.

"You still believe that killing's not a good business! I know that! I can feel that! Please don't get carried away with the action of an irresponsible character like that one today!"

"You're right. I'm sorry," I said, and was about to walk away when Saeed approached me.

159

"Do you wanna come with me?" he asked me.

We remembered that we hadn't had lunch and reminded the rest of our group. It seemed nobody had thought about it before. Now the other young men, including Farouk, jumped to their feet and followed us as we headed for the small bibito in the garage compound. It had run out of food so we had to go outside to the town to eat. We found a good restaurant and ate a big meal. Farouk was still in a state of shock. He would laugh out loud to himself sometimes. We would join in to encourage him to get it out of his system. As we ate and talked we eventually got talking about the day's incident.

"When I heard the shot I thought at first it was Mohamed," Bustale said.

"Mohamed?" I asked.

Bustale grew silent as Farouk looked at him. I noticed Farouk staring at Bustale accusingly.

"Something wrong?" I asked.

"Later," said Farouk. "I'll tell you later, Ali."

We finished eating and took more food for the women and children. On the way to the garage Farouk told me what I had already guessed, that Mohamed was a Darood. My comment to him was that it was not his fault that he was a Darood no more than it was Falis's fault being Darood. I knew that Farouk knew that my stepmother Falis, too, was a Darood. We decided not to let anyone else know about them. Not because we couldn't trust them but because we couldn't afford any mistakes. We laughed at the silliness of tribalism.

"Is Falis really a Darood?" asked Mohamed at last in a voice of relief.

"Yes," I assured him.

When we got back to the garage I introduced Mohamed to Falis who also hadn't known there was another Darood in our car. They talked intimately as the rest ate in the dark cold garage. I watched them in the dark and remembered the Daroods I'd killed during the war. I remembered how they had suffered and, unlike in the movies, how they fell to the ground immediately they were hit. I also remembered what they'd done to my uncles and to our maid, Mona. I cried silently in the dark and lay down on my bag to sleep. I didn't know who should be blamed for the terrible misfortunes. It's as though bigger forces were actually ruling my life.

# 34

I was awakened at about five the next morning by the noise of those people who say their morning prayers. I found myself covered with an old piece of red blanket. I looked around me. Some people were doing the ritual washing of their limbs in preparation for prayers, some were already praying. Others were still sleeping or just lying there awake. Drivers and mechanics were working on the vehicles to make sure they were ready for the journey ahead. I lit a cigarette and stood up. I was staring at the red blanket when I heard a woman's voice.

"It's ours, Ali" she said. It was Jamila.

"Thanks," I said and gave the blanket to her.

"Iftin saw you shivering with cold and she thought to cover you with her blanket," Jamila continued. Iftin was her daughter.

"That's very kind of her." I looked around to see Iftin. She was not anywhere in sight.

"What about her?" I asked. "I mean it must have been cold for her, too."

"Women have more tolerance for hardships than men," the woman said proudly.

"Thank you again," I said and smiled. "And thanks to Iftin of course."

Jamila smiled too.

"Where is everybody?" I asked.

"Water," she said. "They're fetching water from the river."

I found two bottles, each of about two litres capacity, and took off for the river. It was still dark but the sky was reddening with the new sun rising in the Heavens and I decided to enjoy the beauty of nature before fetching the water. I wandered through the bush and puffed on a cigarette. After about five minutes of wandering around I heard someone calling my name. I looked about me and saw nobody. The call was repeated. "Here," the voice said.

I saw a young girl of about my own age lying on the grass in the bush. All I could see was that she was smiling and her long black curls were stretched behind her on the ground. I walked towards her and stood over her. She was wearing a cream coloured diraa which matched the colour of her light brown skin. She was not wearing a bra so the erect brown nipples of her full breasts were visible through the transparent diraa. They seemed to grow bigger as I watched them.

"Good morning, Iftin," I greeted her.

"Hello," she said and sat up. She must have noticed how my eyes were fixed on her breasts because she pulled her diraa to the front so that it hung loose enough for the nipples not to protrude. That, however, displayed her breasts to better effect. I could see them hang on her chest as ripe mangoes hang from the tree branches.

"You must have gone the wrong way," she added.

"Why do you say that?" I asked. Her breasts swung as she fidgeted to sit properly.

"Because I can see you wanted to fetch some water and the river is not in the direction you were going."

"Oh," I said and put the two bottles on the ground. "I decided to enjoy the early morning beauty before I fetched water." I noticed there were cigarette butts squeezed into the grass beside her. "What about you?" I asked. "Are you lost or are you on some other mission?"

"I was smoking." she said as she looked at the cigarette butts beside her. "And I was also enjoying the beauty of the morning." She smiled again. "You want to sit?" she added.

I sat beside her without a word.

"Thanks for the blanket," I said.

She reached for a packet of Marlboros behind her and without even looking at me she said, "Don't mention it."

162

She took a cigarette and offered me one too. I took it and fumbled in my pockets in search of matches.

"Here," she said holding a flaming matchstick out to me. I looked at her face as her eyes concentrated to light the cigarette between my lips. She had an oval face with very fine eyebrows and big, beautiful, almost red lips which reached their utmost beauty when she blew out the cigarette smoke. I felt a thrill running through my body.

"You were shivering," she said as she put the matchstick out, still without looking at my eyes.

"Me?" I said. "No, I'm not!"

"I mean this morning." Then she looked at me with the kindest eyes I had ever seen. "You were trembling with cold when I covered you with the blanket."

"That's very kind of you," I said. "Thank you again."

We smoked silently for a while when she said:

"Feel like walking around?"

"Sure."

We stood up. She held her Marlboro packet and I was holding my two bottles. We walked silently through the bush.

"My mother doesn't know I smoke," she said looking at her cigarettes.

"I can understand that."

"What I mean is, don't mention it in front of her."

"Sure." I threw the end of my cigarette on the ground before me and stepped on it in passing. "How long have you been smoking?" I asked.

"I don't know." She threw her cigarette ahead of her thoughtfully but didn't step on it.

"I don't know," she repeated, still thoughtful. "Two or three years, I guess."

"I started when I was eleven," I volunteered.

"And how old are you now?"

"Eighteen."

"I'm seventeen."

We walked through the bush in silence, accompanied by the sound of our footsteps, and the noise of birdsong in the background. We reached a place where the grass was as tall as our knees. I picked a yellow flower and gave it to her without speaking. She took it and smiled. We kept on walking. She smelt the flower and turned to me.

"Let's sit for a while," she suggested. We sat on the wet grass, still silent. I lay down. She joined me. I stared at the sky which was now getting lighter. She stared at the yellow flower which she held in front of her. I didn't know where to start.

"Do you have a boyfriend?" I asked.

"No." She was still staring at the flower as if seeing a flower for the first time. Would she ask me whether I had a girlfriend or not? I was not sure whether I would mention the girl I left behind whom I was almost sure I would never see again in my life.

"What about you?" she asked.

"What about me?"

"Do you have a girlfriend?"

I was silent for a moment before I said:

"No."

She placed the flower in between her breasts and put her hands flat down by her sides. She was now staring at the sky. I glanced at her left hand which was very close to my right one. I placed my hand on hers. My heart pounded. She turned to me completely expressionless. She lay on her left side and placed her right hand on my hand. She squeezed my hand and I squeezed hers. She held herself up and reached to kiss my lips. She kissed me lightly but as she moved to go back to her lying position I grabbed her by the waist and kissed her hard. She came on top of me and we kissed again. We kissed very passionately for a very long time. I lifted her head with both my hands and held it in front of mine. We both found ourselves smiling.

"You know something?" I asked.

"What?"

"You're beautiful," I said.

"I know."

We burst out laughing, then I noticed the sun was full up and the sky was not red any more.

"What time is it?" I asked.

164

She got off me, glanced at her watch and said, "Almost six-thirty."

We stood up and faced one another.

"I'm glad we met," I said.

"So am I."

"Well," I said. "I have to get some water from the river."

She nodded.

"You want to come along?"

"No," she said. "I think I want to go back. I'll see you later."

"Sure."

People at the garage were already in the middle of breakfast when I brought the water. They were being served from the small bibito. I put the bottles on the ground and joined the queue. I bought myself tea and anjeelo, and settled down with Farouk and Bustale who were sitting on chairs borrowed from the bibito. I saw Iftin watching me from where she sat with her mother and sister. We exchanged knowing smiles and resumed eating. After breakfast it was time to start getting ready to hit the road again. Some people went to the town centre to buy last minute things for the journey, but others resumed sleeping until everybody was ready. Vehicles were being checked for oil, tyres and water, and re-loaded with peoples' effects. I joined a group who sat around and talked about nothing and everything. Farouk and Mohamed had gone to the town, Tuke was working on the car, but everyone else from our car was gathered near one tree. Arabo with her youngest son on her lap was sleeping. Saeed, Bustale, Faduma, Iftin and I were sitting together and talking. My stepmothers and the rest of the women were also sitting or lying under the tree and chatting. Iftin and I exchanged secret smiles every now and then, but avoided talking directly to one another in case anyone should suspect something. It was not exactly forbidden to have a relationship with the other sex, but there was a bit of a taboo attached, especially for the girl.

As a matter of fact we had a strange sort of mentality in our country to relationships. Everybody messed around yet society pretended it didn't happen. All young people went out in the evenings in search of partners, and parents knew about it. Boys were allowed to bring girls home and have something going. Girls were also allowed to bring boys home, but mothers would always keep a close eye on what they were doing. The young couple were not allowed too much privacy. If they were alone in a room the mother or other female family members would keep calling in on them every now and then, carrying soft drinks or tea, or with some sort of silly excuse. The idea was that they should not be allowed more than a few kisses, though mothers wouldn't even admit to allowing that much. No mother would admit to her daughter kissing boys in her home. Fathers were not much different. A father wouldn't care much about the small things, but if he knew his daughter was really messing around he would do anything to deny it. But get this, he would brag about how many women his sons brought home. Boys were also allowed to go out any time, without permission from parents, whereas girls should have some sort of excuse for going out.

Anyway, by about eleven o'clock we were all ready. The elderly, the responsible adults, the children and the luggage were all aboard. The vehicles began lining up on the highway, which took about an hour. When all sixty-three vehicles were in line the rest of the people took their seats. No one tried to take someone else's seat. At last, at about one o'clock we all took off for the next town of Jowhar.

# 35

In the good old days Jowhar was less than forty-five minutes from Balaad. For a variety of reasons it now took all afternoon for us to reach it, for the highway had been absolutely destroyed by the tanks which had been coming down from up-country to devastate the capital city. and we also had to travel very carefully for we were all overloaded. Another reason was that we stopped just about every ten minutes or so because something either fell off a vehicle or else a child, and sometimes a grown up, had to take a leak, or even worse a vehicle would break down. We had to wait for one another because it was almost impossible to pass in that long line of vehicles and also it was dangerous to be left alone. As our Toyota was somewhere in the middle of the convoy we didn't have much of a choice anyway. With an average speed of not more than twenty kilometres an hour, it was almost five o'clock when we reached Jowhar.

Jowhar was not very different from Balaad. Just like Balaad it was along the Shabelle River. It had the same rich black soil and its people also lived from their farm products. But while Balaad was famous for its cotton, Jowhar was famous for its good sugar-cane, and our only sugar factory was located there. Jowhar was twice or maybe even three times as big as Balaad. Unlike on my previous visit of a few months ago, Jowhar was now as dark as the rest of the country and without electricity.

We found a huge empty space just at the beginning of the town, and parked all sixty-three vehicles there, having decided to spend the night in Jowhar. My stepmothers couldn't wait to see their children so they rushed me to my father's house, accompanied also by Zeinab, Anab, Faduma and Iftin. The old couple were sitting in front of the house when we arrived.

"Hello, Uncle Jimaale," I greeted them. I always spoke to the man because of his better ears.

"Who is it?" he asked narrowing his eyes as usual.

"It's Ali Farah," said Haleemo, his wife.

They greeted and welcomed us.

"Where are the children?" my stepmother Anab asked.

"They just went to bed," said Jimaale. "It's been dangerous these last days," he explained. "Everybody has forgotten all about God's words. They all went crazy. I didn't want the children to be in danger so I told them never to go out of the house."

Both my stepmothers went inside as the man finished his words. Old Haleemo followed saying, "Let me light the kerosene lamps for you."

167

The rest of the women followed. I waited with Jimaale.

"Thank God you're still alive," he said to me.

"*Alhamd lilah*," I said.

"*Alhamd lilah*," he echoed. "We're too old to be killed. They're after the young, not people like us."

I saw Haleemo waving lighted lamps in the daash.

"Ali! Ali!" My brothers Nasir and Ahmed came running from inside.

"Hi," I held Nasir up and Ahmed clung to my hand. "Very good, very good. You took care of yourselves."

"There were two children killed across the street," Nasir said.

I looked at him.

"It's true," he added. "Ask Ahmed if you think I'm lying."

"I believe you."

My stepmothers waited at the door while I talked to the children. The rest of the women were already inside. I could see some of their limbs as they spread themselves out in the daash. I noticed two long beautiful legs as I put Nasir down.

"Let's go inside," I said. Everybody followed including the old couple.

The women pulled themselves together as I entered. The beautiful legs belonged to Iftin. She was still wearing the same cream coloured diraa as this morning. Haleemo made us tea and Jimaale brought us some mattresses but no one seemed interested, for we had already stretched ourselves out on the ground. It was a relief after being squeezed into the crowded Toyota. I sat close to Iftin and we talked and touched each other while the rest were busy in conversation with the elderly couple. Her sister Faduma glanced at us over her shoulders every now and then. She smiled and resumed her conversation. After tea I excused myself.

"I have to go," I declared.

"Why?" said Iftin. "I mean where?"

"To my uncles' house."

"He's visiting his mother," my stepmother Anab explained.

"Say hello from us," said Falis.

"I will."

I departed and disappeared into the dark streets. It was by now after nine o'clock.

The door was not locked so I just pushed it open. There was no lamp in the daash and I couldn't see much. Gradually I could make out the figure of a woman sitting on a chair alone somewhere in the middle of the daash.

"Ali!" shouted the woman, it was my mother. "Ali!" she repeated. "I'm grateful to God that you're still alive!"

"Mum!"

She repeated over and over again how glad she was to see me, how horrible it had been after the tragic deaths of the rest of her brothers. It was the first time for a long time that I had remembered my uncles' deaths. I told her about my plans of leaving the country and begged her to come along. She refused. She said she couldn't think about leaving her country, and was too old for it. But she gave me her blessing to go ahead, and wished me good luck.

"Where's Grandpa?" I asked her.

"He's lying down."

"I have some money from Hassan for the family."

"Then let's try to talk to him."

We went inside the room where the old man was sleeping. Mother called him but there was no answer. I called him and he grumbled and sat up. He looked so ill and downcast that I could hardly recognize him as Grandpa. He held my hand tightly as he spoke very softly, almost in a whisper. He was not making much sense either. He was mixing up all kinds of names. He called me with the names of his deceased sons most of the time, but sometimes he called me by names I'd never even heard of. Twice he called me by my own name. I didn't mind it at all. I told him all about my plans but I doubt if he even listened to me; he kept rambling on about his sons while I was talking. The couple of times he addressed me correctly he was saying:

"Be careful, Ali. People have lost their minds. They have lost their religion and common sense. Your mother cannot afford to lose you as well."

"Yes, Grandpa," was all I could manage.

"I think we should leave him in peace," mother whispered to me at last and I bid him good-bye. I gave him the three hundred thousand shillings from Hassan.

"Money," was all he said. "Money. Only money. What am I going to do with money?"

I kissed him on the hands and left him still sitting up in the bed and staring at the pile of notes.

"He's been like that since the boys were killed," Mum said when we stepped into the daash, and then she started weeping. She hugged me and held me until the tears stopped rolling down her cheeks.

Mum and I talked for a little longer in the daash. She made me a very good dish of stew and rice. She also gave me milk. After dinner she went back to her room and told me to wait. After a moment she came back with her purse.

"Do you have enough money for your journey?" she asked, fumbling in her purse.

"Yes," I said. "I do."

"Here," she said holding out her hand, "take this. You'll need it."

"No, Mum. I have enough money. Believe me."

"Take this money," she insisted. "I don't know what to do with money any more. Besides you might just need it. You never know."

I took the money. It looked so much.

"It's one million shillings," she added.

"Thank you, Mum."

"Do you want to sleep here or…"

"No, Mum. I can't do that. I don't know when exactly we're leaving. I'd better stay with the rest of the crowd."

"Yes, you're right," she agreed and kissed me on the forehead. "You'd better hurry if you want to get some sleep," she added looking at her watch under the dim moon. "It's after ten o'clock."

I bade her goodbye and departed.

Almost everybody was already asleep when I arrived at the other house. Only Iftin and Zeinab were chatting in the almost dark daash when I came in. I had a feeling that I was one of the issues that had been under discussion. I greeted them and sat between the two ladies.

"I could use some body heat," I said as I took the warm spot.

"We could use some, too," said Iftin. "So how was your mother?"

"Fine," I said. "My Grandpa was not feeling so well though."

"Well," said Zeinab. "I guess I should be going to bed. Good night."

"Good night," I said. "Sleep well."

"Take care of that pretty girl, Ali," she added as she left us alone.

"I will."

We were the only ones left in the daash. We started kissing as soon as Zeinab has gone inside the house. After long kisses like earlier that day, I put my hand under her diraa and touched her thighs.

"Let's wait for a while!" she whispered. "People are still awake!"

We lay down under the dim moonlight.

"What have you and Zeinab been talking about?" I asked. She invited herself to a cigarette from the packet of Benson & Hedges in my hand without answering my question. I lit it for her. She inhaled deeply and blew out to the dark sky.

"Nothing in particular," she said at last. "Girls' stuff, you know."

I pulled her to me and pressed her warm body against mine. She held me tightly and laid her head on my hand as a pillow. We caressed one another silently for a while before she said:

"Zeinab thinks you're a wonderful guy."

"I don't care what she thinks of me," I said. "What do you think of me?"

"I think you're a very wonderful guy."

I waited no more. I don't know how and when but I found myself on top of her. We kissed for a short time before I pulled her diraa upwards so I could feel her body. She was mumbling something but all I could really hear was our loud breathing as

171

our bodies touched. I sucked at her hard erect breasts as I pulled her underwear down to her feet. She flicked it aside and unzipped my pants. I slipped them down and left them on the ground. I held both of her long legs in the air and thrust into where her thighs met. She groaned and I shivered.

I was still lying on top of her when Jimaale came out and headed across the courtyard for the toilet. We froze. I covered Iftin's lips with my hand and whispered:

"Just stay quiet! He doesn't see very well!"

We hurriedly snatched up our clothes which were scattered on the ground and dressed very quietly when the old man had disappeared behind the small wooden door of the toilet.

"I can't find my underwear," she said.

"Hush," I whispered. "Be careful – he's got very good ears."

I looked for her panties and found them almost in front of the door to the room where the old couple slept. We chuckled and she slipped into them. We heard the click of the toilet door being opened and we lit our cigarettes and leaned against the wall.

"Who's there?" the man asked as he approached his door.

"It's me, Uncle," I said. "Ali."

"You have a long day ahead of you, Ali. You should be going to bed," he suggested.

"Yes."

I watched the old man stumble over the doorstep as he entered his room. We smoked silently for a while before she asked me, "So what did you do during the war?"

"You don't want to know."

"Yes, I do," she insisted.

"Well…I was killing people." Strangely enough the only victim I remembered was the hostage I shot when he tried to escape from me. "What about you?" I asked. "What have you been doing? Running from one city to another?"

"No," she said without looking at me. "I was taking care of people."

"Taking care of people?"

"Yes, the wounded people." She looked at me now. "I was a nurse."

172

"A nurse?" I said. "What a contrast!" I thought.

"Hmmm."

"A USC nurse or a real one?"

The term "USC" was used when somebody had become something during the USC war. You would hear terms like USC driver, USC soldier, USC nurse etc. when referring to these people.

"A real one," she smiled. "I'd just started to work at the Digfeer Hospital when the war broke out."

"You must surely have seen some human suffering, then?"

"I sure did."

"Well, at least you weren't shot since you weren't in a battlefield." I didn't know what else to say.

"Actually I was wounded."

"Wounded? What for?"

"For helping the wrong people."

"Tribalism," I snapped.

"Tribalism."

We went to bed at four o'clock that morning.

# 36

My head was heavy with sleep when the old couple woke us up just after six. I wouldn't have got up if it was not for the fact that I was the only able-bodied male of our family at home.

"Ali," said my stepmother Anab as she shook me by the shoulder. "I think you should check the car. We don't know when we're supposed to be leaving, and they don't know where we are."

"Let the others do it," I mumbled turning to the wall.

"The women?" she asked in a sarcastic voice.

I hate women, I thought to myself. Why do they act as though they're cripples? I got up from the mattress and staggered out of the room. Falis and the children were still sleeping. The old couple were drinking their morning tea in the daash and I could hear the noise of the rest of the women in the other room. They were just getting up, it seemed.

"You got up at last," said Haleemo. The old man shaded his eyes from the morning sun with his hand as he looked at me.

"Good morning," I said rubbing my eyes as I passed them and went out of the small wooden door to the street.

Before I got around to asking anything I was told that we would spend a second night in Jowhar. I was so tired and grateful. Farouk and Saeed came back to the house with me. Farouk said he should know where we were so that he would be able to fetch us at any time. Saeed wanted to see his girlfriend Zeinab and he teased me that I had taken all the girls with me without telling anyone.

The women were awake when we came home. Saeed said he would stay there for a while with his girlfriend. We watched my little brothers chasing after one another in the daash. Farouk said he hadn't had much sleep the previous night, and the kids were getting on his tired nerves. So I suggested that we go to my mother's where we could both get as much sleep as we wanted. We told the rest of the crowd we would fetch them the following morning, then we departed.

Mum was very happy that I was going to be able to stay another night. She made us a good breakfast of fried liver and onions with tomato sauce and French bread rolls. We told her not to wake us up even if we slept for a week, and went to bed.

"What about lunch?" she asked.

"Forget it."

We slept through the day. About midnight, however, I awoke with pains in my stomach. I was starving. I looked around and saw a gas lantern burning on a table and Farouk still sleeping and snoring. I looked at him as he slept. His chest was bare and he seemed much fatter than I had thought. I smiled at the sight and sound of him, and remembered strange theories I'd heard in childhood about fat people. I stood up and slipped out of the room into the daash where I found Mum sitting silently on the same chair she had sat on the night before.

"Mum?" I said.

"Yes, son," she said.

"What time is it?"

"About midnight."

"I couldn't sleep."

"I expect," she said rising from the chair, "you're hungry."

"Starving," I answered. "Have you got any food?"

"Yes," she said straightening her bra. "The dinner I made for you boys is still there in the kitchen."

She walked towards the kitchen as I went back to the room to wake Farouk up. He had already been woken by my voice and was putting his shirt on. When we came out, I dangling the gas lamp in my hand, Mum had already served the dinner. We sat on a mattress in the daash and ate what she had prepared by the dim light of the lamp. It was warm red beans cooked with rice and fresh butter. We drank warm milk. As we finished the meal we grew sleepy again, as though from liquor, and went straight back to bed. We asked to be woken up before six the next morning.

## 37

We told Mum not to bother with breakfast for it was too early. She looked so pale from worrying about everything. We said good-bye to her and left as soon as we had had a cup of tea. Just before seven we arrived at the spot where all the cars were parked, and found everybody was ready. Mrs. Shukri, it seemed, was particularly impatient for our arrival.

"What took you so long?" she asked as she saw us coming.

We soon found out why she had been growing so anxious. We had a new job to do. The rumour was that there were some marauding gangs operating in the countryside, to the north of the town, along the road we would be travelling. They robbed and, if necessary, raped and killed to get what they wanted. They preyed on the people who were fleeing to the North and West because they were carrying money and goods and, especially in the case of women, gold. The bandit gangs didn't care which tribe you belonged to. These gangs were Hawiyas, it was said. They had started out as anti-Daroods, stopping any Darood who was fleeing from the capital. But, it was also said, they had acquired a taste for the loot they could get from the frightened travellers, so now their strategy was to stop everybody regardless of tribe. They were outlaws.

Each vehicle, it had been agreed already, would have to be responsible for the safety of its own passengers. That meant that we had to hire other gangs from the city who could protect us from the outlaw bands. The people from our car discussed the matter and found it a little difficult to find a solution. First, we hardly knew anybody in the town except for my mother and Grandpa, who were themselves guests in the town. And secondly, most of us were either women or too young to be of use. It was the job of older men – elders – to understand matters relating to tribes and tribalism. We found it necessary to get advice. Farouk and I took off and headed for my father's house to talk to Jimaale.

We told the old man the situation. He listened very carefully then told us to wait for him. He didn't say where he was going, but we imagined and hoped that he was going to meet some people who could do something for us. He didn't take long. When Jimaale came back he had two young men with him who were in their twenties and armed with kalashnikovs. Jimaale introduced them as being close tribesmen of mine. They would do anything to protect us, he said. Their names were Ismael and Deeq.

Anyway, at about noon all the vehicles were ready to depart despite the fact that many hadn't been successful in hiring bodyguards. The reason why some couldn't find bodyguards, it was said, was that they had some famous or infamous Daroods in their party; the hired bodyguards did not want to have any uneccesary clashes with the gangs because they themselves didn't have any argument with them -- after all, they were also only interested in the money they would get as payment. They didn't want to fight, they said, but they didn't want to say they were being hired either, for that would bring about troubles in sharing the money. All they wanted to use as their excuse for protecting us was that we were Hawiyas and therefore shouldn't be killed by other Hawiyas.

My two little brothers found a place in the children's corner. We found room for Ismael and Deeq in the crowded Toyota. Their guns dangled from their shoulders. Ismael sat on top of the cabin above the driver and Deeq hung from the back of the vehicle, with Tuke. The two men bargained about the money. First they said they would charge half a million shillings each, but after a long wrangle they reduced it to half a million total. Other than that they were very quiet and said almost nothing.

We drove off at about twelve. In an hour we were completely out of the town and nothing had happened. At about two o'clock, however, all the vehicles stopped and our breath stopped with them. We couldn't see what was going on up front because we were in the middle of the line. None of us wanted to admit the possibility that we had been stopped by the gangs. We soothed ourselves with the probability that one of the front vehicles had broken down. Five minutes passed by, and what seemed like five years of our lives passed with it. We couldn't ignore it any more, so we, all the boys except Farouk, got down from the car to take a look. The natural thing would have been to take a walk to see what was going on. Instead we stood near the Toyota and looked around. We were in the middle of nowhere. Everything was green except for the tarmacked road. Dense thorn bush ran along both sides of the road as if to form walls. Beyond the road were farms, and thin rivulets of water taken from the river ran through them. There were some huts scattered here and there but I saw no people. There was the noise of engines whirring and people talking almost in whispers. It seemed that we, the young men who had got down, all wished that we would be rooted to the ground so that we wouldn't have to walk up to the front to witness what our wild imaginations were telling us was going on. Our two bodyguards merely followed us, with their guns swaying in their hands, as we sauntered up to the front. A middle-aged man who looked rich and confident descended from a bus behind us and joined us in the march. Soon the man was leading the march and we reached the front vehicle which was a Fiat lorry overloaded with people and their possessions from beds to rags. To our surprise we saw nothing unusual. The man went over to the driver's window.

"What happened?" he asked.

The driver pointed with his head in a sideways direction without saying a word. We followed his eyes and saw a young boy not more than sixteen years old standing with a gun aimed at the driver. Another young man of about nineteen appeared from nowhere and aimed his gun towards us. We all grew extraordinarily quiet. I was just thinking that it didn't seem too hopeless, when I saw that there was a long line of armed men behind the bushes lying on the ground with their guns covering our line of vehicles. I froze. My small hope disappeared. A middle-aged man with frightening eyes suddenly appeared from the bushes. He was wearing two machineguns and a pistol as he approached the driver. He was not aiming any of his guns and he walked briskly. He looked like the boss. But before he could speak to the driver the wealthy-looking man who was leading us spoke to him.

"What is it you want from us?" asked the man. "Why did you stop us?"

"Who are you?" asked the gunman.

"I am the Ugaas."

"You're exactly what I was looking for."

Ugaas meant tribal chief.

"Come with me," he ordered the Ugaas as he walked back towards the bush. We made an attempt to follow but we were stopped by the two young men who pushed us with their guns. Their faces were sullen and shiny with sweat. It was easy to tell that all the members of the gang were what we call 'from the bush', not from the city. You could tell from their behaviour and things that they were people from the countryside. Their accent was non-Mogadishan and their clothes were out of fashion.

"Only the Ugaas can come with me," explained the boss.

"Can I at least bring some of my men?" requested the Ugaas.

"Not more than three."

It seemed that we would soon have things under control since the gangs were willing to negotiate. The Ugaas got three of his men and they began talks with the gang leader. A group of spectators from among the travellers joined us and we watched at a distance as the men engaged in what became increasingly heated arguments.

"What do you mean everybody must get down?" we heard the Ugaas ask in a raised voice. "Why don't you say what you want from us and then we can see what we can do?"

"I said tell your people to get down from the cars!" the boss man shouted. The two gunmen beside us held their guns tight and aimed them with a new enthusiasm. The younger one grew more excited as he swayed his gun.

"But that's impossible!" the Ugaas yelled back. "It would take us all afternoon to do that! We don't have that much time to lose!"

Another man appeared from among the men in the ambush. He too walked briskly as he approached the Ugaas,

"Who the hell do you think you are to get in the way of our business, eh?" he said as he came right in front of the Ugaas, standing so close that the Ugaas could only focus on the man's angry face. Then he turned to his boss and said: "Don't get into a discussion with him. Just give him your orders and tell him to keep his suggestions to himself."

"Get back to your position," ordered the boss quietly. The man went back in line and lay down with his gun pointing menacingly at the Ugaas.

"Why don't you tell us what you want so we can give it to you?" asked one of the Ugaas's men.

"That will make things easier for all of us," added the Ugaas.

"OK, OK," agreed the boss. "I want each and every gun you guys have on your vehicles."

"That's impossible!" said the Ugaas almost angrily.

"We're not that stupid to give up all our guns when we both know what you have in your dirty minds to do after that. Why don't you get to the point and tell us what you want from us?"

The boss looked at the Ugaas with a you'll-pay-for-that-attitude expression, and then looked at the two young men beside us as though giving them silent orders.

"Look," the Ugaas tried again. "We all know that you're after money. Say the amount you want and let's discuss it."

The younger of the two general's men drew a grenade out of his pocket and pulled out the pin with his teeth. He walked towards the cars as though to stand in the midst of them. A man came out of the bushes shouting to the boy. The boy was still holding the grenade in his hands but I knew sooner or later it would have to explode so I ran back to our car passing him on the way. My stepmother Anab and a few other people were standing near the car. I kept an eye on the boy as I ran.

"A bomb will explode!" I shouted. "Everybody run!"

"Oh my God," screamed everybody.

The man was chasing after the boy, who was now running in our direction.

"Get out of the car everybody!" I screamed again climbing up on to the Toyota. Everybody rushed out. I jumped down, ran a few steps and threw myself to the ground on my belly.

BOM! The grenade exploded. People screamed. Dust covered the whole world. Pieces of things could be seen flying through the air. I froze at first but when I realized that gunshots were following the grenade I stood up and attempted to run. I collided into all kind of people and things and fell down on the road. I realised it was the road because my knees hurt as I fell. People ran over me, screaming. Some fell as they stumbled over me. Others just stumbled and kept on running. The gunfire didn't stop. I stood up and ran around looking for my family.

"Ahmed! Nasir!" I called for my brothers. "Anab! Falis!" I called my stepmothers.

I could hardly hear my own voice, let alone be heard,

because of the horrifying gunshots and human cries. I found Falis as I fled. I grabbed her by the hand and fled with her.

"Where are the boys?" she screamed.

"I thought they were with you," I gasped.

She turned to run towards the scene. I held her back.

"Let me go! I have to find the boys!"

I ran on, dragging her by the hand. We stopped under a tree and hid ourselves behind the trunk.

"Let me go!" she screamed again trying to free herself from my grip.

"Wait here! I'll find them!"

I ran back to the place from which the people were fleeing.

"Ahmed! Nasir!" I called.

I saw the gunmen coming up from their positions. I fled back to the tree where my stepmother lay trembling with fear.

"Let's run with the crowd!" she begged.

"That's not a good idea," I said. "We must stay here."

She changed her mind when she saw that the gunmen were chasing after the big crowd of people and firing on them. She held my hand tight and rooted herself to the ground. People were falling down in great numbers. Other gunmen ransacked and plundered the vehicles which were so close to our tree that we were afraid the gunmen on the vehicles would see us.

"Keep your head down," I told Falis as we stayed frozen to the spot.

We watched as the men took televisions and video-recorders, bags and purses, even boxes of spaghetti. They left nothing that was of value either to themselves or to us. The group who had chased after the people started to come back to get a share of the booty. Soon all of them were carrying things into the bushes and the firing died down. Now I could hear women wailing, children screaming, old men weeping. People started to come back after realising that the gunmen were no longer chasing them. We watched the people and looked for my brothers among the crowd. But my brothers were not any-where in sight.

"Where are they?" asked Falis.

"I don't know."

The gangs were still firing their guns as they carried away our belongings, but not as much as before and not at any particular thing. It was as though they wanted to deter anyone from following them or something. But no one dared to do anything about it. Some of the people who came back stood with us under the tree. Others watched the scene at a greater distance. Suddenly a tank appeared coming towards us from the opposite direction. It was so fast and throwing up dust all over the place. There was a sudden change of mood. Everywhere grew silent. The gangs stopped firing. We all watched the wonderful machine in awe. As if by a miracle the gangs started to run away. The tank veered off the road and chased after them into the bushes. People held their breath. The noise of the tank suddenly stopped. Silence took its place. Suddenly there was hope in the atmosphere, hope to live after all. It was not anything you could see, it was just this powerful feeling inside. People didn't rush back to their vehicles. Nor did they look at each other. It was as if everybody pushed out all the air from their lungs, then took a great breath in. It was as though their blood began to circulate once again. Sweet life knocked on our door. The breeze of freedom blew around us. The people were still rooted to the spot when in what seemed like a couple of minutes the wonderful invention roared back into view. It was then that the people did something physical. We all clapped. Clapped like little children whose Indian film hero had saved the heroine. A man wearing a mask pushed his head out of the little hole on the tank.

"Get back to your vehicles!" the man shouted as he waved his hand towards the line of vehicles on the highway. "Get back to your cars quickly!"

The noise resumed. Wailing, screaming, crying. You name it. It was perfectly horrible. People were running up and down calling for their loved ones, or climbing into their vehicles. I found myself standing alone under the tree. My stepmother was gone.

I looked around me for a moment before making my way to our car and something caught my attention. A woman in her thirties was trying to make her way to the vehicles like everybody else but was falling further and further behind. Her limbs seemed unwilling to do what was required of them and she flopped to the ground. Even though I was sick with fear I went to her aid.

"Hurry! Hurry!" the tank man was still saying. "Get back to your damn vehicles!."

She was about five hundred yards from me and twice that distance to the vehicles. As I got closer I concluded that she'd been wounded.

"Is it your legs?" I asked when I reached her.

"No," she said feebly. "I…"

"Where did the bullet hit you?" I asked again.

"It wasn't a bullet," she said, managing a faint smile. "It's not a bullet. I just gave birth this morning."

I could tell she was a Darood from her accent. But she wasn't a Darood to me now. It was as though the whole tribe bullshit didn't matter anymore. It's like we belonged to the same tribe, the tribe who'd just been robbed.

"You had a baby!" I was shocked, partly because I wasn't prepared for that answer and partly because I didn't know how to be of help. I didn't know anything about giving birth – all I knew was that new mothers always limped for days in hospital, and for more days when they came home. At least my step-mothers did. A friend of mine whose father was a doctor once told me that this was because of the circumcision thing that was done to girls, and not necessarily because of the labour. My stepmothers, however, disagreed. They said that it was nature, with or without circumcision. But that didn't help me now.

"Can you stand up?" I asked.

"Yes, I think so," she murmured, "but I doubt if I can walk."

It was hopeless. I stood there for a moment wondering whether she would mind being dragged along the ground. I decided to pull her whether she liked it or not when a young man came running towards us.

"Ubah!" wailed the man. "Are you OK?"

We carried the woman together. I took the legs and he took the head. All the way to her vehicle she kept on repeating insults against my tribe. When we were at her vehicle, which was a bus, the woman thanked me but didn't know what to say when I, for what reason I don't know, told her that I was a Hawiye. As I jogged along the long line of vehicles to get back to my Toyota I realised for the first time how serious had been the incident. In almost every car I passed there were signs of disaster. People were bleeding, women sobbed and clung to their dead. Men yelled to bring things under control. I saw men dragging dead bodies and women trailing after them. As I got closer to our car I realised that there was trouble there too. Most of my group were standing on the ground like the passengers of other cars. Almost all of the women and some men were crying. My stepmothers were screaming and people were trying to restrain them and get them into the car while at the same time trying to cover the scene with a piece of cloth. No one had noticed me coming. They were fully occupied with the appalling scene before them. I joined them there and froze. My two baby brothers were the scene. Ahmed's innocent body lay on the sun-boiled road. He was cut to pieces. His right arm and the lower part of his right leg were severed. The rest of his body was burned from the explosion. Only his head was recognizable. Nasir's body lay on its back on the sandy ground beside the road. His mouth and eyes were wide open and there was a large hole through his tiny chest. He had apparently been shot in the back. The rest of his body was as fine as ever. Not burned like Ahmed. One single thing occupied my odd little head again. My gun. I wanted to have my gun again. I wanted to chase these men who killed my baby brothers, and kill them one by one. I wanted to get revenge. That's all I could think of, revenge. This goddam situation! These goddam thoughts.

"Please hurry up! Hurry up!" ordered the tankmen again.

We wrapped the bodies of my two brothers in a piece of cloth then placed the bundle inside the Toyota so that we could at least give them a burial. My step mothers, still screaming hysterically, clung to one another, and the rest of the women clung to them and sobbed with them. The children would shed no more tears; their eyes were as dry as glass, red as blood, and fixed and unblinking as the eyes of a cat in a fight. The men simply swallowed their tears like I did, as custom expected. I cannot pretend to describe how I felt. Blood, pain, fear and all climbed into our car on that hot, sad afternoon. We drove off at three o'clock. The tank led us away.

# 38

Only God the Almighty could know the full extent of the disaster to our convoy, but our car was probably typical of the situation on cars throughout the convoy. Jamila was shot in the left ankle and was still bleeding. A new man in his fifties who was seriously wounded had joined our car. He'd probably been unable to find his own car, but no one asked questions. He sat beside me. One of his legs was totally smashed from receiving a chain of bullets. He said he had also been hit in the back and the bullet had got lodged in him. He was very fat so maybe that's why the bullet didn't go through. Anyhow, every time the car jumped on the rough road the man moaned close to my ear, and held his breath while pressing his lips together. His left hand occasionally gripped me tight and the other went to his stomach.

The bodies of my two baby brothers covered with the big piece of red cloth lay on the floor of the car. None of us said anything. It was quiet except for the man's moaning and the women's sobbing and the engine's roaring. Eyes were blankly staring, trying not to fix on things that ordinary people in ordinary circumstances don't usually see. I watched the ground outside passing us by so swiftly as the car speeded on. I couldn't tell what the rest of the men were watching, except when we would all look at the Soviet-built tank which appeared and disappeared every now and then apparently guarding us. It roared past our vehicle, went all the way to the front, all the way to the last vehicle and came back again and again. The machine was so wonderful. It crushed all the trees in its path whether big or small, tall or short, without any problem whatsoever. It didn't even need a road at all. It needed only terra firma and a fine driver. It was something good to have as a friend but not as an enemy. After a while we grew bored with watching it and went back to blank staring. The wounded man must have grown sick of the noise of silence which had taken over since he met us, or perhaps he felt sorry for us and wanted to help, or perhaps he wanted to distract himself from the excruciating pain he was in, because I became aware that he was repeating something and was trying to talk to me.

"I just asked you what your name was?" He managed a kind of smile as he clenched his teeth during the inquiry.

"Ali," I answered.

"You're a fine boy," he added, and as he tried to tap my shoulder the car made another jerk and he withdrew his hand immediately and moaned. That was the last time he tried to say anything to anybody. I thought his tiny puffy eyes looked sleepy as though he was drunk.

We stopped every five kilometres or so to bury the dead. We buried Ahmed and Nasir at the third stop, for their mothers would cling to them whenever anything to do with burial was mentioned. As we buried them their mothers regained some energy and started crying more than ever. We also received information on the number of casualties. Twenty-six people, including six children, killed and thirteen wounded.

At about five o'clock the situation took another turn. Suddenly we stopped. No one knew why and no one seemed interested. We felt safe with this powerful friend of ours, the Tank. After a moment, however, we found out the bad news. It was the tank men who'd stopped us and who wanted to hold us to ransom in their turn. It seemed they had only saved us so that they themselves could loot us.

They wanted our money, we were told, and any weapons we had. The Ugaas and his men tried their talking once again. This time the Ugaas didn't seem as self-confident. Maybe he was remembering what his arrogance had done for us. Or maybe he was intimidated by the powerful tank like the rest of us were. Whatever the reason, this time the Ugaas begged. But that didn't change matters. The people who had gathered to look on watched the Ugaas and his men bargain in vain. It was clear that the tank men were not letting us go unless their conditions were met. An idea hit me. I spoke to the two young men who were being paid to guard us up to the next town. I told them that if they wanted to be paid the remainder of the money my family had agreed on for getting us there safely, then they had better do something about the situation we were in. The threat worked and Ismael and Deeq walked over to one of the three tank men and took him to a nearby tree to talk. I couldn't hear what they were saying but I could tell they were serious from their gestures. After five minutes or so the tank man walked to his companions who were still arguing with the Ugaas. The three of them talked briefly and then went over to our bodyguards. It seemed they recognized one another for they shook hands. The Ugaas waited and the focus was changed towards the bodyguards who now seemed our best hope, as they seemed to be on friendly terms with the gang. They all walked towards our car and all eyes of the spectators followed them.

"Are you sure they are Hawiyas?" one of the tank men was saying as they approached our Toyota, "Because that's what they all say, but I'm not so sure."

"Of course I'm sure," said Ismael, one of our guards. "I never lied to you, did I?"

The five men were all carrying the same brand of gun. They first eyed the group of us who were standing beside the car, but we satisfied their suspicious looks. Then they peered inside the car where the women and the wounded man were. Unlike the previous gang these had accents and clothes which marked them out as pure city people.

When he saw the wounded man, the leader smiled sarcastically. "Now I can tell you're all Hawiyas," he joked. "Hello, Lieutenant," he said to our latest passenger, "Do you remember me?"

The man moaned with pain before opening his eyes. Then

his face stiffened as he saw the tall tank man who was addressing him.

"Yes, Captain," said Mr. Fatman, "But I thought you were dead long ago."

"I bet you did," said the tall man beckoning the other to the ground, "but I knew *you* were alive."

The fat man tried to get out but couldn't.

"I also knew I'd be lucky enough to see you like this one day," the tall man added. "Get down!"

The fat man tried, and I made a move to help him but the tall man held me by the shoulder saying:

"Don't bother."

He himself grabbed the wounded man by the collar and dragged him out of the car. The man fell heavily to the ground, partly because of his weight and condition, and partly because of the force that had been used against him. The tall man stood over him triumphantly and shot him twice in the chest.

"Who else is Hawiye" the tall man sneered as he looked at my stepmothers.

"Don't touch these women!" I said. "They are the wives of Mr. Farah Geeddi!"

The tall man and the rest of his crew eyed me suspiciously.

"Who the hell are you?" he asked me.

"I'm his son."

"I don't believe it," he said. "You mean Farah the Traveller's son?"

"Yes!" I said. Traveller was the nickname of my father.

"Count your ancestors if you're not lying," he commanded me.

"Ali, Farah, Geeddi, Abdi, Hussein, Mahadalle......"

"Enough!" he said. "Enough!"

We were all silent for a moment before the man continued:

"I'm glad I didn't make a mistake there," he admitted. "Traveller is not a man whose family I dare touch. I'm sure he'd feel the same about me." He grabbed me, "Listen!" he continued, "you must tell your people who you are! You young whippersnappers are all the same, you're a disgrace, you're animals.

What do you think would have happened today if you hadn't told us your clan identity?"

I said nothing.

"Tell your father about this," he requested. "My name is Captain Siyad. They call me Captain Cook. I was the first man who discovered where the Daroods hide. Hear?"

I nodded.

"Is the car your father's?" he asked.

"Yes," I lied.

"Listen" he now talked to his gang, "collect the ransom money from every other car except this one, do you hear?"

The men nodded as they turned away to carry out the order.

"I don't kill Daroods," he said to me, "unless I know that they personally abused my people. But I'll not let them get away with the money and the gold they're carrying in their bags. That's why I saved you from those gangs back there. Understand?"

"But there are no Daroods with us," I pleaded.

"You don't know anything." And with that, the tall man in the green military uniform marched away.

They went through every car except ours. We watched them from our spot as they took the money from every other car. Then they let them go one by one. At last at about six o'clock all the vehicles were released and once again we were on the road.

# 39

We arrived at the town of Buulo Burte where we paid off the bodyguards, and decided to spend the night there. The town was so small that our vehicles filled the town centre. Our Toyota was parked somewhere near a restaurant so we decided to have dinner before sleeping. Even though we were all dead tired it was only the children who were able to sleep. I sat on the edge of one of the blankets that we had spread out on the ground. I could hear the noise of the nearby restaurant and the low conversations of the people around the vehicles. I could see young armed men going up and down the streets of the town like police patrols. They looked at us in passing as though we had come from another planet, but they didn't talk to us or bother us.

I thought about what had really happened in my life during the last few months which now seemed longer than all the rest of my life previous to that. Pictures of people, places and incidents would come to mind. I wanted to think about those pictures of my past but I couldn't keep them in my mind long enough. They disappeared as fast as they came. Perhaps my brain was too tired to think but perhaps part of me wanted to forget. While still struggling with my inability to concentrate, my attention was drawn to a scene which was taking place in a dark area in front of the restaurant. Several young men who were all armed were arguing about something. I watched them. With the help of the lights of a passing lorry I recognised that two of them were Ismael and Deeq, the two guards who had accompanied us from Jowhar and were supposed to have gone long ago. I opened my eyes wider to try and see better. It became clear to me that the five were divided into two opposing sides, Ismael and Deeq on one side and the other three on the other. The two sides started pushing one another as if the three wanted to go somewhere and the two were not letting them. I stood up without saying anything to anyone and got a little closer to the scene.

"I don't want to hurt any Hawiyas," one of the three was saying, "all I want is the car!"

"But the people in the car are Hawiyas and if you take their car in a situation like this you're hurting them!" Ismael argued.

Another of the three said, "But according to my information the car belongs to Gadaburses!"

Now I was pretty sure they were talking about our car. They wanted to take our car and leave us in the middle of nowhere. I had to do something because the guys sounded very determined. I approached them, and they stopped talking as they saw me coming.

"Good evening," I said. No one answered.

"Does any one of you happen to know a man by the name of Farah the Traveller?" I asked.

"Of course," said the first one of the three. "What about him?"

"The car you are talking about is his," I said without any introductions. "I thought you should know that before you take it."

They eyed me without a word.

"Go ahead and take it if you want." I continued. "But I promise you I'll do everything in my power to make you pay if you touch that car or its passengers."

"Who the hell are you?" asked another.

"I'm his son and the rest of the people in the car are our family," I concluded and walked away.

"Wait a minute!" said the first. "You can't intimidate us! If..."

"I'm not," I cut him short. "I'm only telling you the true nature of this business in case you happen not to know it already."

"What're you going to do?"

"I'm going to defend my family," I said. "You're only three with three guns and we're more than twenty with more than twenty guns." I lied. "If you think you're in the middle of your people so do I. If you think you're bulletproof then let's see." I kept on walking and bluffing and went back to sit silently on the blanket where I was earlier. They didn't follow me. Most of the people were by now lying down, whether sleeping or not. I sat there alone and hoped and prayed that the trick had worked. After a quarter of an hour of smoking like a chimney and secretly stealing glances at the situation every ten seconds or so, hoping I was the winner, Ismael walked towards me. I stood up.

"They want to talk to you, Ali," he told me. "I think they're scared to touch the car but I also think they didn't like your attitude."

"What should I do?" I asked.

"Back off a bit," he advised, "be sort of apologetic, you know."

We walked back to the scene. The three youths waited.

"Listen," the first one said. I could see he was pissed off.

"We were misinformed," he explained. "We'd never dream of confiscating the car if we'd known who the owner was. We're sorry."

"It's OK," I said. "No harm done. And I'm sorry for my roughness. I must have got carried away in my anger."

And that was that. We were left alone. I didn't tell anybody about the incident of that night.

# 40

At six o'clock the following morning we left Buulo Burte. In a couple more hours we reached the middle of Hiiraan region, another Hawiye-dominated area. We stopped on the outskirts of the region's capital, Beledweyne, where we had our lunch in safety. Representatives from every car, mainly elderly and respected men, the Ugaas and his men, and a few women, including Shukri as the owner of our car, gathered for some discussions on security matters. They discussed the geography of the country, who lived where and the risks that should be avoided and the ones that could be taken. Since most of the people were either Gadaburses or Isaaqs, the decision was to avoid continuing on the main road north, which led through the last region of the Hawiyas and then through other Somalia regions. Instead, they decided to take a route through Ethiopia to Djibouti. In the parts of Ethiopia that we would travel through, the dominant population was Somali, because before the European colonizers gave it to Ethiopia as a present or a bribe, it was a part of Somalia. The Somali tribes in these areas were, according to the representatives, less dangerous because, it was argued, they were not as well informed as their counterparts in the main territory as to who was who, and so they were less likely to follow the rotten political games based on tribal connections, even though they were aware of what was going on in the mother country.

Anyway just after two o'clock we hit the road. All the vehicles, except those of the Isaaqs and a few Hawiyas, took the route through Ethiopia. We journeyed in silence, the kind of silence when people look at one another now and then and wear faint and sad smiles on rock-dry lips. The kind of silence when people say out-of-nowhere and meaningless sentences like "The car is not fast enough," or "Isn't the road good?". For no one wanted to remember or discuss the awful past which overshadowed their lives together. No one mentioned words like "safety" or "war" or "love" or "hatred" or anything of meaning. It seemed we all wanted to leave our memories behind. Far behind where no one could ever reach them. To bury them in a deep, deep hole in the middle of the Indian Ocean or the Pacific or whichever deep waters would take on the burden. The women sat staring at nothing with their hands to their cheeks which still showed the strain of the tears they had shed over the recent past. The men's Adam's apples moved up and down as though they were endlessly swallowing invisible food, and their eyes slowly rolled from this side to that as though secretly watching a slow motion tennis match. The silence grew deeper as the day grew darker and darker, until all we could see were the lights of the vehicles behind us, which went up and down as they ascended or descended the hills we left behind. Sometime early in that dark evening the now smaller convoy settled for the night on a large plain just beyond the small town of Farjanno. The weather was now a little chilly and wet but it didn't bother us at all. Neither were we any more fearful of dying by the bullet at the mercy of crazy gangs which might turn up at any moment. Each group found its place on the plain and ate whatever food they had. My group had dates and biscuits. We were soon snoring away our exhaustion, helped by the clean air which was still fresh from the rain.

# 41

The landscape changed as we continued our trek the following morning, The road was more mountainous. Sometimes the vehicles seemed as if they could only roll backwards down the steep slopes, but they didn't. It was not savannah grassland any more. Forests and taller trees dominated the land. We were stopped a couple of times by gangs, however. The first gang, on the outskirts of the town of Shilaabo, were looking for Hawiyas. And the second gang, who caught up with us when we were having a break in Qabribayah, were looking for Isaaqs. It was weird that they were looking for Isaaqs for as far as I was aware the Isaaqs were not in the war. At least not officially. Neither of the gangs, though, was successful. Both gangs were small compared to the large or heavily armed ones we'd encountered earlier, and the size of our caravan of vehicles seemed to daunt them. Both times our car declared that we were all pure Gadaburses, so Saeed and I were saved by our Gadaburse travel companions.

About five that evening another incident took place. This time we were only five vehicles because we had left the rest of the cars far behind. They were too big to take the short cuts we did to avoid the mountains. We were all small practical cars, two small Japanese buses, two Toyota four-wheel-drives and a small Mazda. The street was blocked by a number of big barrels, and as we slowed down to see what the matter was, a gang of men appeared from the sides of the street. They surrounded us and pointed their guns. We stayed in our seats. Somebody shouted something that sounded to us like a declaration of war.

"That's Amharic!" somebody in our car exclaimed. "They're Amharas!"

The word Amhara is synonymous with Ethiopian in Somali, and had a lot of negative meanings for Somalis, what with our two countries having different religions, and because we'd fought over our borders since way back in time. Anyhow, one of the bad meanings connected with Amhara and which had got famous during the Somalo-Ethiopian war in the 1970s was that Amharas ate their meat raw. I don't really know how or for how long they cook their meat, but that was the story that went around.

Anyhow, this idea was later transformed by the children into something worse. Oh, how I love what goes on in children's heads. You know what they said about these poor Amharas. You know what we children changed it to? We said that Amharas ate human flesh, with hot spices and all. (And you know what else we said? We also said that Jews didn't look like human beings.) It sounds really crazy. I know now it's not true, but then I really believed it. At least I know that Amharas don't eat human flesh, because I once met a guy from Ethiopia. He was two years or so older than me and his Dad was married to a Somali woman from the old town. She wasn't his Mum though. Anyway, this guy, his name was Tasfai or something, was really smart. He's the one who taught me to walk on my hands. I was about ten at the time, but I still remember. Anyway, I asked him one day if Amharas eat human flesh and the guy just laughed at me. It was pretty embarrassing. He knew what people said, though. He told me this was just war propaganda. He was really smart. He knew politics and all and he was only twelve. I think it's because his Dad was political or something, because they'd had to leave their country. Anway, for Heaven's sake, that Tasfai guy didn't even eat ordinary meat. He said they were vegetarians or something. But I'm still curious about the Jewish thing. I know that's not true either, but I have to see for myself to really get it out of my head. Thing is I never saw a Jew in my entire life, at least not knowingly. I'd really like to meet one one day. Anyway, we were all scared to death when that Amhara guy shouted in his language.

"I said nobody move!" one of the men said now in Somali.

We obeyed and stayed still.

"Bring all your luggage down!"

We all brought out the luggage from our cars on to the ground. Now I could tell from their complexion and language that the gang were a mixture of Somalis and Ethiopians – nine or ten men in plain clothes whose ages were between eighteen and thirty.

"Open them up!" ordered a strongly-built short man of about twenty-eight or so, who was Somali and seemed to be the boss. "Very slowly!"

We opened the bags and stood aside. The short man spoke with the others in Amharic for a while.

"Now," he continued, "I want you to come here together. All of you! Come on, move it! Come right here beside me!"

We did as we were told. The short man watched us triumphantly while the rest pointed their guns without saying anything. We were about forty or so in number when we came together. Almost half were women and children, the other half mainly young men, with five elderly men also among us. No one dared to speak.

"Sit down and put your hands on your heads!" The short man ordered again.

We sat like a flock of thirsty sheep and placed our hands on top of our heads without a word. All the gang members were now standing in front of us. All were pointing their guns except the short man who now hung his gun loosely on his shoulder. The only audible noise was the heavy steps of the short man's boots as he marched up and down without a word, like a Mafia boss in the movies who is about to murder his victims in cold blood after he had got all the secrets they had to tell. The silence grew so audible around us that I felt I would be relieved if I shouted. Fortunately, after a couple of minutes of that noisy silence my friend Saeed, who was sitting beside me in the front row, interrupted it.

"Would you please take what you want and leave us alone?" He pleaded. "Shut up, asshole!" the short man said. He walked towards us and we lowered our heads and watched the ground to avoid any eye contact which might cause more trouble than we already had. As I continued staring into the wet, red sand, a big dusty black boot appeared in view. I still didn't look up for I could tell the rest of the story – it was that the short man was standing over Saeed. I prayed that the man wouldn't talk about tribes for both I and Saeed were outsiders and the most

196

probable guess was that the men were either Daroods or Gadaburses, judging from their accent. My prayers were accepted.

"Did you speak to me?" the short man asked in a tone of authority. He didn't get any answer though. "Stand up!" he ordered and Saeed was at once on his feet.

A very tall skinny man, who could have been mistaken for a living ghost any night, spoke to the short man in Amharic. The short man listened carefully as the lanky figure said whatever it was he was saying. The message was short, sharp and important because the short man gave new orders to his men and forgot all about Saeed. The men divided up, and half of them stayed in their places while the other half went to the lined-up luggage near the Mazda. It contained two video-recorders, one television, five or six stereos and radios, one typewriter, and all kinds of bags varying from samsonite suitcases to large travel bags. They started with the bags. They searched them and took everything useful out and put it on the ground. If a bag proved to contain only useful things they took the whole bag and put it beside the other chosen materials. It took them about ten minutes to sort things out and then the men surrounded us when they had finished their task. The short man had put on his bossy manner once again. This time I wasn't worried because it was clear to me the men were simply gangs who didn't belong to any particular tribe.

"Stand up!" he said as he pointed at me.

"Me?"

"All of you!"

We all stood up. He ordered his men to search our pockets. We had all our pockets emptied. They took everything. Everything. Bracelets, necklaces, spectacles, watches and money, even some of our clothing. But not *my* money. I hid that in my shoe. I learned that from my brother Hassan. He was really good at hiding all kinds of things, especially money. I'll always remember how he once hid some cigarettes. It was this time that Dad came from Germany – or Italy – or wherever he told us he went. Anyway, Hassan and I and my friend Musa were smoking a cigarette behind Musa's house when Dad appeared from nowhere. Luckily, we were sharing one single cigarette, and at that moment Hassan was taking a puff. Dad said 'hello' to us as he passed by, and boy, you should have heard how loud our hearts were thumping in our chests. Anyway, you know what Hassan did? He hid the whole goddam burning cigarette in his mouth. He even managed an odd sort of smile. Man, that Hassan could really hide things. Anyway, when I thought the guy had done searching he came up with another trick. He chose eight, of the youngest, I'd say.

"Stand over there!" he ordered us and pointed towards the luggage.

We did. He inspected us curiously for a while before he spoke to *me*.

"Your shoes," he whispered in my ear. Man, this man was psychic.

I looked at my brand new sneakers and thought about my money. I desperately needed a plan to trick him, but all my stupid little head could think of was the money instead of a plan.

"My shoes?" was all I could repeat.

"Yes, your shoes!" he shouted. "Take off your shoes and put them in that goddam bag!"

I obeyed him painfully. He eyed the new shoes for a while and apparently being satisfied that they were new gave one final order.

"Carry these things over to the hill!" he said pointed across to the the right. I even thought of telling him that there were nine hundred US fucking dollars in the stupid shoes, but I didn't. The guy was robbing me for heaven's sake. So was I supposed to help him find *my* money? Anyway, the eight of us and four of the gunmen carried the possessions away. My load was a heavy black handbag on my right shoulder, a smaller white one in my right hand and two small radios in my left hand. None of them belonged to our car, at least. My shoulder hurt and my fingers ached with the weight but I didn't even dream of putting them on the ground for I saw what happened to Mohamed when he tried to do it. The tall ghost-like figure hit him hard on the right kidney with the butt of his gun. Mohamed moaned with pain.

"Move on!" shouted the figure and put an extra bag on Mohamed's shoulder as a punishment. Mohamed moved on swaying with the unbalanced weight on his body as we climbed up the hill.

"Put them here!" ordered the short man when we were at the top of the hill. We placed our possessions on the ground and waited for more orders.

"Now, get back to your cars!" the short man ordered. That was the only order everybody was waiting for, and therefore, with all the energy we had left inside us, we rushed back to our cars. As I was running with the rest I was still thinking about the goddam money and all. Not only because I'd lost it, but also because I was afraid the stupid short man wouldn't even find it. What a waste. The gang didn't follow us, neither did they shoot at us. We hurried into our seats and drove off without a word of complaint. We could see them as they disappeared to the other side of the hill. It was just after six in the evening.

## 42

We found we had nothing left but some small change in a purse of Anab's which had been in the car, and a little food and water. Never mind, we were still breathing and we still had the rest of our gasoline.

At about midnight we arrived in a small town and since the small town was asleep we went straight to one end and slept there. When we woke the following morning the town already had the news of our presence. The local people, mostly women and children, surrounded us to see if they happened to know any one, or to ask us about the situation in Somalia, or to know which tribes we belonged to, or to help us if we needed anything from the town, or simply to trade. The people of Farjanno were gentle and they welcomed us wholeheartedly.

Even though the people in this Ethiopian-ruled town were Somalis, they acted more like Ethiopians. They wore Ethiopian garments, ate Ethiopian food and spoke both Amharic and Somali. When we drove into the town centre we noticed that most of the men were soldiers. There were Ethiopian soldiers and to my surprise also USC soldiers. However none of them bothered us except to ask a few questions about our general situation and plans. At least the USC soldiers acted like professional soldiers and not like those outlaws and bandits we had met on the way. They talked to us decently and without either prejudice or favour. We learned that the USC had dozens of military lorries parked in the middle of the town.

Anyway, we had our breakfast in a small café, and ate something called 'dafi'. It looks like the Somali anjeelo pancake but is bigger and more spicy and they put some red and yellow sauces on top which made it look something like pizza. The food was cheap and good, and we spent all the money we had left. As we ate breakfast the Ethiopian soldiers searched what bit of luggage we had left. They also made a thorough search of our vehicles. They said it was for security reasons but since we carried nothing illegal we were not concerned. At about eleven o'clock that morning we hit the road again. This time we were accompanied by Ethiopian and USC soldiers who were going to another town. They said it was stupid to go alone when we were all going in the same direction. They offered us protection against the gangs which they knew could be lying in wait. They said there were incidents almost every day since the Somali civil war started. They led and we followed. We would stop every now and then whenever we came to places well known for illegal road blocks, and wait until they had checked that the road ahead was clear.

We journeyed through the night and the following day, still stopping every now and then. The third day we stopped to rest at about midday in the middle of nowhere. Here we shared out the remaining food that any of us in the group had left. Some had bread, others had only water like us, and some had nothing. The soldiers contributed powdered milk and some dafi. We shared everything and we had a little energy once again.

We resumed our journey late in the afternoon and continued through the night and the following day without any sleep other than the naps we took in the cars. Then at about ten o'clock that night something happened. The vehicles in front had stopped and our car suddenly reduced speed and came to a halt with the rest. Before we had even bothered to think about what could have gone wrong, however, there was gunfire and soon we were in the middle of another war.

"Turn all your lights off!" the USC soldiers in the front shouted, "and get out of the cars!"

The Ethiopian soldiers shouted the same orders, I suppose, in their own language. We did as we were told.

Everybody, except for poor old Mrs. Jamila and the children, because she was wounded and all, jumped out of the car into the dark bushes to hide. I was lying on my belly under a tree and Farouk was beside me. He was standing somewhere like two yards from me with his hands on his ears.

"Farouk!" I yelled, "lie down!"

He didn't seem to hear me so I rolled over and threw him to the ground in my direction.

"I said lie down!" I repeated. "Are you nuts?"

He lay down beside me without a word. He was shaking and I could hear his heavy breath before he buried his head in the ground. By now I could see the battle was between our protectors – the USC and the Ethiopian soldiers who escorted us – on one side, and an unknown invisible enemy in the bushes on the other. Our escorts were taking positions as the enemy fired like hell. Soon both parties were firing equally furiously. The bullets were like rain, I swear. They shone in the dark like small stars but they dropped like rain. It was hard to tell for sure, but it seemed the enemy was in the bushes on the right, and after five or so long minutes the shooting subsided and our escorts had seen off the invisible enemy.

"Get back to your cars!" they ordered us. We hurried back to our vehicles and soon were on the road again. Eight people were killed. Apart from an Ethiopian soldier and two USC soldiers, the rest were innocent travellers. Nobody from our car was among the dead.

We continued our trek. I don't think anyone slept that night. Not because of fear, which was a regular part of our lives, but we had another problem. A problem which overshadowed fear. Hunger. Hunger – the biggest enemy of all mankind, the mother of all human ills, the cause of diseases, theft, robbery and so forth – was our sole problem now. We'd had nothing much to eat for almost four days, and to aggravate the problem we'd now run out of water. Our stomachs had shrunk to nothing, and simply to breathe was an effort, let alone to move around. Our heads hit the sides of the car as the vehicle swayed on the rough road. My saliva was as sticky as chewing gum and it was easier not to swallow than to try and ease the thirst.

Anyway some time around three o'clock in the morning we arrived at another village and spent the rest of the night there. Some men and women who could speak the Ethiopian language went into the village to call for help. By seven o'clock our prayers were answered when a water truck belonging to the military pulled up. Suddenly there were signs of life in our camp, and people chased after the lorry. I wanted to join the crowd to get a drop of water but I couldn't stand up. My legs disobeyed me, and I was left to watch the activity from where I lay.

The lorry driver was unsuccessfully trying to calm the people who were now becoming violent. He shouted something in Amharic which had no effect whatsoever on the mob. The lorry never really stopped properly and the crowd never drank properly either. Women, men and children were running with all kinds of jugs and pots to catch the water from the tap of the lorry which was now open. Some managed to fill their jugs and run back to where their loved ones lay like me on the ground for lack of energy, some drank with their bare hands, some old people and children chasing the lorry failed to get anything. Most of the water was pouring on to the ground. Soon a second water lorry pulled up. Everybody was yelling "There's enough water for all of us! Slow down!" but nobody did, not even those who said it. But in ten minutes or so the situation had calmed down and people started to help the rest of us who lay on the ground. Everybody was running with water to the helpless. Mohamed came running to me with a big jugful. He splashed half of it on top of me. I was drowning. Not only with the cool water but also with joy and happiness. He held my head and helped me to drink.

"Don't drink too much!" he was saying. "Don't drink too much!"

I kept on drinking it like milk until my stomach hurt. I lay down.

"Are you OK?" he asked.

I nodded and gave a weak smile again. As I tried to say something I threw up.

He put his hand on my back as I poured water on to the ground. "You're going to be fine," he said. "It happened to me too. It's because your stomach's empty and you drank too much too fast. Nothing else."

He teased me about how cool I'd looked when we first met. My clothing, glasses, walkman and all. He said there was a big contrast between my appearance now and then. He was trying to amuse me, and I have to admit it helped me get back into a better mood. I felt my energy returning as I took a mouthful of water every now and then.

"Let's do something about food," I declared at last when I felt good enough to talk, and we went back to join the crowd.

## 43

The general situation of these several hundred travellers was like this: most people were sick and some not even strong enough to stand on their feet. The few who still had some energy left were busy being useful to the rest. They brought water, cigarettes and food to their nearest ones. We were now sort of sub-divided into small groups, with each vehicle acting like a family. Each family had to take care of themselves and they did so in different ways. Some, though very few families, still had a little money left so they used it to buy food and other necessities from the local people. Some families knew people in the village and therefore were saved. Others could at least speak the local language and were helped by the Ethiopians. Some, however, were less fortunate like my family. They had no money. They spoke no Amharic. And they knew no one in the small village. But still they had to do something to survive. We couldn't give up after all we had been through. I don't know how other unfortunate families survived but this is what my family did. Mohamed, Tuke, Iftin and I were the only ones in our family capable of walking. The rest were too weak, and the children were very sick. The four of us went into the village looking for ideas for feeding ourselves and the rest of the family. We were not going anywhere in particular, we were simply acting according to the Somali proverb which says: 'Being active is the key to all success'. And we knew God was on our side. After walking around the village for a while and speaking with a few of the local people in English and with mime, we were directed to a Somali woman who was living at the other end of the village. She was a huge woman of about fifty, and was washing clothes in front of her one-room hut. She first spoke in Amharic to us but when she found out our nationality she spoke in Somali.

"I heard there were some Somalis who arrived here last night," she said, "but I thought they'd already gone."

We waited.

"Now what can I do for you?" she asked. "Are you looking for somebody?"

"Not really," Mohamed spoke. "We were looking for some help."

"We're starving and we have no money at all," I added.

"Oh! Poor children," she said and hurried to her hut, drying her wet hands on the way with the hem of her garment. We waited in silence and hope. She came back with a plate of dafi and a kettle of warm tea.

"Here," she said. "This might help you a little while I prepare some lunch for you."

There were about ten to fifteen pieces of dafi on the plate. Each of us grabbed a piece as soon as she handed us the plate. Tuke took the rest to the others back at the Toyota.

"That's why his name is Tuke," Mohamed observed as the young man ran off with a new pair of hopeful legs. "He's always active."

We reminisced about how Tuke had run around fixing the car while the rest of us sat back, dozens of times during the trek. The woman asked questions and our answers seemed to increase her concern. She nodded admiringly as we told her how we had made it through.

"God was on your side," she would say every now and then. "God is always on the side of the weak."

We told her that she shouldn't think of trying to feed all of our family members for we were too many. But she insisted she would. She said she didn't care a bit even if it meant she would be broke for the rest of the month.

"I can borrow some money and pay it back when I get my wage," she said.

"Do you work?" Mohamed asked.

"Work!" she exclaimed. "There's no work for women in this small village. There's hardly any even in Addis Ababa."

Mohamed said nothing. Iftin nodded.

"My husband does," she added. "He's in the army."

She watched us drink the tea for a moment before she added: "He's Ethiopian."

Tuke came back running. We all looked at him.

"We've got a new idea," he declared. "It's about lunch."

"I'm making lunch for you," the woman said. "All of you."

Tuke was silent. He looked at us for an explanation.

"Let's hear your idea," Iftin said.

"We've just got some money," he said.

"How?" we all asked.

"Shukri and Anab had hidden some of their gold necklaces." We waited.

"And they just sold them to a local woman."

"For how much?" asked Iftin.

"I don't know," he said, "but they said there's enough to feed the people and all until we reach Djibouti."

"What do we do?" Mohamed asked the woman. "I mean, is there any place we can buy food?" Before the woman said anything Tuke continued.

"They're now buying rice and meat and all we need is a place to cook. Somebody who can let us use their kitchen things, you know."

"That's no problem at all," said the woman. And so it was arranged. On our way back Tuke produced cigarettes. While Anab, Iftin and Zeinab went off to cook, the rest of us waited with indescribable joy and impatience. I felt like being alone for a moment and went to the other side of the Toyota to smoke a cigarette. I listened to the innocent, hopeful voices in conversation on the other side of the car, and smiled with happiness. Random thoughts came into my head. I remembered my two little brothers for the first time in days. I remembered my days and nights in the war back home in Somalia. I wondered who was really responsible for this agony and the uncountable sufferings. How much blame should I throw on myself? My weak self who couldn't even say no to war like my uncle Hassan did? My cruel self who killed men and women and God knows who else? Should I blame people like my father who, by overthrowing the corrupt government had brought about this situation? Or the government itself who had forced people like my father to resist in the first place? Or perhaps the people behind the scenes who had kept such a government in power over the long miserable years? Or should the blame be on those men and women who had invented the tribes, weapons, governments, politics and all? Or was it God the Almighty who gave some people too much power and others too little? I decided to blame all of them.

"Food is coming very soon," someone said from the other side of the car but which sounded from the other side of the world. I thought of how precious was food, though it had never crossed my mind before and now seemed to mean existence. It seemed food was the ultimate goal of all mankind. The invisible ingredient of their happiness. For the first time in my life, too, I respected and cherished how my old man had struggled in his own way to put food on our table over the years while all I had been able to see was his failure to make my own selfish little dreams come true.

"Ali!" somebody called me. "Food time, Ali!" the male voice repeated. I stood up and Saeed was there beside me. "We have to go to Asha's house to eat the food," he explained.

"Asha?"

"Yes, the woman whose kitchen we were using."

"Of course," I said.

So we went to Asha's house, and now the grassy place beside the house, under a big tree which I hadn't noticed before, was being furnished with blankets and mattresses by Iftin. She was placing the last piece on the ground when we arrived. Anab and Zeinab were carrying large oval enamel plates of white rice and others full of grilled and boiled meat. They arranged them on the ground in the centre of the blankets. We stood aside and watched the delicious food in front us. Even though we we were meant to feel happy, and even though inside we really did, the atmosphere was somehow more like a funeral. We were as silent as rocks as our hungry eyes fixed upon the juicy plates of food before us. Anab put down the last plate, which was tomato salad, and broke the funereal silence. "Help yourselves," she smiled, and our hands reached into the steaming plates, and people were talking and getting noisy as hell now. Each dish was for a group of two or three.

"And there's more in the kitchen when you need it," Anab added.

I was already in the middle of finishing a big piece of meat as she spoke. My partners were Saeed and Tuke, and we ate like wild dogs who have just killed a deer for lunch. Except for some of the women – who were a little shy and were eating like human beings – all of us were eating as though we had just discovered the word FOOD. Some of the children even threw up from eating too fast. Anyway the lunch went very successfully. We all waited for tea, except Tuke who had to check the car's engine and its other parts. That Tuke! Man, we wouldn't have been anywhere without him. Anyway, the tea came in a quarter of an hour and we finished drinking in half an hour or so. By about three o'clock the feast was over, and by half past it was officially over, after we'd washed all the dishes and so on.

"Thank you Asha," Shukri concluded. "Thank you for everything. If you ever come to Djibouti I want you to visit me. That's my home town, you know. I live there." She handed the woman a piece of paper. "Here's my telephone and address. It would be very nice of you to come and see me in better times."

"But I can't read," the woman said shyly as she pondered on the paper. "Can't I ask around for you in Djibouti?"

Shukri smiled politely and we all chuckled. I am not sure of why the rest thought this was funny but I have a suspicion that we had the same thing in mind. There was this famous play in Mogadishu in which the main character is from the countryside. He comes to the city for the first time searching for his rich brother, but he doesn't know his address. He keeps asking everywhere for him by name, but of course everybody laughs at him because no one looks for some one in the city when all one has is a name. At last he gives up, saying "City people are dumb – they don't even know their neighbours."

"You don't have to be able to read," Shukri explained. "Just bring this piece of paper with you when you come to Djibouti. Then ask someone to show you this address or to telephone this number. It's not very difficult."

## 44

It was about five o'clock by the time we left the village. We were in good spirits, all except for Mohamed who had some problem with his stomach because he'd eaten too much and too fast. Late that evening we arrived in a town called Dhagah-buur where we spent half an hour drinking tea and buying more cigarettes. Some of the travellers, mainly Daroods, ended their journey there because it was their destination, as it was for the Ethiopian and USC soldiers who'd been our escort. We thanked them and drove away in the dark. We drove through the night, and early the following morning we arrived at a town called Jigjigga, where we decided to take some rest and have lunch.

Just after lunch we were standing beside our Toyota ready to leave, and waiting for the rest of the group including Shukri who were still having lunch, when some Ethiopian policemen approached us. They were five, including one who could speak Somali and who interpreted for the senior officer.

"He wants to know where the driver of this car is," he translated.

"I'm the driver," said Farouk.

"He's asking for the car documents."

Farouk opened the car and brought out the papers. The officer looked through the papers for a while and then said, "These papers are not right."

"What's wrong with them?" asked Tuke.

The officer spoke to his interpreter with some anger in his voice.

"The officer only wants to speak with the driver," the man translated.

"These papers are not right," he repeated.

"What's wrong with them?" Farouk asked.

"Is the car yours?" the officer inquired.

"Yes," said Farouk. "I mean it's my mother's. She's now having lunch."

"Do you have any proof?"

"Yes," said Farouk. "You have it in your hands."

"I told you these papers are not right," the officer repeated. "Do you have any other proof?"

"No."

"This car is not yours or your mother's."

"Then whose car is it?"

"It's stolen," concluded the officer. "We've received a list of illegal vehicles and we believe this car is one of them."

"Where's the list?" asked Farouk, "and who made these false allegations?"

The officer and his four accomplices ignored us and started to speak together in their language. We waited in silence.

"You'll have to come with us to the police station," the officer said at last. "That's where the lists are."

We followed him in silence as he led us to a nearby building.

"Wait outside," he told us.

He came back in a few minutes with a pile of papers in his hand.

"It's not in this list," he admitted.

We were relieved for a while before he added, "But that doesn't prove your car's legitimate. We'll have to take it to Addis Ababa for further investigation."

"Addis Ababa!"

"I'm sorry."

And that was that. Nothing could change his mind even though both parties knew that the car was legitimate – some of us knew the car long before that day, some of us even knew when the car had been bought, more than five years earlier. Shukri on hearing the news came to the police station. To our surprise she spoke in fluent Amharic and entered into heated arguments with the men. But that didn't change anything either, and she was mad as hell. The final decision was that the car should be taken to Addis Ababa first thing in the morning, and nobody could alter that. We were also forced to stay in this town another night.

## 45

We didn't want to spend too much money so we decided not to look for a hotel or some place to sleep. What we did was, we brought the mattresses, pillows, blankets and all out from the car and spread them on the ground around the car. There was enough room for everyone. The damn town didn't have much light and it was pitch-black. That was OK, though. I mean, some people can't sleep if there's too much light, although I wasn't one of them. My brother Hassan's like that though. That guy couldn't sleep if there was a light within a million miles. He just couldn't. We always had trouble because we always shared a room. He's the most terrible room-mate you could get. Not because he's scruffy and very untidy and all, like me, but he's the worst room-mate I ever had. He couldn't sleep if there was a light somewhere from the other end of the world, and he couldn't sleep if you were making *any* noise. I mean you couldn't go to the WC without him waking up. He's such a light sleeper he could wake up if you moved your *finger*, and what's more, he couldn't go back to sleep easily if you woke him up. But otherwise he's OK. Anyway, I was saying that it was a dark night, and fine, too, and we should have been able to sleep easily, but we didn't. We didn't only guard the car more than usual that night but we also discussed what had made the so-called officer stick to his deliberately false conclusion. We decided that he simply wanted our car. We knew that he was wrong about its identity and all, and we knew that there was no Somali government right now to exercise authority against criminal activity even if it had been a stolen vehicle. I personally knew that more than twenty stolen cars were in my uncles' garage, let alone countless other possessions which had been taken legally or illegally from their owners. Second, any Somali administration would have first started to impose some law in the territories it controlled, not in Ethiopia. All these things led us to the only logical and comprehensible conclusion: that he was determined to take our car. We also came to the conclusion that he had no intention of going to Addis Ababa, although he said that it was the only place that the car's real identity could be checked. Addis was almost as far away as Somalia.

Anyway, it was about midnight when most people started lying down to sleep, although Mrs. Jamila and her children had gone to bed earlier. Soon everybody was lying down. Almost everybody, except for Iftin who wasn't there at all. Tuke and I and another guy, I think it was Saeed, were talking about how life in Djibouti would be and everything, when I became aware of Iftin's absence. It's funny in a way, I mean, remembering someone at a time like that and in the dark. I don't know why it happened. Anyhow, I stood up and pretended that I was looking for my cigarettes, which I knew were in my pocket, but I was in fact looking around for her. I could've asked about her whereabouts but I didn't. I looked in all directions for her while standing on my spot but couldn't see her anywhere. I walked around to the other side of the car but she wasn't there either. My eyes had got used to the dark by now, and saw some one sitting alone twenty yards or so away. I knew that was Iftin even though all I could see was a shape. I walked towards the figure, then stopped when I was a little way off, just to make sure.

"Come on, Ali," the figure said. "It's me – Iftin."

I walked some more and stopped right in front of her.

"Hi, there," I said. "Why're you sitting alone in the dark?" I almost regretted the question, though I'm not sure why.

"No reason," she said and she held my hand. "I'm just thinking."

Now I was getting a little worried. I really was. I always hated it when girls got melancholy. I just can't stand it.

"Sit beside me," she said. "Here."

She was pulling my hand down to make me sit beside her.

"I'll sit here instead," I said and sat on the ground in front of her.

She started caressing my hand, only this time I didn't like it. Not because I don't respond to such things, because I'm a hot bastard, but somehow *this* wasn't sexy at all. I'm always lucky attracting girls, but I almost always have a problem with them at the end, especially if they become mournful or something like that.

"You know what I was thinking about?" she asked.

I didn't say anything. I *knew* what she was thinking about, though. That's the whole trouble. I just knew it.

"I was thinking about you," she added. "Have you been thinking about me, too?"

I still didn't say anything. I didn't know what to say. I really didn't. Before, I wanted to hold her and kiss her and all, but now I didn't even feel like touching her. I guess I wasn't ready for such a serious conversation, if you want to know the truth. Funny thing is, many of my friends wouldn't mind serious conversations of that sort but I would. It's always like that with me. Like this girl, her name's Shukri, who's a friend of Mona's. Oh, good old Mona. I don't want to talk about it now. Anyway, this girl, Shukri, was really pretty and everything and I wanted her so much, I remember. But when I finally managed to get something arranged, and we were seeing each other and we were about to do it, she got all serious and wanted me to promise to be her boyfriend. The trouble was, I already had a girlfriend. I was very honest about it, but she was mad as hell when I turned her down. When I later told my friends about it, they all laughed at me, except Musa. They thought I should lie like a madman. But I couldn't. That's me. I just couldn't.

"I'm talking to you," Iftin repeated. "Did you think about me?"

Trouble was I didn't think about her. I didn't even think much about my two dead baby brothers, for God's sake. I really didn't think much about anything lately. I liked her and I liked her breasts and everything, but that's all really. I think the only time I missed her was tonight when I found out she wasn't sitting around the place. But here I was, I came looking for her and all, and all she wants to do is have this melancholic coversation. I don't understand why most girls don't just forget the sad part and look on the bright side.

"I don't know if I was thinking about you or not, Iftin," I answered at last. "I really don't." Now I was being a bastard. I knew it.

"Not even a single thought?" I could see she was disappointed now.

"Yes," I said. "I mean ... tonight, for example. I thought about you."

We were silent for a while. I could feel she wasn't buying it.

213

"Listen," I started, "I like you. I really like you."

"All you need is sex, isn't it?" she asked as though torturing me.

I didn't know what to say. I was really feeling ashamed of myself now, I admit.

"Is that all?" she asked. She was crying now, I could detect it from her voice which was cracking in the dark. "You're using me, all the way, huuh?"

I stood up and took a deep breath. I also lit a cigarette. I was feeling like telling her to stop the bullshit and all, but I couldn't. I thought it's my fault as well.

"Let's go to bed," I said at last out of the blue.

She was now crying. I mean really crying, even though she was not making much of a noise.

"Let's go to bed, now," I repeated. I really didn't know what else to say. I even tried to put my arm round her shoulder but she wouldn't let me. I wanted to flee the place.

"You go to bed if you want," was all she could say. "Leave me alone."

That's much better. I really wanted to leave the place but I hadn't felt able to leave her in that dark spot alone. I walked back to my mattress feeling sick inside.

Most of them were asleep by now – I mean snoring and all. Only Tuke was really awake. I lay down near him.

"Where were you?" he asked.

"I went out for a walk," I told him. "Couldn't you sleep either?"

"No," he said. "I was sleeping, but I thought I heard somebody behind the car and I figured I should check."

"I'm really so tired," I told him. "I've got to go to sleep, if you don't mind."

"No," he said. "I'm also very sleepy."

"Good night, then."

"G'night."

The officer and his men came at eight o'clock sharp the following morning as expected. We were all awake and standing around in groups. I was standing to one side of the car and Iftin was standing to the other, and in case you're interested, we

214

were just stealing a glance at each other every now and then. I was really sorry for what happened but I couldn't have done anything else. Anyway, those thoughts were going through my head when the officer and his team appeared. They'd already had their breakfast, you could tell because they were fresh and full of energy, and we meanwhile were starving.

"The car will be taken to Addis at two o'clock," the Officer informed us without even bothering to say good morning or anything. "Only the driver need come with us," he added and he walked away. "I'll be back to get the car soon. Have your breakfast first," he concluded, as though he could give a damn about our well-being.

Farouk was a nervous wreck. He was a hopeless case. He was so scared that he decided to make his escape before the officer came back. We tried to convince him that he didn't have to accompany the officer, and that the officer wouldn't mind if he told him to take the goddam car and go without him. But Farouk wouldn't take the chance. He caught the first vehicle that was leaving for the next major town.

The officer smiled when he returned and saw the car still parked there.

"Where're the keys?" he asked.

Tuke handed him the keys.

"And where's the driver?"

"He left town."

"Where did he go?"

"He went back to Somalia," we lied.

"Ah! I knew his papers were somehow not correct," he smiled.

The officer handed the keys to one of his men and spoke in Amharic. The man unlocked the car and got inside. The car wouldn't start. He tried again and again but the engine just wouldn't start.

"What did you do to the car?" he asked.

"Nothing," said Tuke.

"Why won't it start?"

"I don't know."

# 46

At about midday that same day, we decided to abandon our car
and everything. What we did was, thanks to Mrs. Shukri, we
hired a lorry and a driver, and left Jigjigga, all except except
for Mohamed who found some relatives in Jigjigga and decided to stay there. During the ride we learned, from Tuke, that
Farouk had removed some pieces from the car's engine before
leaving. It would cost them a fortune to get it moving again,
Tuke explained proudly. Shukri vowed that she would get her
car back as soon as she was financially back on her feet again.
It was with a little bit of triumph that we sat in the Fiat lorry
which was to bring us safely to the ancient Somali port city of
Zeila early on the following morning.

# 47

At Zeila Shukri again surprised us by making quite a splash in
the town. As we reached the bus and truck station we found
Farouk there waiting for us. We also found that a crowd was
gathering around to greet Shukri. She suddenly seemed like a
forgotten princess. Everybody knew her and everybody was at
her disposal, rich and poor alike. They included many businessmen and women of the town, who welcomed her and
poured out sympathy over her recent troubles. Shukri, we soon
realised, was herself a rich businesswoman. We learned that
she had made her fortune by trading goods back and forth
between Djibouti, Somalia and Ethiopia. All kinds of things she
traded, from sweets and cloth to equipment and utensils. She
did business in Zeila, Addis Ababa, Djibouti and Mogadishu

and she was known to, and knew, powerful people in all of these places.

Our travelling group, except for my family, now considered themselves to be home one way or another, either because they were indeed from Zeila or because they were able to find some relatives and tribespeople here. Iftin also stayed at Zeila. Just as people were saying good-bye and good luck and everything to one another, Iftin came over to me. I was shaking like a leaf, I swear, when I saw her heading towards me. We didn't have much time, and she was really very nice about it. She told me she'd rushed things a bit, and she apologized like a madman. I was so relieved, you can't imagine, and after we got back to normal I asked her if I could see her again. I really did. I swear to God. She told me she knew Djibouti like the back of her hand and all, and promised she'd *find* me. She was such a smart ass, I admit, but she's also a very nice girl. Maybe she was just getting rid of me, but I accepted her promise anyway.

Later that day those of us who knew nobody in Zeila, that is my little Darood-Hawiye family – me and Falis and Anab – were invited along with Shukri and her family to an enormous meal at a large house in the middle of the town, which house, we learned, was owned by Shukri. Over lunch we were informed that a boat was waiting to take us the short sea journey up the coast to Djibouti, leaving at three o'clock that afternoon. Shukri promised us that she was sending instructions for us to be taken care of in Djibouti until we could find a place. But my stepmother Anab told her that would not be necessary. In Djibouti we would go to her brother Erik's house.

## 48

As the boat sailed to Djibouti that afternoon, my memories sailed back to where I came from. I thought of my father. I wondered where Dad was and how he was doing. I missed him more than at any other time in my entire life. I knew I always loved him and I never doubted that he loved me too, but I just couldn't help thinking that he'd let me down somehow. I thought about my life for the last few months, and I wondered how much of everything that had happened to me lately was somehow his fault. I felt guilty thinking this way, but I couldn't help thinking that Dad had let me down, over and over again. I hated blaming him this way but I just couldn't help it. I was feeling sorry for him and I was also mad at him. I ...

"How far's Djibouti, Captain."

"Not very far."

...I really was sorry for him because he was all alone somewhere, and couldn't see his family. And I was mad at him, mad as hell because *he* is the one who'd put me through the hell I was in during the last few months. I mean if it hadn't been for his politics, and if he hadn't told me that I'd have to fight for my people and all. If only he and his friends hadn't make that USC thing, and if he hadn't gone on about civil wars and tribalism and...

"I can see some buildings!"

"That's the city of Djibouti!"

...and... and if our president and his friends hadn't run the country like they did. If only...

The sight of Djibouti as we came nearer overcame my thoughts. It was so grand that I cried, right there in the middle of everybody. Tears rolled down my cheeks, and the funny thing was that I was glad about that. I really was, I swear. I was glad that I cried in that boat with everybody watching me and all.